About the author

Audrey Pembroke was born and grew up in the Purbeck stone quarrying area of Dorset. With her imagination nourished by her parents and grandmother telling her stories, and several great-aunts and uncles she developed a feel for the past.

Having spent several years in Australia, she began serious writing on her return to Purbeck. She has travelled extensively, with a fascination for the history of each country she has visited.

Hearts on Fire is Audrey's third historical novel to be published and she has a fourth in the pipe-line. She lives in her home town of Swanage with her husband.

Also by Audrey Pembroke

Maid of Purbeck
Hearts of Stone

Hearts on Fire

Audrey Pembroke

Matador
9 Priory Business Park,
Wistow Road, Kibworth Beauchamp,
Leicestershire. LE8 0RX
Tel: 0116 279 2299
Email: books@troubador.co.uk
Web: www.troubador.co.uk/matador
Twitter: @matadorbooks

ISBN 978 1788032 629

British Library Cataloguing in Publication Data.
A catalogue record for this book is available from the British Library.

Printed and bound by CPI Group (UK) Ltd, Croydon, CR0 4YY
Typeset in 11pt Aldine401 BT by Troubador Publishing Ltd, Leicester, UK

Matador is an imprint of Troubador Publishing Ltd

The image on the back cover is taken from a sketch by Will Dyson, 1934. Courtesty of the
Trade Union Congress and Tolpuddle Martyrs' Trust

To
Jenny, Victor Thomas and Karen

Acknowledgements

I would like to thank the members of my creative writing group for their patient listening and advice; Bob Walters for taking the time to read my manuscript and suggesting improvements; Tom de Witt, Manager of The Tolpuddle Martyrs' Museum for his help and interest; my husband Mark for helping with household chores and sallying forth each week to do the shopping.

The Freers

Henry Warren 1797 = Charlotte Annereaux
 d. 1833 | d 1813
 |
 Amelia 1816 = William Freer
  1797 | d 1832

Will	Charlotte	boy stillborn	Tommy
1815	1817	1820	1825

The Maltravers

The Honourable Anthony and Mrs Maltravers
 |

Alice = Sir Hugh Lackford   The Honourable Simon = Jane Audley
  No issue

The Lackfords

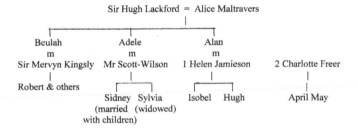

```
                    Sir Hugh Lackford  =  Alice Maltravers
                                      |
      ┌───────────────────────────────┼────────────────┐
   Beulah                          Adele              Alan
      m                              m                  m
Sir Mervyn Kingsly           Mr Scott-Wilson    1 Helen Jamieson         2 Charlotte Freer
      |                              |                  |                        |
Robert & others            ┌─────────┴─────┐    ┌───────┴────┐                   |
                        Sidney      Sylvia   Isobel      Hugh             April May
                       (married    (widowed
                       with children)
```

Prologue

August 1834

∽

Close confinement meant having to contend with five other convicts sharing a berth less than six feet square, and avoid being trampled on. The rattling of chains never ceased, day or night. While his companions complained, bitterly bemoaning their fate, Abe Manuel suffered his discomfort in silence. He was being transported for life, ironically on the ship he'd once served as Mate. After her requisition, *Esmerelda* had been fitted out for transportation at Deptford. But Abe was a survivor.

One of ten children he'd grown tired of the poverty and misery of village life, scratching a living by cutting turf and furze for fuel. One day, he swore, he would get back at his 'betters', the greedy landowners who kept his kind poor with their ever increasing enclosures. At seventeen he joined a travelling fair and worked his way to London. Ignorant and inexperienced, he was soon press-ganged into His Majesty's Navy. Life at sea toughened him until he became ruthless in the art of self-preservation. During the slump after the Peace of 1815 smuggling became rife and he slipped wantonly into the illicit trade then in its heyday. He knew how to land a boat, and welcomed the challenge of climbing a cliff on a dark night. It was owed to him and his like, he thought, to get away with their free trade.

He'd enjoyed outwitting the government's revenue officials for years – until that fateful day, last year, when the young Princess Victoria arrived in the south-coast town of Swanwick. The planned landing of contraband while the whole town was engrossed in the royal visit had gone awry thanks to informant Horace Skinner.

If Will Freer hadn't bumped into that weasel, and got wounded, he, Abe, wouldn't have had to get rid of Skinner and might still be free. He'd saved the lad from bleeding to death on account of his grandfather, Henry Warren, being a ringleader of the gang. After directing the crew to dispose of Skinner in brutal fashion, throwing him over the cliff to make his death look like an accident, he'd sailed away. The gang had no idea what happened ashore, but when their signals were never answered it was clear something was wrong. In the end they were caught by the King's Navy.

Abe growled to himself. Each latter stage of his life was worse than the one before. On their arrest he and the others were stripped, searched, put in irons and had their heads shaved. Locked up together in a cold damp prison, on a meagre diet of bad bread and water with only straw on the floor for sleeping, several of them succumbed to prison fever. Their captain was hanged but Abe was sent in chains on a dark midwinter's night to await transportation in the misery of a prison hulk somewhere on the Thames. Even he was astounded to see the number of prisoners, stripped and donning the hulk livery. Irons riveted on their legs finally broke most men's spirits.

But not Abe. He wasted no energy on self-pity, or self-loathing. Instead he kept a sly lookout for any chance of escape. The best behaved convicts were called to work on the gun wharf, one way to get fresh air and keep up strength. So he kept himself to himself, uncomplaining and avoiding quarrels. One look, or snarl from him and he was left alone. He endured the foul conditions and meagre rations for month after month, feeding on the hate and anger that smouldered in his breast. Going over in his mind what must have gone wrong, not knowing enraged him. He should have let that young quarryman die. Someone must have blabbed to the authorities. He didn't believe it of either Warren or his partner Maltravers, they had too much at stake. If it wasn't the lad, could it have been Biddy Cauldon, the old hag who hid their contraband in her cellar – or even her dullard whelp of a granddaughter? Or the squire's groom who lent them horses when his master was away?

With such thoughts Abe nursed his grievances, and determined to bide his time. His obsession to escape never lessened.

Esmerelda's hold was so crowded it was impossible to lie down and sleep. Abe knew things could only get worse on scant daily rations that were bad and salty. With over 100 days sailing ahead, half of them would be dead before they reached their destination. He did not intend to be among them.

Now, four days out of Woolwich, *Esmerelda* was battling a wild summer storm. Abe scowled in contempt at the miserable wretches around him. Most were thieves and pickpockets, not hardened sea dogs like him. Being thrown around as the ship rose and sank on the raging sea, vomiting was rife. It was difficult for men hampered by leg irons to scramble for the leather buckets provided for sanitation, and spilled contents made the boards slippery. Abe steeled himself against the stench.

As the hours passed with no let up from the howling gale, there was no telling if it were night or day in this hell-hole. For the umpteenth time Abe swore, and lashed out with both feet at some wretch who fell over him. He was about to belabour the man with his fists when he noticed a change in the ship's motion. He knew every inch of her, every spar, and every timber of her hull. It felt like she was being pushed sideways, causing her to wallow as well as being tossed about. She must be blown off course – but where?

Abe ceased to hear men's oaths and groans or chains rattling as he considered what must be happening on deck. Then came the sound of heavy bolts being drawn. A crew member opened the door to peer in by the light of a lantern. 'Prisoner number 168!' he yelled.

Abe started, it was his number. He clambered to his feet.

'That's me,' he growled.

'You're to come with me. Cap'n wants a word.'

The man stood back as Abe made his way clumsily to the door, cursing any obstacle that tripped him. He was clanking his way up the steep gangway steps by the time the sailor had re-bolted the hold.

As he emerged into daylight it took Abe a few moments to accustom his eyes but he welcomed the wind and salty spray on his face. He clung to a rail, blinking, as *Esmerelda* lurched drunkenly, then he clambered up the steps to the forecastle where the worried looking captain stood. Land was in sight on the port side, and from the violent sou'westerly Abe knew it had to be France.

There was respect rather than sarcasm in the way Captain Ross spoke:

'We're just east of Boulogne, Mr Manuel. I believe you know these waters?'

Abe nodded, 'Aye, Cap'n, I'm familiar with the landmarks.'

He guessed what the captain wanted. Here was his chance …

'Can you guide us into harbour?'

Abe squinted up at the men clinging for dear life in the rigging as they awaited orders. 'Not in these leg irons, I can't.'

The captain roared for the blacksmith, and Abe grunted in painful relief as his shackles came off.

'Reef the mainsail,' he yelled, 'and set the top foresail!'

With the familiar feel of the wheel in his hands he felt he was in charge. Tacking against the wind, he knew just where to steer. It couldn't have been better if he'd planned it. While the captain supervised the crew in their precarious positions, Abe edged the ship shoreward, and steered her into the shallow waters of a sand bar. *Esmerelda* shuddered to a halt as she ran aground, and settled firmly in quicksand.

Abe let loose a string of oaths, blaming the 'accident' on the swells.

'When the tide comes in with this sea, we'll all drown,' bellowed the mate.

'We're a half-mile from shore, I could swim it with a rope,' Abe suggested. 'Look at the crowd gathering on the beach. They'll help with the rescue-'

'Rescue?' The captain's face blanched. 'How the hell can I free two hundred convicts? I'm responsible for getting them to Botany Bay!'

'Somebody should try and get ashore to alert the French authorities,' barked the mate. 'Their militia would take care of the prisoners.'

'Aye, Cap'n,' put in Abe, yelling. 'By the time they make shore there'll be no fight left in 'em.'

'Who speaks French? You Mister Mate?' The captain looked round as the mate shook his head, but got no response from the rest of his crew.

'I know enough of the lingo to ask someone to send for the soldiers,' Abe persisted.

Captain Ross looked doubtful. 'How do I know I can trust ye-'

'If you don't do somethin' soon,' Abe snarled, 'there won't be time to unshackle the poor buggers afore she breaks in two!' Stuck fast, *Esmerelda* had no defence against the buffeting wind and waves. To Abe she was like an old mate whom he'd rather see die than suffer the indignities of her present use.

The crowd on the beach grew larger. Abe realised the watchers on shore couldn't know the stricken ship was full of convicts. A heated discussion had begun between the captain, his mate, and the ship's surgeon. 'I have no authority to release the prisoners,' Captain Ross yelled, 'I will not abandon ship!'

While the officers and crew argued against the captain's obstinacy, Abe took his chance to slip unseen over the side.

Though a strong swimmer, Abe could only dog-paddle through the huge swells, his lungs bursting with the effort. At last, fighting exhaustion, and nausea from swallowing mouthfuls of sea water he gained the shore. He managed to cling to his senses until he'd dragged himself across the sand away from the watchers to hide behind a fisherman's hut. There he sank into blissful un-consciousness

When he came to, wet and shivering with cold, he saw the tide was in. The ship was broken in two, and men still sought survivors amid the billowing waves. Abe felt no remorse for lost souls, only for the fate of *Esmerelda*.

He braced himself to wait for the storm to subside. Then he would steal a boat with oars and a sail. He'd often rowed from Cherbourg to some sandy cove or rocky ledge between Weymouth and the Isle of Wight with small cargoes. Boulogne to Hastings was less distance, but he'd need a calm sea to row it alone. He'd think about what to do when he reached the English coast while he was crossing the Channel. First he must find food and clothes, and regain his strength.

Chapter One

Springtime 1834

∽

'Where you off to maid, all done up in yer best bonnet an' smotherin' yerself in rose-water? T'ain't Sunday.'

Hunched in her rocking-chair by the fire, puffing at her clay pipe, Biddy Cauldon pulled her shawl closer around her bony shoulders and squinted at her granddaughter.

'No, 'tis Saturday after Easter.'

Hetty Cauldon turned from the small mirror propped up on the kitchen window ledge and sighed at her grandmother. 'I told you *ages* ago I was goin' to Charlie Freer's weddin'. Anyway,' she added, 'this bonnet be the only bit of *best* I've got. I wouldn't have that if Miss Charlie hadn't sold it to me cheap at the Whit Tuesday Fair last year. 'tis hardly bein' all dressed up!'

She turned back to the mirror and tied the satin ribbons in a lop-sided bow beneath her chin. It made her face less plain, and since she'd worked for Charlie's ma she'd learnt that her wide smile helped her looks. With the sun shining at the end of March this was her first chance to wear her bonnet on a day other than Sunday. She smiled at herself now, glad her gran wasn't coming. The old woman was slow these days, and Hetty meant to squeeze in at the back of the church.

She'd heard Mrs Freer, in the bonnet shop one day, discussing arrangements with her business partner Mrs Maltravers.

'It's a shame Charlotte has no father to give her away,' Jane Maltravers remarked. Both middle-aged ladies were widows, and with her eldest son away Amelia Freer was wondering who might escort her daughter up the aisle.

'Charlie wants Sam Roper to take her father's place,' said Amelia.

Jane raised her eyebrows, 'The blacksmith?'

'I think he would be happy to oblige, he's been a good friend to our family ever since my poor William was killed in the quarry.'

Jane nodded sympathetically.

'The ideal person would be your eldest son. I assume you have written to Will about his sister getting married?'

'Of course,' said Amelia clasping her hands. 'But I don't know if it's safe yet for him to return. I just hope he's learned his lesson.'

Will had left home under a cloud but with Squire's blessing, to avoid the hue and cry over the smashed smuggling ring he'd been involved in; he went to London to work as a stone mason.

'I'll have a word with my nephew,' Jane said. She was Sir Alan's aunt by marriage. 'I'm sure he'll know.'

That was weeks ago, and Hetty hadn't heard nor thought any more about it. Now, with a sudden twinge of conscience she forced a smile.

'You sure you don't want to come, Gran? We could wait outside for the bride and groom to come out of ch–'

'No I *don't!*' Biddy Cauldon waved her pipe at Hetty. 'I got no time for that hoighty-toighty miss what's bin tryin' to turn a sow's ear into a silk purse!'

Hetty felt her face grow red. She was well aware

her peasant build and uneducated ways were lowly in comparison with her well-bred employers.

'For goodness sake, Gran, Charlie only got me a job in her ma's shop. It's not her what's teaching me manners, an' how to talk proper! Why've you got to be so naasty all the time, you horrid old woman?'

Biddy cackled and sucked on her pipe clearly amused to hear her granddaughter lapse into her old way of speaking.

Hetty grabbed her woollen shawl, and threw it around her shoulders. With a last glare at Biddy, she slammed out of the cottage. Still simmering, she followed the path beside the stream that flowed towards the Parish Church.

Hetty's mood gradually improved. She loved this time of year when the woods were full of primroses and violets, when daisies and golden celandines starred the banks and wrens and yellowhammers were busy at their nests in the hedgerows.

At fifteen she was enjoying life now she was no longer a shabby household drudge, nor looked down on by folk. She knew what they thought, that it wasn't surprising she was the way she was, living with that awful old woman. Poor little bugger, never knew her ma or pa, and spending her early years in the orphanage. Then she got in with those Freers …

Oh aah, Hetty thought, brightening. Thanks to Mrs Freer teaching her the art of straw-plait folk had begun to respect her, especially after Princess Victoria visited Swanwick last summer. Hetty had sat up all night with her employer, plaiting straw for the special bonnet for Squire to present to the princess. It was the most important time in Hetty's life, so why did Granny Cauldon resent her attempts to better herself?

Hetty mentioned as much one day to Mrs Maltravers –

who was much nicer and looked ten years younger now her wicked rogue of a husband was dead.

'Try not to mind, dear,' Jane Maltravers had said. 'Old people get like that sometimes.'

Did everyone get bitter and twisted, Hetty wondered, when they get old? Her gran never liked anybody, mean old thing, especially Will and Charlie Freer who Biddy blamed when the smuggling racket she profited from got smashed. The ring-leaders, unbeknown at the time to Hetty's employers, were Mrs Freer's father Henry Warren, and the *Honourable* Simon Maltravers. Her gran also thrived on the respect of those who bought her potions and lotions, and who feared her 'evil eye'. Even the preventive men avoided her.

Huh, if only they knew! Charlie Freer was the only one beside herself who knew Biddy wasn't really cross-eyed. She pretended by wearing a black patch to give folks the impression she had the power to cast spells.

The smuggling went on right under Squire's nose, but things were never so bad until old Skinner's death. Mrs Freer hadn't known Will was involved until he was falsely charged with the coastguard's murder. Then the *honourable Mr* had caused Mr Warren to be shot dead when the old man tried to save his grandson. But Maltravers got his come-uppance – horribly crushed to death by a loaded stone wagon whilst trying to escape justice. Sir Alan, as magistrate, had Will acquitted and packed him off to London.

Now Squire was marrying Will's sister, who was *years* younger, he and the Freers were again the talk of the town. The Parish Church would be packed.

★

Charlie Freer opened the door of her room in the house that once was her grandfather's, and glanced at the tall clock on the landing. There was still no sign of Sam Roper. The moment Charlie both desired, and was apprehensive of, had arrived at last, for she'd hoped to be married at Christmas. Still, her one regret was that neither her father or grandfather were there to see her wedded to her beloved squire.

Sir Alan had come to see her and Ma the very day her brother went away, intimating that no further questions would be asked concerning Will's part in the 'trade'. That's when he suggested they postpone their wedding until Easter.

'Isobel wants to be your bride's maid,' he reminded her. 'We'd never be forgiven if the children can't come.' Both his children, Isobel and Hugh from his first marriage, were at boarding school. 'Also,' he'd added gently, 'your mother needs time to grieve for her father.'

To Amelia he said, 'You realise the authorities will sequester *Esmerelda,* as she was used to smuggle contraband. 'I'd advise you not to appeal against it.'

Amelia nodded, 'Losing my father's ship is a small price to pay for Will's freedom, and I've more than enough to do.' Henry Warren had left everything to Will on condition he looked after her. 'There's the shop to run, and teaching girls to plait straw, as well as Father's house and shire stables to manage while Will's away – then there's the quarry ...'

Ma was only too glad to sell her stone to the merchants and let them worry about conveying it to where it was needed. It had taken His Majesty's Navy two months to catch the gang, who must surely have met their fate by now. Charlie shuddered at the thought. Those who weren't hanged were being transported to Botany Bay.

Hearing the front door open and shut, she peered over the banisters.

'Is that you, Ma? Is Sam with you?'

'He's not coming,' said the man behind her mother. 'He's to be Friend of the Groom.'

Charlie recognised her brother's voice and screamed, 'Will – oh Will!'

Hoisting the skirts of her wedding gown to her knees, she ran down to greet him. Her little brother, Tommy, was already there; his smug expression told Charlie he'd known Will was coming.

'Steady on, maid!' Will laughed as Charlie threw her arms around his neck and hugged him tight. 'You're strangling me, not to mention spoilin' me weddin' finery!'

She stood back to look at him. 'Oh Will – Look, Ma, the silk shirt and striped trousers he's always hankered after!'

'Come now,' said Amelia, dabbing Charlie's wet cheeks with her hand-kerchief. 'Save your tears of joy for later. You're spoiling your looks, maid – and stop *that*!'

Charlie was wiping her nose with the back of her hand.

Tommy sniggered and Will chuckled, 'That's my sis, about to become Charlotte, Lady Lackford, and still behaving like a pauper!'

Charlie stopped sniffling and berated him in sisterly fashion. 'Why didn't you let me know you were coming, you – !'

'It was our secret,' said Amelia, putting an arm around Tommy's shoulders. 'Sir Alan wanted to surprise you. That's why he made you wait 'til Easter. Will's had success in London, and with justice done he can come home when he likes.'

Charlie felt a surge of love for her husband-to-be. How like him, to make sure of her complete happiness by delaying the nuptials until it was safe for Will to return.

★

A triumphal arch of greenery and flowers adorned the church gate and a banner displayed the mottoes "Long Life, Health and Happiness" and "God Bless You". Hetty edged her way through the crowd on the church lawn where, it seemed, the whole of Swanwick had come to witness the stylish wedding.

Inside the church, its usual mustiness was smothered by the fragrance of primroses and daffodils on the window ledges, and evergreens entwining the altar rails. Amelia and Jane had taken great pains over the decorations.

Most pews were full but there was some space near the back where the Server's wife sat with her two children. As Hetty approached she saw the woman look up, as if to see whether Biddy was with her. Apparently satisfied she wasn't, she motioned to her children.

'Move up you two, make room for Hetty.'

When Hetty smiled, and said 'Thank you,' she received a polite nod in reply. The tiny act of respect pleased her. Folks might not give her a second glance, but they never shied away as they did from old Granny Cauldon.

She looked to see who was up front. Sir Alan, with layers of lace cravat spilling down the front of his crimson velvet jacket, sat with his friends and relations in the pew to the right of the aisle. Beside him stood Sam Roper. The burly blacksmith looked smarter than Hetty ever remembered, despite his gap-toothed smile.

Behind them sat Jane Maltravers with her father who leaned across the aisle to speak to Mrs Freer. Turning towards the sound of a baby wailing, Hetty saw the kitchen maid from the Hall rocking her two month old infant in her arms. Maisie had wedded Squire's head groom, just in time.

All Squire's employees sat on the Lackford side. The gardener's wife was looking over Maisie's shoulder, probably offering motherly advice.

Seeing Maisie's maternal side made Hetty wistful. How lovely to be a baby with a *real* mother who *loves* you. If the child was still crying Hetty couldn't hear, for the organist let out all the stops and began to play Mendelssohn's fashionable new march for brides entering church. The whole congregation stood as one, heads turning for a glimpse of the bride. Hetty could see everything although at first she had eyes only for Charlie.

Charlotte Freer looked radiant and demure in gleaming ivory satin. Buttoned to the neck the bodice was overlaid with lace and the long puffed sleeves, also edged with lace, were gorgeous. Hetty had never seen anything like it. Charlie's raven-dark hair was swept up at the back and pinned with a circlet of orange blossoms. Attached to it a veil of Honiton lace floated behind her as she glided down the aisle on her brother's arm.

'Doesn't she look beautiful?' the Server's wife murmured with a tremor in her voice. 'Her father would have been so proud.'

Hetty nodded, then as brother and sister passed by she sucked in her breath. She barely recognised Will. He looked so smart and confident in the dark blue cut-away tailed coat he wore over the silk shirt – and so dashing with a stripe down the side of each tight trouser leg. He wore shiny black shoes, and carried a black top hat. With his head held high he seemed taller, and older than Hetty remembered. People were whispering 'My, don't Will Freer look a dandy!'

No wonder he looked so proud!

Will and Charlie were preceded by the parson and followed by Isobel and Hugh Lackford as bride's maid and page boy. Tommy had rebelled against being made to look a sissy, as he saw it. Then came Sir Alan's niece as maid of honour. Hetty recognised the young widow whom she'd once seen when she worked at Lackford Hall. Mistress

Sylvia was all in black then. Today, dressed in pale blue and with her flaxen hair in ringlets, she looked stunning.

Hetty craned her neck to watch as the procession reached the altar where Will unhanded Charlie. A sunbeam slanting through the window lit up Sir Alan's hair like burnished gold when he turned to smile down at his bride.

'Dearly beloved,' the parson began, 'we are gathered here ... '

Hetty joined in the sighs and whispers of admiration that reverberated around the ancient stone walls, and dared to dream of such a moment for herself. Only not on such a grand scale of course. After the ceremony she joined the crowd throwing rice over the couple and yelling congratulations. She followed the procession to Lackford Hall where a feast was laid out on trestle tables. Sir Alan had arranged for outside staff to do the catering.

The bride and groom stood at the door to welcome their guests who then rushed for a place on the benches provided. Hetty held back feeling shy and uncertain.

'Hetty, go and squeeze in between Ma and Tommy.' Charlie smiled encouragingly, 'They'll look after you.'

Hetty gasped, 'Oh, I couldn't, not on the top table!' The Freers were sitting there with Sir Alan's relations, chatting easily while their youngsters tucked in heartily. Mistress Sylvia, she noticed, had Will's undivided attention.

Charlie had turned to welcome more guests, and Hetty's new-found confidence waned. She wanted to run away until she felt a tug on her sleeve.

It was Maisie.

'Sit down yer, Hetty, an' help me with baby. My Dick's getting the best carriage ready.'

Hetty was surprised. But then Maisie seemed much nicer since she became Mrs Farmer. Tidier, too, apart from the stray wisp of blond hair straying from beneath her broderie anglaise bonnet.

Always willing to be friends with anyone who was kind to her, Hetty sat down. They took it in turns to hold the child so their hands were free to stuff food in their mouths.

'Your baby's a real cherub,' said Hetty, cradling the soft, milky-sweet smelling bundle in her arms. 'What's his name?'

'Arthur, after the Duke of Wellington.' Maisie smiled, 'Dick wanted him named after somebody famous. Anyway, where did you learn to handle a baby like that?'

Hetty began crooning softly when the child stirred. 'In the orphanage,' she murmured. 'I used to help in the nursery 'til I was nine and me Gran took me out to work for Squire—'

She paused and bit back the words *until you got me the sack*.

Maisie seemed to guess her thoughts.

'Look, Hetty,' she began, flushing. 'I'm sorry 'bout getting you in trouble over them logs that time. Can we let bygones be bygones?'

'All right,' Hetty wasn't one to bear a grudge, 'if you'll let me see young Arthur sometimes.' She couldn't remember feeling so happy, despite disdainful looks from Mrs Biggins the Cook.

'Aah, don' ee worry about she,' said Maisie, grinning. 'Mrs Biggins be annoyed she cain't order me about no more 'cause I'm to be Charlie's personal maid when her gets back. Cook'll have to train up another kitchen maid, and wot's more—' Maisie elbowed Hetty in the ribs and chuckled, 'Her'll be under a new housekeeper when our Lady Lackford's had time to hire one.'

Hetty laughed, feeling at ease once more.

She stared dreamily after the newly-weds when Dick Farmer drove them away on the first stage of the journey that would take them on a grand tour of the Continent. I wish I could be a beautiful bride with a nice rich man to cherish me, she thought wistfully.

Later, she began to tell her gran all about it.

'I'll never forget Charlie Freer's weddin–'

Biddy interrupted her enthusiastic flow. 'Was it a religious ceremony – or a pantomime?'

For once Hetty didn't rise to the bait. 'Oh, Gran, it was a wonderful weddin'!' She twirled round in delight. 'Like it should be, all beautiful, and hallowed–'

'Aah, *weddins* perhaps,' the old woman cackled, 'I don't know of many *marriages* that stay hallowed.' She watched Hetty gazing ecstatically at the ceiling, her hands clasped tight to her chest. 'Don'ee let it go to yer head, maid, and 'tis no use moonin' about Will Freer. He might 'ave bettered hisself in Lonnon, but that's why he ain't likely to look twice at you!'

The remark was like a slap in the face, but Hetty clung to the joys of the day.

'What makes you think I'm hankerin' after Will Freer?'

'The look on yer face when you mention him,' was the tart reply.

'Well I was surprised to see him so changed,' said Hetty. 'Everybody was – ask who you like, if you don't believe me!' Will was surly and unsociable before he went away. She saw her gran flinch, trust the old witch to spoil her day!

'I know I'm plain, but Mrs Maltravers an' Amelia Freer be teaching me things. They both say my hair's lovely. It's auburn, and I got nice green eyes. They said "beauty's only skin deep," and 'tis what's inside that –'

'I just don't want 'ee to be disappointed, expectin' too much.' Biddy snorted, 'You ain't just plain. You'm a base-born –'

'I'm a *what*? Gran, you'm just sayin' that to annoy me. You said you put me in the orphanage because I had no ma or pa–'

'Aah, when you was a babe. But you'm growed up now, an' old 'nuff to know better.'

'Better! How can being baseborn be better'n being an orphan?'

'That ain't what I mean. Listen, maid, yer ma were real flighty. She never knew who yer father was, and when I threw her out she ran off wi' a gang o' gypsies! S'far as I was concerned she were dead. You was left in a basket on me doorstep, an' I couldn't cope wi' a wailin' babe.'

Hetty felt suddenly weak at the knees and clung to the back of a chair for support. As if growing up an orphan wasn't hard enough. Now she was being told she'd been born out of wedlock. Gritting her teeth against the urge to cry she blinked back tears of shame and frustration. To think she'd never been wanted – abandoned as a babe, and dumped in that institution until she was old enough to earn her keep. She clenched her fists, wanting to hit out at somebody – the mother she never knew – the father who cared even less. But there was only this spiteful old witch of a grandmother who she put up with because she had nowhere else to go.

'Fancy tellin' me now!' she finally burst out. 'Just when I'm getting on, wi' folks liking me you have to spoil everything! 'tis your fault, you should've brought me ma up proper. You might not like the Freers but if it weren't for them you and me would be in the workhouse!'

'Aah! Now smuggling's finished – thanks to your precious Freers!'

Hetty refused to listen. 'The trouble with you, Gran, yer insides be rotten – accordin' to the poison that comes out when you open yer mouth!'

She ran upstairs to her attic and flung herself on her bed, sobbing.

Chapter Two

∽

I'm a *bastard*! The word gnawed at her insides. All she'd ever wanted was to be loved and needed – to be important to someone. Now she knew it wasn't just because she was plain and Biddy's grandchild that folk had avoided her. They must have known about her ma. She felt as if the progress she'd made over recent months was melting away.

And yet … Sir Alan was a good man. Since that business with Maltravers, when she'd helped save Charlie's life, Squire knew she was no thief–

She sat up and wiped her eyes with the back of her hands. Whatever else I am, I'm no thief. I'm better than that, and now I'm earnin' me own living folks respect me. Mrs Freer values my work, the customers talk to me and I've got friends. There's Maisie and her babe, then Sandy and me, we understand each other. Sandy Mason, an apprentice at the Freer quarry had come from the same orphanage.

Hetty grabbed the brush from the wide window sill that served as a dressing table and brushed her hair with long hard strokes. No-one, especially not her gran, was going to get the better of her any more. Even so, she knew the silly old fool was right. It was no good getting ideas about Will. At nineteen he was his own man and would soon go back to London. And … yet …

She'd never before thought such things. It was seeing

Will so changed, Hetty told herself, that made her notice him.

Despite this devastating blow, the normal romantic feelings of a young girl took over. Hetty's heart lifted at the thought that Will Freer would be with his family in church tomorrow.

Will did attend morning service but the Freers sat with Mrs Maltravers and the well-tailored Lackford relations. Hetty received smiles from Amelia and Jane but Will was too busy talking to Sylvia to notice her.

After the service, while the grown-ups chatted, Isobel and Hugh played games with Tommy Freer and Sandy. Hearing Tommy imitate Hugh's educated speech made Hetty painfully aware of her own backwardness.

'What you starin' at?'

Maisie's sudden question made Hetty jump. She became hot with embarrassment. 'Oh – them Scott-Wilsons is all here, I see,' she blustered, 'I was just wonderin' where be the rest o'the quality?'

'My Dick said he heard Sir Alan telling Cook that Lord an' Lady Kingsly couldn't come–' Maisie lowered her voice, 'Truth is, his eldest sister don't think Charlie be good 'nuff fer Sir Alan. Cook reckons ol' Beulah Kingsly frowned on Charlie actin' like a common midwife when she helped birth me baby!' Maisie smirked as she elbowed Hetty in the ribs. 'Charlie didn't care, she just grinned an' said she can manage very well wi'out 'em!'

'Now she's married to his lordship,' said Hetty, 'she'll have to act more like a lady. But 'tis nice to know she's still one of us at heart.'

'I must hurry back now,' Maisie said, 'and feed Arthur before I help Mrs Hart serve at table.' Mrs Hart was the gardener's wife. 'Sir Alan's relations are staying for lunch so her girls will mind Arthur, and help Cook in the kitchen.'

'My daughter will have her work cut out, running such a large household and employing new staff,' said Amelia Freer. She'd gladly accepted Jane's invitation to Sunday lunch. Sir Alan had left his aunt in charge of Lackford Hall while he and Charlie were abroad. The Scott-Wilsons, and Jane's father Luke Audley, a widower and retired banker now living with his daughter, were there too.

Amelia was missing Charlie already. It occurred to her during the ceremony how different her own wedding had been, twenty years ago. Will was already born when the ship's captain in Weymouth had married her and William Freer with only Aunt Mary and her cook as witnesses. A 'shotgun wedding' some called it, but she'd denied position and wealth to marry for love against her father's wishes. Now her Charlotte had gone chaste to the altar, surrounded by folk who knew and liked her. Amelia had shed tears of joy and pride. It was only natural, she told herself, to feel apprehensive because her daughter was marrying into Society.

At least Charlie had blue blood in her veins, for Amelia herself was the daughter of a French aristocrat. She got on especially well with Sylvia, whose husband died from influenza, for *Maman* died young from cholera many years ago.

'Mrs Biggins will enjoy ordering a new scullery maid around,' Jane was saying. 'She wasn't too pleased to have Maisie as her equal.'

'I hope Cook and Charlie will get along,' said Amelia. 'Sir Alan was wise to advertise for a housekeeper. Now Mrs B won't have to take orders direct from Charlie – oh dear, there I go again. I must get used to her being Lady Charlotte!'

Mr and Mrs Scott-Wilson murmured understandingly while Sylvia smiled and said, 'She'll always be Charlie to those close to her.'

'But not in public,' Hugh stated pompously, his fair curls shaking as he tilted his nose.

Isobel gave him a withering look, 'She will to me. I shall whisper her name–'

'Don't start, you two,' interrupted their great-aunt Jane. 'If you've finished, take Tom and Sandy with you and go for a walk or something.'

The youngsters made their escape, and Jane turned to Amelia. 'Charlotte will be fine. I can advise her, and the steward will take care things are in order.'

'Yes, of course,' said Amelia. 'I suppose I'm nervous my Charlie isn't up to being Sir Alan's new Lady ... what's so amusing?'

Jane and the Scott-Wilsons were smiling at each other. Less gaunt, and having lost her pinched look, Jane often laughed these days, and now she twinkled at Amelia.

'It amuses me to hear you call my nephew "Sir". You have the right to call him by name, he is your son-in-law!'

'You too, Will,' Sylvia said with a disarming smile. 'You are Uncle Alan's brother-in-law.'

'Oh my,' said Amelia, laughing with the others. She'd forgotten what life was like in society, having spent so long struggling against poverty. Thanks to her father's legacy and her daughter's marriage, she'd risen socially. But like Charlie, her one regret was that neither William nor her father could share her good fortune.

Her thoughts were echoed by Will as they retired to the withdrawing room. 'I wish Granddad Warren could have been here to see it,' he said, soberly.

Amelia looked at him. He'd grown taller and broader since he'd been away but, she noticed affectionately, he still had his thatch of tawny hair. Apart from brief exchanges with Sylvia he'd been quiet during the meal.

'Is something bothering you, Will?' Aren't you happy to be home? I suppose life is more exciting in London.'

Will's mouth twisted in a grimace.

'London takes a bit of getting used to,' he said, 'and I miss home, but it's not that, Ma. I do want to settle down and take some of the workload off your hands, but I can't – yet.'

'Why not, my son?'

'There's a big demonstration being planned in support of the Tolpuddle men.' He raised his eyebrows quizzically, 'You've heard of them?'

'Well, yes, who hasn't? But –' Amelia, startled by the sudden change in topic was glad that Sylvia intervened.

'You mean those farm labourers who were recently tried at Dorchester for conspiracy?' Her blue eyes were large with concern.

Will nodded, encouraged by her interest.

'Yes, but they're no more conspirators than you, or Ma. They're good Christian men trying to support their families.'

'But dissenters,' said Mr Scott-Wilson, 'which doesn't help their case. I've been following it in *The Times,* and I agree their crime could hardly be said to justify their sentence. Seven years transportation is extremely severe.'

Relieved that Sylvia's father was sympathetic, Will said, 'I'm glad you can see it, sir. I believe the Tolpuddle men's only crime was ignorance of the law in taking their oath of loyalty to the friendly society they started. That's hardly disturbing the public peace!'

Mr Scott-Wilson frowned.

'I think Squire Frampton feared outbreaks of arson like those of three years ago when farmers received threatening letters.'

He meant the so-called peasants' revolt of a few years

ago – the 'Captain Swing' movement. Partly influenced by the unrest in France when the French King Charles X was deposed, but mostly fired by the British government's Enclosures Acts, the movement was spontaneous, and disorganised. Villagers lost the right to graze their pigs, sheep and cows on common land so were forced to sell their animals. It was impossible to support their families on the pittance paid for working someone else's land. When a severe winter followed the very poor harvest of 1829 broken-hearted men were driven by starvation into seeming madness. Haystacks and barns were fired when farmers refused to pay them enough to live on, riots occurred right across the south, and 500 Dorsetshire labourers were among those transported. Children were hanged for stealing, or taking wood for fuel. Even a petty thing like pulling a turnip from a field to gnaw on was punished by years in prison. All this raced through Will's mind as, enraged at the injustice meted out to fellow workers, he tried to form a reply to Mr Scott-Wilson's reasoning.

'But not from these Tolpuddle men,' he persisted. 'After their masters promised to raise their wages they actually lowered them by another shilling! How else can labourers help themselves peacefully but by banding together?' He looked earnestly at the faces of his listeners. 'Those men were almost reduced to stealing to feed their families.'

He turned to Amelia, 'That's why I couldn't leave London until the last minute. I went to Monday's meeting at the National Institute. There were *thousands* protesting against their sentence.'

'You care about these men,' said Jane Maltravers. 'Do you know them?'

'No, but they're Dorset men like me, they live only about 20 miles from here.'

Will glanced at his mother, 'Squire Frampton is behind this business,' he added bitterly. 'It was his crony Judge

Williams who directed the jury to find the labourers guilty. The jury were all farmers and magistrates who signed the arrest warrants. And their foreman was Lord Melbourne's brother-in-law. Took 'em twenty minutes to return their verdict! What chance did the poor buggers have?'

'Frampton ... Williams?' Amelia looked bewildered.

'They're powerful men, Ma,' said Will, his eyes darkening stormily as he tried to swallow his anger, 'They have connections in government, and Frampton would have been my judge if Maltravers had made that false charge of murder stick. I owe a debt of gratitude to Sir Al – er my brother-in-law.'

He looked at Jane, and murmured an apology for dragging her late husband into the discussion. Jane gave a dismissive shake of her head and said, 'The law is so harsh.'

'It's fear that makes men cruel.' Mr Scott-Wilson coughed, and patted his ample stomach. 'The government is jittery about combinations because they fear the unrest on the Continent will spread to our country. Workers in Paris, Lyons and Brussels are all rebelling.'

'So the Dorchester labourers have been made an example of to warn other would-be conspirators,' said Luke Audley.

'As if that makes it all right,' Will muttered. 'Now they're rotting in prison hulks at Portsmouth while they await transportation. Ma, I must go back. The London Central Dorchester Committee have prepared petitions, and I'm collecting signatures.'

'Will, do be careful,' pleaded Amelia. 'If you get caught up in riots –' Her son had escaped the law once, he might not be so fortunate another time.

'It's all right Ma,' said Will, 'the protests will be peaceful. Besides, funds will be raised to support the prisoners' families.'

'Of course,' exclaimed Sylvia. 'How else will they live and pay rent without their breadwinners? I'll sign your petition, Will. So would Uncle Alan if he were here.'

'Thank you, Mistress Sylvia,' said Will. Her understanding cooled the temper he was at pains to control. Like her uncle she had compassion for ordinary folk.

'I hope you're right about peaceful demonstrations,' said Adele Scott-Wilson, Sylvia's mother.

'No one wants riots,' said Will forcefully. 'Desperate people burning ricks and smashing machines that take away their jobs won't help the Tolpuddle men. We want only to see justice done.'

'The sentiment is commendable,' said Mr Scott-Wilson, 'I admire your sense of fair play. You may bring your petition to me – but you must realise the authorities will take precautions against any kind of disorder.'

Early next day Will took his petition to the Hall and obtained signatures from the staff, and the Scott-Wilsons who were leaving for London.

'I wish you well,' said Sylvia's father, 'but take care my boy.'

'I will, sir. And thank you.'

Will went around the village and the quarries. For the people who couldn't write, he printed their names beside each mark.

'What about you, Hetty,' he said when he called in at the Amelia Jane Boutique. 'Will you make your mark?'

'I can do better'n that,' said Hetty, shyly, but with pride. She carefully signed her name, 'Hetty Cauldon,' then added 'shop assistant.' Knowing he thought his ma employed her only to clean the shop, she looked up at him for a sign of approval.

'Well, I'll be …' Will chuckled in surprise. His own schooling finished when he was ten and he'd had to study for himself in his spare time. He understood the struggle Hetty must be having. 'I take my hat off to you, Hetty. Thank you,' he added, 'everyone counts in this cause.'

To Hetty it was praise enough. She gave him her wide grin and smiled long after he left. He'd made her feel important.

When Will said goodbye to Amelia, he hugged and kissed his mother. 'I wish I could stay and help you, Ma, but ...'

'Don't worry about me, my son,' said Amelia. 'You've seen how Hetty is coming on, she's a real help. She's good at figures, she can count money and give change.'

'I noticed,' said Will.

'Luke takes care of the stable accounts,' Amelia went on, 'and Jane will be back when your sister returns from abroad. You just look after yourself and come home when you can.'

Will squeezed her hands in his, 'I'll come home for good when it's all over Ma, I promise.'

Chapter Three

The affair of the Dorchester labourers was a national concern, as was the unrest in France. During April the public outcry reached its peak. Hetty studied avidly the papers Mr Audley brought into the shop, trying hard to understand what was happening. She could at least read the headlines.

'Your Will spoke true,' she heard Jane say to Amelia. 'The protest meetings were quite orderly.'

'Yes, but the government will never admit to the injustice,' said Amelia.

By April 3rd most newspapers were defending the cause of the *six poor, misguided, ignorant labourers* even calling them martyrs. Then, when a serious riot broke out in Lyons through French trade unionists interfering with the trial of some associates, Amelia feared for Charlie and Sir Alan's safety.

'Why couldn't they have gone to Scotland, or the Channel Islands rather than the Continent?' she worried.

Jane laid a comforting hand on her arm, 'I'm sure Alan will keep them both safe. He's an experienced traveller.'

Only two days later, despite all the efforts to save the Dorchester labourers their sentence was hastily carried out, and the convict ship sailed from Plymouth.

'The government has panicked,' said Jane, 'and hope the protests will stop.'

'Then they're wrong,' said Amelia, 'according to Will. Listen–' She picked up the letter she'd been reading. '*The agitation will go on until they are pardoned. There are protest meetings in all the towns, and our petition is so big the government can't ignore it! When the mass rally goes ahead I shall be there.*'

Added now to Amelia's concern for the newlyweds was her fear for Will's safety. The newspapers told how, in Leeds, 3,000 workers struck in one day because their masters refused to employ trade unionists. Rioters in Oldham were dispersed by lancers and those arrested received long prison sentences. When the trade unions announced they would bring a monster petition to the King on behalf of the Tolpuddle men, the government armed police officers and swore in 5,000 special constables. She'd been so happy lately, Amelia reflected. The bonnet shop was booming, her only daughter had married well and there were no financial worries. Now all these dreadful affairs could turn her world upside down. She sighed wistfully when Luke Audley tried to console her.

'Your children are a credit to you, the way you've brought them up,' he said. 'But you can't live their lives for them.'

In London the big demonstration went ahead on 21st April. Will rose early and met Sylvia near Copenhagen House, an old gabled mansion on the City outskirts. Here roads converged from all over the metropolis on to a huge field. The road was lined by trade unionists while more of them crowded on to the field, their crimson and blue banners marked with the insignias of the various lodges. There were smart tailors, less jaunty-looking smiths and metal workers, coal heavers in frocks and fantails, even poverty stricken silk weavers lent their support.

Will felt awed by such a large assembly. 'Just look at 'em all!'

Sylvia nodded, 'It's humbling,' she said quietly. 'There are not many here who can afford to miss a day's pay.'

'Something must come of it,' said Will hopefully.

The shops had all closed but muffin men and pie sellers mingled with the crowds and ale stalls had been set up. When a rocket signalled the protest to begin Will joined the marchers while Sylvia stood with the watchers.

A big wooden roller, on which the huge petition was wound, was fixed in an iron frame borne on a light wagon covered in red and blue calico. It needed twelve men to carry it. The Central Committee of the metropolitan Trade Union headed the procession with its founder, Robert Owen, on horseback. Among the leaders were two more champions of the cause, MPs Joseph Hume and Doctor Wade.

Will sensed a strangeness in the atmosphere. All the spectators jamming the route stood in silence. Only the rhythmic sound of marching feet could be heard. His chest swelled with pride to be part of this momentous occasion.

Six abreast 30,000 men wound their way into the City, past the Smallpox Hospital to the Foundling Hospital in Guilford Street, and on across the heart of London until they reached the Home Office. Five delegates carried the petition inside while the main procession marched on across Westminster Bridge to Kennington Common. Here Will waited for Sylvia who was among the crowd following the procession. It wasn't until late in the day that they heard what actually happened.

They were turned away!' Will wrote home with a hand shaking from anger. *'Lord Melbourne didn't like the way the petition was presented, and accused us of threatening behaviour. There would have been a riot if the men with the petition hadn't left by the back door to avoid the crowds! Luckily the marchers knew it would take time for the petition to be put before the King and had dispersed on the Common.'*

The newspapers praised the orderly way in which the march was carried out. In Swanwick, Luke Audley and Jane came into the shop together to show Amelia a copy of a trade union paper.

'Look at this—' Luke pointed to a paragraph which read: *'Last Monday was a day in Britain's history which long will be remembered; for labour put its hat upon its head and walked towards the throne.'*

'Grand words,' Amelia said, 'but it's too late for the Tolpuddle men.'

'The King could have them brought back,' said Luke. 'The petition will have been presented to him by now.'

'If he's not influenced by Melbourne's attitude,' countered Amelia. 'That man disapproves of dissenters as much as trade unions. Those labourers were all chapel goers.

'Will won't come home yet. He says the unions will go on badgering the politicians until something *is* done. Meanwhile he has plenty of work at his stonemason's yard in Pimlico.'

'Well, he's come to no harm,' said Luke, 'and he's gaining valuable experience in the building trade.'

'Our Lady Charlotte will soon be home,' said Jane, changing the subject. 'She'll have other things to talk about.' Isobel and Hugh had returned to school for the summer term, and she was glad to be back helping Amelia in the shop. 'Aren't you looking forward to hearing about her travels?'

'Yes,' said Amelia, 'but they intend to visit the Kingslys before coming to Swanwick.'

Jane smiled knowingly. 'In that case she will be looking forward to her homecoming as much as you.'

★

The Lackfords arrived at the house of Lord and Lady Kingsly in Chelsea at the beginning of May. The Scott-Wilsons were invited to dine with them, and Sylvia brought Will.

Happy as he was to be with Sylvia, Will went for Charlie's sake too. He guessed it wasn't his sister's choice to attend, knowing how Lady Kingsly disapproved of her younger brother's second marriage. No doubt Sir Alan hoped to reconcile Beulah to his new wife.

Will had thought his grandfather's house in Swanwick was grand compared with the quarryman's cottage where he grew up, but the Kingslys' mansion rivalled even Lackford Hall. It was three storeys high with a basement where the servants worked, and an attic where they slept. The butler ushered them into the drawing room which smelt of beeswax polish and fresh cut flowers. They were greeted by their hosts and a generous whiff of lavender from Lady Beulah's plump bosom.

'So you're the quarryman my brother saved from the gallows,' Beulah said airily when Sylvia introduced Will.

Will pretended to assume her ladyship's remark was a feeble attempt at a quip. He had no intention of kow-towing to the woman. He gave her a tight-lipped smile then gazed in awe around the room whose large windows were curtained with blue velvet drapes and silken pull cords.

'Do sit down.' Beulah gestured magnanimously to a plush couch and easy chairs around the ornate marble-surround fireplace. 'I'm sure Alan won't be long.'

She spoke as if Sir Alan were coming alone, his wife irrelevant. Aware of her looking him up and down Will deliberately crossed his legs and plonked both feet on the gleaming brass fender. She can like it or lump it, he thought, now I'm one of the family. Behind the fireguard a log crackled and sent sparks shooting up the chimney.

Above the mantelpiece hung a mirror surrounded by family portraits.

Will was glad when his sister and Sir Alan arrived, despite the tepid welcome Beulah gave them. After greeting her brother coolly she offered Charlie a limp hand. Lord Kingsly was more effusive, giving her a peck on the cheek.

'I am glad you brought my brother along,' Charlie said to the Scott-Wilsons who gave her a warm welcome and asked how she'd enjoyed the Continent.

Lord Kingsly steered the conversation away from the newlyweds' time abroad to the unsettled state of their own country. Will knew which side the affluent Kingslys were on and groaned inwardly when Beulah began to belittle working men.

'Don't talk to me about trade unions,' she cried, 'their lack of consideration is deplorable – honestly, such inconvenience!'

'Beulah,' Sir Alan asked, 'what has upset you?'

'Why, the tailors' strike – haven't you heard?'

'Hardly. We arrived at Dover yesterday, glad to be away from the terrible happenings in France. We had to avoid Lyons and Paris altogether.'

'It must have been dreadful,' said Sylvia. 'The papers said there were thousands of people killed in those riots.' She glanced at Will and added, 'The protests here have been most orderly.'

'You say that,' cried Beulah, clearly more concerned with her own affairs. 'Thirteen thousand people are out of work in the metropolis alone. I shall have nothing to wear to the King's birthday dinner!'

Will bridled. Journeymen tailors, who were kept by overseers they called 'sweaters', worked long hours with barely enough food to feed a child.

Just in time he saw Charlie eyeing him with a glimmer

of a smile, and realised his sister viewed Lady Kingsly as a form of entertainment. All Beulah cared about was creating a good impression on anyone who was richer than she. And for why? If only the foolish woman could see herself!

Will swallowed his resentment, determined not to spoil the newlyweds' visit. He abhorred those of his 'betters' who thought only of themselves. 'tis a pity the lack of imagination's not a crime, he thought. I'd transport the whole lot of 'em.

'Hrmph.' Lord Kingsly coughed uncomfortably. 'I'm more concerned with the stability of the country if things are not dealt with–'

Beulah sniffed. 'I just hope the tailors will see sense and return to work soon. I must have a new gown for the Grand Music Festival in June. It's at Westminster Abbey, and their majesties are bound to attend. Shall you come, Alan?'

She directed the question directly at her brother, making it clear Charlie's presence was unimportant.

'Possibly,' murmured Alan, glancing at his wife. The look he gave her conveyed desire and affection. 'We shall see.'

He clearly adored Charlie, and the thought that he would talk it over with her pleased Will. But he was angered when, following the other men to the smoking room, he heard Beulah say to Charlie, 'You realise that when you bear a child it cannot inherit a title?'

The bitch, Will thought. As if Charlie cared about titles! Still, it must be a bitter pill for Beulah to swallow, having to own a common quarryman's daughter as a sister-in-law. He noticed Sylvia and her mother looked uncomfortable, but it would have been rude to argue with their hostess. He lingered near the door pretending to study a painting, ready to intervene. Then Charlie's answer made him grin.

'Should that happy day come,' she began, 'I shall

remember we are all Dorset born. Nothing can change that. As for inheritance, my children will inherit all the love and care that Alan and I can give. I know Isobel and Hugh will be delighted to have baby brothers and sisters.'

She leaned back in her easy chair, surveying Beulah through half-closed lids.

'If we don't have children it won't be for lack of trying I assure you!'

Oh aah still the same old Charlie, Will thought, smothering a chuckle as he went to join the other men.

Later, when they had a moment alone, he asked Sylvia, 'Why is Beulah so hard to get on with?'

'Try not to mind my aunt,' said Sylvia. 'She was very fond of Uncle Alan's first wife. She could never see any wrong in her.'

'She does't know about Lady Helen's affair with Maltravers?'

Sylvia shook her head, murmuring, 'She has no idea Helen was unfaithful, nor does Mother. Uncle Alan doesn't want the embarrassment of his sisters knowing he was cuckolded, and because Maltravers died there was no trial or public scandal. Also, Beulah is the eldest in the family, and Mother says she felt left out when Uncle Alan was born.'

Will nodded.

'I can understand that. Alan was bound to be the centre of attention being the only son and heir. Your Uncle Mervyn is kinder, and I like your parents. They're both fair-minded.'

Sylvia smiled, 'I'm glad you understand. Anyway,' she added, 'my parents like your sister, because Charlie has blotted out the past and made Uncle Alan and my cousins happy.'

Chapter Four

Life went on as usual for Hetty and those around her. Amelia's business was doing well, her quarry foreman reported that Sandy Mason was a willing apprentice and making good progress, and her youngest son, Tommy, was school marm Martha Hyer's top pupil.

'He should go to one of Dorchester's more advanced schools,' Martha told Amelia in the shop one day. 'Tommy is particularly good at drawing, as well as arithmetic.'

'But we expected him to learn about the stone trade,' said Amelia doubtfully. 'He ought to have something to fall back on.'

The school mistress nodded, 'I know,' she said, fixing her gaze on Amelia. 'He could also have a bright future as an engineer, or an architect. He's so interested in Sir Christopher Wren it may be he's destined to build with stone rather than spend his life producing it.'

Amelia's eyebrows lifted, 'I'm glad you mentioned it,' she said. 'I'll discuss it with Will when he's home again.'

Martha nodded with satisfaction. 'Well, you have time to think about it.'

'And I shall,' said Amelia. She could afford to send Tommy away to school if that's what he wanted.

Hetty was now adept at straw plait work. She began to

teach village girls in the cellar beneath the shop, giving them work to take home. She was entrusted with money to pay them, and once a week she went round collecting the items they made. When Amelia increased her wages Hetty saved the extra coppers.

'Ive had enough of me gran's penny-pinching,' she told Maisie when she met the young mother on her way home. 'I enjoy me independence.'

One day, Luke Audley came into the shop. It wasn't busy, and he found Amelia correcting Hetty's grammar.

'Aah, I wish I could be a fine lady like you,' Hetty was saying, 'but tain't no good, Ma'am. I cain't get it right.'

'You will if you try harder,' said Amelia, smiling at Luke. 'Never mind, that will do for today.' She rolled her eyes at the ceiling as Hetty went out on her errands. 'That maid will keep saying "I be" instead of "I am".'

'She's a funny little thing,' said Luke. 'She enjoys responsibility, but is still shy.'

'Only with her betters,' said Amelia. 'She sticks up for herself when the village children tease her because she hasn't been to school. She told me the other day that none of them is rude to her more than once, "Because I be bigger'n they," she said.'

Luke chuckled. 'You can't spare her the time to attend school?'

'Jane and I discussed it,' said Amelia, 'but we thought she'd be a sitting duck for the other pupils' teasing. Besides, she has enough to do looking after Biddy and catching up with housework in the evenings.'

'Hm,' said Luke thoughtfully, 'all work and no play –. Tell you what, if you could spare her for an hour before closing time perhaps she could come to me at Underhill Manor. I'd enjoy tutoring her and it's not far out of her way.'

'That's an excellent idea,' said Amelia. 'I'd like to see

Hetty make more of herself. She's a good girl at heart, she has a good memory and knows all about growing things when she chats to the customers.'

Hetty was eager to learn. She and Mr Audley got on well, and Jane grew fond of her. Once an outsider herself, thanks to her husband's unpopularity, Jane knew what it was to be lonely. Having paid off Maltravers' gambling debts with her father's help and income from her quarries, respect for her in the community had grown. She never tried to press leases on the quarrymen as her husband had. Hearing Hetty singing at her work one day Jane encouraged her to join the church singers. 'We can ignore the funny looks together,' she said, making Hetty laugh.

It was true the Freers and Lackfords had a reputation, Hetty thought. Folk took notice when any of them were around. She occasionally overheard remarks such as '... that rogue's widow', meaning Jane, being 'well in with them Freers.' Once in the bakery she overheard Mrs Smith tell the baker's wife that being seventeen years younger than Squire, Charlie must have married him for position and money. Mrs Smith had six children and another on the way. Springing to her friend's defence, Hetty snapped, 'Better to be an old man's darlin' than a young man's slave!' Now folks watched their tongues with her.

Jane taught Hetty how to make new skirts and dresses from the unwanted clothes she and Amelia gave her.

In the shop Hetty had to mind her p's and q's, and to sound her h's. Yet try as she might she was hard put to shorten her vowels and lapsed into broad vernacular if she was upset. When her gran sneered at her efforts to better herself, she found her self-control still wanting.

'Why shouldn't I wash my hair on Saturdays?' she cried.

'I need to look me best in the shop, an' 'specially now I'm one o' the church singers.'

Biddy shrugged and sucked on her pipe. 'So where'd you git the money for they new clothes?' she bickered. 'If you be cheaten me wi' your wages—'

'Me new clothes, as you call 'em, ain't cost nothin'. They be altered hand-me-downs from Jane and Amelia. So stop judging' me by yer own rotten standards!'

'Oh aah! Where'd you git talk like that from, eh? Miss o-so-clever. An' 'tis Jane and Amelia now, is it?' Biddy gave an unpleasant cackle, 'Thee's getting conceited, maid!'

Hetty felt her cheeks burning. 'No I ain't! I always say Mrs, or Ma'am to their faces 'cause I respect 'em. But 'tis all right to other folk, especially now they got their new sign up for *The Amelia Jane Boutique*.'

She didn't bother to explain that Amelia used the French word for shop in memory of her 'aristo' mother who escaped from France during the terrible reign of terror. Instead she towelled her hair fiercely, pretending not to hear her gran's sarcastic remarks.

She told Maisie about it next time she called to see Arthur, but Maisie was busy.

'Don't take no notice,' she said, bustling around her kitchen. 'And if folk think Amelia Freer's getting stuck up 'twill give 'em something else to talk about.' Maisie's husband Dick, who never used to be tidy, now expected to see the house well kept, and his meal on the table when he came in. 'I don't know how I'll cope,' she added, 'when Charlie comes back and I have to work for her, too.'

'Knowing her she'll let you bring little Arthur with you,' said Hetty confidently.

Everyone looked forward to the Whit Tuesday Fair, and while Amelia and Jane tended their stall Hetty helped her gran in the fortune teller's tent. For the first time that evening she dressed up for the dance to be held in the upper room of the Dun Cow Inn. She donned a peacock-blue gown that set off her chestnut brown hair and put on her Sunday shoes. As usual Biddy's caustic comments made her prickly.

'You don't like seeing folks enjoy themselves do you, Gran? You'd rather they had ailments you can sell 'em pills and potions for.'

'Speakin' o' pills an' potions, 'tis 'bout time you learned a bit about it. Me old eyes ain't so good as they used ter be.'

As if she didn't have enough to do! Hetty sighed, but refused to be made to feel guilty. She bid her gran a cheery good night and left.

Nevertheless she was still shy in public and at the dance she was happy just to watch until, nudged by Sam Roper, Sandy Mason approached her. Blushing to the roots of his hair, for which he was nicknamed, Sandy dipped his head politely, 'Will you dance with me, Hetty?'

At thirteen he was tall as her, and equally bashful in company. He feels safe asking me, Hetty thought. He was probably as self-conscious about his freckles as she was about her plainness. She gave him her wide grin. 'I'll be glad to, Sandy.'

Soon, despite Sandy's hobnail boots, they became oblivious to anyone watching them practise the steps.

Luke Audley and Sam Roper were the most eligible males present. They gave all the unpartnered ladies a turn around the dance floor, even crusty Martha Hyer. Behind her fan Amelia nudged Jane, 'I believe your father's got his eye on Martha.'

'Perhaps.' Jane smiled. 'And how many times have you danced with Sam?'

'Oh, once or twice,' said Amelia dismissively, and

nodded at Tommy dancing with a classmate. Then it was time for a progressive reel when everyone partnered everyone else.

By the end of the evening Hetty was more flushed and happy than she'd ever been. It was midnight when Jane and her father drove her home in their pony trap.

'You looked lovely tonight,' Jane told her. 'And it's good to see you enjoying yourself with friends your own age.'

Hetty's self esteem soared, and not until they put her down near her cottage did she think of her gran. Tonight, having tasted real happiness, she felt sorry Biddy couldn't enjoy life more. She crept in quietly, hoping Biddy was asleep, but out of the darkness came the old woman's voice.

'What you skulkin' around for? I b'ain't asleep.'

'Oh Gran – you startled me!'

Hetty could see Biddy now, hunched over the fireplace in the glow of the dying embers, her white hair straggling from beneath her kerchief. Hetty felt a sliver of pity. Her gran was a lonely old woman.

'You needn't have waited up for me.'

'I had to make sure you got home all right. Nobody else cares about ye.'

'Mrs Maltravers and her dad brought me home,' said Hetty. 'There's lots of people who like me now. They respect me 'cause I'm good at me job.'

'Aah, they likes ye, but who really cares about ye – 'cepts me? Fools, the lot of 'em!'

Hetty was learning to take Biddy's sourness lightly thanks to Jane, and Luke especially. He'd encouraged her to confide in him. He said a sense of humour was the best way to combat adverse remarks whoever made them. Now she barked a laugh at the thought that the old crone actually cared about her.

'You got a funny way of showing it,' she said. 'I'm going on to bed. Thanks for waitin' up.' She had no intention of ending up bitter and twisted like her gran.

Biddy grunted as Hetty ran upstairs. Thic maid was getting too uppity.

'Oh aah,' she muttered, taking a last draw of her pipe. 'I were young an' happy once – until my pore Harold got drowned. Bloody gover'ment – fools the lot of 'em!'

Harry Cauldon had been up cliff fetching out the big stone needed during the French war. Stone was needed urgently for bigger docks, and defence towers along the south coast. One day they were loading a stone barge while the sea was choppy. As he guided a lowered block into the boat Harold lost his balance and fell overboard. He couldn't swim and was drowned, despite frantic efforts to save him. Biddy was left to bring up their baby daughter alone. Resentful of the government she grew bitter, and with her knowledge of herbs and remedies gained a reputation for witchcraft. She'd never believed in schooling, and being hard up made her miserly. When her chance came to make easy money by hiding smuggled goods she'd seen it as revenge on the government, robbing them of taxes as they'd robbed her of a husband. Anyway, what were taxes if not daylight robbery?

Incapable of expressing affection, Biddy allowed her daughter to run wild, for the less Maud knew about smuggling, the better. Then the girl got pregnant and never knew which lad was the father. Furious at the disgrace, Biddy threw her out. Talk was Maud fell in with a band of gypsies, but Biddy cared nothing about her daughter until the day she found baby Hetty on her doorstep. It was too much. Pleading poverty, she'd taken the child to the orphanage.

Biddy sighed, tapped out her pipe in the hearth and put it on the mantle-piece. Oh, she cared about Hetty, enough to worry what would happen to the maid when she was gone. What chance did a baseborn have, gettin' mixed up wi' the quality and their high-falutin' ways?

Chapter Five

∽

'I'm sorry you and Alan had to miss the Fair,' said Amelia when Charlie came to see her on her return home. 'It wasn't the same without you.'

Charlie smiled, 'I wouldn't want Biddy telling my fortune. I've had enough doom and gloom from Lady Kingsly.' She told her mother about the visit to Alan's relations, adding, 'But it was better than having them at Lackford Hall. I think Beulah is jealous that a common quarry maid was presented to royalty when she wasn't.'

'Especially as she went all the way to Lyme last year to see the Princess,' said Amelia, 'little knowing their royal highnesses were coming to Swanwick. What about the Scott-Wilsons, you get on all right with them?'

'Quite well,' Charlie replied. 'Adele is pleased for me. She's so different from Beulah, and I like Sylvia. She and Will both support the cause for the Tolpuddle men. She even went to that April demonstration, and she brought Will to the Kingsly's dinner.'

'Oh dear,' Amelia said. She gave Charlie a swift and anxious glance. 'I hope he won't get any false notions.'

'He worships the ground Sylvia walks on,' Charlie said, laughing. 'Thanks to Alan she's interested in our local affairs.'

But Amelia worried that Will was setting his sights too

high. 'I fear Will is mistaking this friendship for more than sympathy and understanding of the cause. Is Sylvia not the real attraction?'

'You wouldn't think so,' said Charlie, 'if you'd seen the look on his face when Beulah criticised the government for not doing more to put down the combinations. That woman's convinced those poor labourers deserve their sentence – thinks nothing could be worse than their existence.'

'And what does your husband think? I hope it won't become a bone of contention between you.'

Charlie shook her head thoughtfully, 'Beulah will always look down on me. She frowns on us mixing with common folk, as she calls them. But Alan knows I'm still a quarry maid at heart and he understands working men. Now that whole towns are growing up around the new industries he says the workers need more representation in Parliament. Will understands it all better than I do. Thank goodness we shall be away for the summer. We have to settle Isobel at her finishing school on the Continent. Don't worry, Ma,' she added. 'We'll not go near Paris, and Sylvia is coming to Switzerland as Isobel's chaperone.'

Relieved to hear it, Amelia quickly agreed that Will's main concern was his work. 'He'll soon become his own master with all the building going on in London. He tells me his present employer is too tight-fisted.' She changed the subject, 'What about your new housekeeper, and kitchen maid?'

'Mrs Maltravers has given some interviews already. She'll help me make the final choice.' Charlie grinned, 'After I have consulted Mrs B. of course.'

'What about Maisie while you're away?'

'She'll show the newcomers the ropes,' said Charlie, 'and when I return her baby should be sitting up and taking notice. That will make things easier when she comes to work full time. Anyway, she won't have too much to do. Alan wants to winter in London.'

'How fashionable,' said Amelia, delighted. 'He'll make a lady of you yet!'

★

The strikes and combinations continued throughout the summer. In June, workers in Leeds returned to their mills and dressing shops, and Beulah Kingsly had her new gown in time for the Grand Music Festival. Then the shoemakers went on strike. No sooner did one strike finish than another began, and the agitation for the release of the Dorchester labourers went on. Browsing through the papers helped Hetty to practise her reading. She listened when Jane or Mr Audley were talking to Amelia about the national situation to gain a better understanding. She heard Jane mention how some sympathetic MPs were keeping the Dorchester affair before Parliament.

'When Joseph Hume saw some better off people forming unions and administering oaths on their members, he questioned why the law's not enforced on them!'

'That will encourage the protesters,' said Amelia.

'Trouble is,' said Luke, 'the government associates reform with the unrest on the Continent. Members are very unsettled what with all the resignations and changes in leadership.'

Then, after a very hot spell in August, there occurred a week of heavy thunder storms. Swanwick folk were more concerned about their spoiled crops than events in Parliament.

'Good thing 'twasn't like this last year when we had the royal visit,' Hetty said to Amelia one morning as she wiped her boots on the doormat. The rain had cleared, but she was hard put to avoid muddy puddles.

'That's true,' said Amelia. 'It was a good time – and a bad time ...' She sighed, 'Such a lot has happened since then.'

Fearing she'd stirred up bad memories for Charlie's ma, Hetty said quickly, 'Let's hope the weather improves, or we shan't sell any bonnets.'

'Then we'll have to find another use for our straw plait, or some people will be out of work,' Amelia said ominously. 'A poor harvest can only increase the price of straw among other things.'

Hetty could have bitten her tongue. She was about to apologise for being melancholy when the shop bell rang. The post man poked his head round the door. 'Letter for you, Mrs Freer.'

'Thank you Mr Crabb.' Amelia smiled as she closed the door behind him, but her face clouded as she read the letter. When she spoke, Hetty was alarmed at the urgency in her tone. 'Hetty, run and fetch Mrs Maltravers. I must speak to her.'

Hetty obeyed at once, though wondering what was in the letter.

Underhill Manor was on the opposite side of the valley from the quarries. Hetty crossed the stream by the brewery and, heedless of the mud, took a short-cut across the fields. She found Jane in her garden inspecting the storm damage to her flower beds. Hetty delivered her message with panting breath.

'Mrs Freer never said why?'

'No, Ma'am,' Hetty gasped, 'but she looked awful worried.'

'Oh dear, I hope it's not bad news about Will.'

The same thought was in Hetty's mind, but she didn't

like to say so. Jane called her stable boy to saddle up her horse. 'Come Hetty, you shall ride pillion.'

Hetty clung on tight as they cantered up the lane and on to the highway where a line of stone wagons rumbled towards the shore. Jane slowed her horse to a trot and threaded her way past them, nodding to the drivers. They raised their whips in salute to her while staring at Hetty.

Any other time Hetty would have felt important, but now she was too anxious to care.

Jane's horse was up to his flanks in mud when they arrived at the shop.

'Take him to my stables,' Amelia told Hetty. 'Ask Bert to wash him down.' As Hetty hesitated, Amelia added, 'Come straight back, this matter concerns you, too.'

As soon as she'd handed Jane's mount to the ostler Hetty hurried back to the shop. Just in time she remembered her muddy boots and left them in the porch. She was relieved to hear the news was not about Will.

'The letter is from my Aunt Mary's doctor in Dorchester,' Amelia began. 'She's old and he fears she is dying. She was very good to me, giving me a home when Will was born. It was she taught me to plait straw. I must go to her.'

'Your father's death must have been a blow to her,' said Jane. 'Has she no one else?'

Amelia shook her head. 'She never married, her young man was killed in the American War. I wrote to her of course but never said how Father was shot. I told her it was an accident.'

Hetty wondered what all this had to do with her. Then Amelia said, 'Hetty, Mrs Maltravers will take care of the business side of things but you will be in charge of the shop. Can you manage that?'

'Oh yes, ma'am,' Hetty said eagerly. 'You can trust me.'

'I must prepare immediately,' said Amelia. 'The quarry

will have to look after itself until I return, which may not be for some time – oh dear –'

'Don't worry,' said Jane firmly. 'Father and I will see to everything, and Hetty has proved herself most reliable. I will drive you to Frometown tomorrow in time to catch the mail coach to Dorchester. Father will come in at closing time to lock up and see that everything is in order. Now Hetty, fetch my horse if you please.'

Chapter Six

Late summer 1834

⌒

Hetty felt proud and pleased by the responsibility laid on her. Her one regret was having to miss her lessons with Mr Audley. She worked hard, running errands while Jane looked after the shop, and made her outworkers bring their finished pieces in to collect their pay. Having to work all hours she was glad of the light evenings.

Biddy was no help. She still looked to her herbs and medicines and rarely had supper ready when Hetty came in. 'The fire went out while I was asleep,' she would say, or, 'I didn't have enough wood to keep it going.'

Then Hetty would have to re-kindle the fire and cook supper herself as well as tending the garden, and chopping wood for the next day.

'The least you could do is feed the chickens, Gran,' she said, trying not to show how irritable she felt. Biddy would only use it against her. Despite all this she felt useful and important to her employers. She began to plan new uses for plaited straw. Certain items like fans and table mats. Nammet bags for men's tools could be made with cheaper straw, and she devised carrying covers for the earthenware jars of tea or cider the men took with them to work.

Towards the end of August, Hetty was in the shop late

one afternoon sewing together strips of straw plait. When the doorbell tinkled she looked up to see Will Freer standing in the open doorway. Her work fell in her lap as she sat gaping at him. He looked tired, and seemed edgy.

'Where is everybody?' he asked, frowning. 'I called at the house, but no one was home, and at the stables the boy said something about Dorchester.'

'That's right,' said Hetty, flustered, but happy to see Will although he didn't greet her. 'Your ma had to go to her Aunt Mary. I thought she wrote to you.'

'Her letter must have passed me on the road,' said Will. He sat on the chair Hetty pushed towards him without a word of thanks. 'I've been travelling three days by mail coach and carrier cart to get here.'

'Oh,' said Hetty, embarrassed at her own ignorance. She knew little about the long journey from London. 'Can I get you a drink of water?'

'Yes, thanks. Where's Tommy, then?' He sounded like he thought it was her fault there was no one around.

'He's staying with Mrs Maltravers at Underhill Manor 'til your ma gets back,' she said as she filled a tumbler with water at the sink in the corner.

Will took the tumbler she thrust at him as if digesting the information. In a moment he looked at her again. This time he gave her a nod and asked more civilly, 'How long is Ma gone for?'

Hetty shook her head. 'It depends. She heard her Aunt Mary was dying and left in a hurry, because the aunt had been good to her when you were a babe.'

Picturing Will as a baby Hetty risked a smile and his expression softened.

'I knew *of* Aunt Mary,' he said, 'but I don't remember her. I was still a baby when me ma and dad came back here to live.'

Encouraged by this, Hetty asked, 'How long be you home for?

He shrugged, 'I dunno. What about my sister? I suppose she and Sir Alan have already left for the Continent?'

'Right after Miss Isobel's birthday, she's fourteen now.' Seeing his face set into a scowl Hetty understood. 'And Mistress Sylvia's gone with 'em as Miss Isobel's chaperone. Didn't you know?'

His disappointment showed with his clamped lips. Hetty yearned to say, *I'm* pleased to see you. Instead, with forced cheerfulness she said, 'Tommy will be pleased to see you, and your ma would be glad to know you're here. She's worried about the quarry 'cause somebody's got to pay the men's wages.'

Will merely grunted, and Hetty felt lost for something to say. She was relieved to see Luke Audley pass the window. 'Here's Mr Audley,' she cried. 'He's come to lock up – Tommy's with him.'

The doorbell tinkled and the old man stood in the doorway beaming. 'Will, what a pleasant surprise!'

Then Tommy shrieked, 'Will!' and leaped on him.

As he swung his young brother around Will's face broke into a grin. Thank goodness, Hetty thought.

'Your mother will be sorry she's missed you,' Luke said as they shook hands. 'Has Hetty told you?'

'Yes,' said Will, 'and I can manage the quarr for a bit–'

'What brings you home?' Luke asked. 'Is it the builders' strike?'

'Partly. I'm only one of thousands who stopped work rather than sign the declaration renouncing trades unions.'

'You're not a unionist, are you?' Luke asked, lifting his coat tails to sit down.

'No.' Will shook his head, 'I don't need to be. Quarrymen have their Ancient Company of Marblers and Stonecutters to protect them.' He added angrily, 'My foreman said they had a trade union fellow come down from up north. He didn't like being talked down to and sent the man on his way. But striking is the only weapon workers have. If merchants can fix their prices, why shouldn't a tradesman have the right to sell his labour at a fair price?'

'A good point, m'boy,' Luke said soberly. 'But workmen unite when their labour is most needed – and that infringes the rights of others. Think of the delay to the hospitals that are being built or improved–'

'People are bound to get hurt when the greedy rich force the workers to fight for their rights.' A muscle twitched in Will's jaw, 'The government abolishes slavery in the West Indies, yet they let their own countrymen starve! Did you know freed slaves are paid more than our labourers?'

Luke bowed his head. 'Truth is,' he said thoughtfully, 'as well as trades' unions the House of Lords is against dissenters – which many workers are.'

'And they're afraid because men have learned there is strength in unity,' Will growled. 'They oppose all the appeals and petitions on behalf of the Tolpuddle men. Well, the workers have to yield or their families will starve. Meanwhile I decided to come home and go round the quarries to see how they're doing.'

'Where will you stay?' asked Luke.

'I could go to your house by the stables and prepare a room for you,' Hetty suggested tentatively, 'and see your bed is aired.'

'No, it's all right, said Will, getting up. 'I'll take our old cottage with Sandy. It's nearer the quarr.'

'Then come to dinner tomorrow evening,' said Luke. 'Jane will want to hear all your news – bring Sandy too.'

Will thanked him, and nodded at Hetty who bobbed a curtsy.

'Everything in order, then Hetty?' Mr Audley smiled, 'Off you go home.'

'Thank you sir,' said Hetty, wishing she could have been invited to Underhill Manor, too. 'Good night.' Leaving him to lock up she followed the path by the stream, back to the cottage in the woods – and Granny Cauldon.

Will bought supper at the pie shop and climbed up the hill to the Freer's old home, his thoughts busy. Mostly he was disappointed at missing Sylvia, but he had plenty to do until she and the Lackfords returned. He would help with the harvest until Ma came home from Dorchester. He could pop into the shop and find out if there was any news about her return. The thought brought Hetty to mind. Finding her in almost sole charge of his ma's shop was a surprise. Once afraid of her own shadow she now seemed quite grown up. Will felt glad his ma had her help.

Next morning he called again at the Warren Stables. His favourite horse Hercules whinnied softly as he fondled the shire's velvety nose.

'Mornin' Will.' Bert the ostler lifted his cap politely.

'How's business?' Will asked him.

'Slowed down a bit since them heavy downpours,' said Bert, 'but it should improve now 'tis dried up. Them horses needed a rest anyway.'

'Why's that?'

'They bin overburdened, zir. They quarriers bin makin' do wi' dree instead o' vour.'

'Because it costs less I suppose,' Will muttered. He hated to see any animal treated badly. 'I'll speak to them about it, I'm going to see them now.'

The men in the Freer quarry were hard at work. Foreman Harris downed his mallet and chisel, clearly pleased to see Will. 'Glad you've come, guv'nor. I have to tell you the present seam of freestone be nigh on finished.'

'When Sir Alan gets back I'll see him about sinking another shaft,' Will promised. 'Meanwhile, the good news is London firms need all the slabs our quarries can provide to pave the city streets. Also, blocks for window sills, and steps for important buildings.'

At neighbouring family quarrs he was concerned by the complaints he heard.

'I thought you'd be glad of more orders,' he said to one owner, a Mr Chapman.

'Oh aah, 'tis all right for you, Will Freer,' the man grumbled. 'Squire don't charge you nothin' for cartin' the stone across his land.'

Will frowned. 'Since when have you been charged? It's our ancient right and custom to dig wherever there's good stone to be fetched out.'

'The farmers ain't disputin' that,' said Chapman, but they'm expectin' another bad harvest. They've already upped the cost o' hirin' their horses and wagons, now they charge us for crossin' their land.'

'That's a new one,' said Will. 'So that's why my horses are being made to struggle.'

Chapman shrugged. 'We have to fill our orders or the merchants'll get their stwun zomewhere else. It don't do us no good to go on strike.'

Everywhere Will went it was the same. The men were hard up with large families to clothe and feed. After the squalor he'd seen in the City Will wanted better for his own folk. He needed to think. Leaving the quarry land behind he climbed to the highest part of the downs. From here he could see the ridge of hills to the north, across east facing Swanwick Bay and around the headland to the open Channel in the south. A fleet of ships lay at anchor in the bay but there was little activity. It wouldn't do.

With his London contacts Will knew he could benefit Swanwick folk. Their stone was good, and the men were skilled in dressing it. Many left home to go and work on cathedrals, or places like Portsmouth to build docks and harbours.

By the time he and Sandy arrived at Underhill Manor that evening Will had decided what to do. 'I've saved a bit of money,' he told Jane Maltravers, 'I can afford to lease the whole of your strip from the cliff down to the highway.'

Jane was agreeably surprised, 'Even though that part of the cliff was used by smugglers?'

Will guessed she was probably thinking of his past involvement. The corners of his mouth turned up as he shrugged. 'That's all water under the bridge. There's still good big stone to be had if we use gunpowder.'

'I hope the farmers won't be upset by your giving quarrymen free access,' Luke warned.

'Too bad. They've got no right to charge for crossing the land and I shall see they don't.' Will didn't care if he sounded arrogant, he wanted fairness for his men.

'All right.' Jane smiled, 'I'll get the papers drawn up and you shall have your own land.'

Sandy looked at Will in admiration. One day he, too, would be his own master. Will had already promised him the job of foreman when he was older.

Hetty looked forward to Will popping into the shop in case of news from his mother. The first letter to arrive was to say the maiden aunt had died and Amelia must stay for the funeral and settle Aunt Mary's affairs.

Sometimes Hetty bumped into Will at the stables as she passed on her way to or from home, or whilst on her rounds. They made small talk about the weather or the harvest until Hetty overcame her shyness. She began to ask him about his work and life in London.

Will was happy to oblige. He told her about the railway being built between London and Birmingham. 'They're building another one to Greenwich village so there's plenty of work for everyone. Do you know, Hetty, thousands of people cross London Bridge every day!'

Hetty blinked and closed her mouth after a huge gasp. So many people were beyond her imagining, let alone the big City itself. He was right, though, she would hate the crowds. But she loved hearing about the omnibuses. 'What a fine sight they must be, with all them horses pulling 'em. Oh Will, I'd love a ride in one.'

'You need plenty of money to afford the fares,' said Will. 'Most of the workers live near their work 'cause they can't afford to ride. That's why their houses are shoved together,' he added. 'There's two or three families living in each one, and they have to share a privy in their tiny back yards. They've hardly room to breathe.'

Hetty pulled a face, 'I don't think I'd like London,' she said. 'Fancy Sir Alan's sisters living there!'

Will's mouth twisted with an ironic chuckle, 'They're all right. They can afford to live further out in big posh houses near nice green parks, where there's ducks and swans on a lake. On fine days they go driving in the parks in their carriages–'

'Oh my, have you seen 'em then?'

'I've been in the Kingsly's mansion ...' He told her about his visit when Charlie and Sir Alan returned from their grand tour. 'Sylvia insisted on taking me along, and I'm glad I was there for me sister's sake.' Will's grey eyes glowed a deep greeny-grey as he spoke about Sylvia. 'Have you ever met her, Hetty?'

'I did once, when I worked at Lackford Hall,' said Hetty, lowering her gaze. She wished Will hadn't mentioned Sylvia, but rather than spoil this newfound friendship she forced herself to add, 'I saw her at your sister's wedding. She looked beautiful, just like a princess.'

Will was smiling now, a shy, lovesick kind of smile, but not for her, Hetty.

'Sylvia is well connected with influential people, but she's no snob. She's as keen to see the Tolpuddle men freed as I am.'

Hetty sighed inwardly. He likes me, she thought, but his heart is on fire with admiration for Sylvia.

Chapter Seven

September 1834

‿

Amelia came home the first week in September feeling exhausted. She gladly accepted Jane's invitation to supper at Underhill. Tommy threw his arms around her neck and hugged her, and when Will arrived with Sandy the reunion was complete.

They plied her with questions about the county town of Dorchester, especially Tommy who was about to start school there.

'I hardly mixed with the fashionable set and their horse racing,' Amelia said, dryly. 'I was with Aunt Mary until she died. Then there was the funeral to organise, her belongings to sort, and arranging about the house which she's left to me. Rather than sell, I've asked an agent to rent it out, with the condition that you're to have lodgings there, Tommy, while you're at school.'

The smile on her face faded as she looked at Will.

'I received Aunt Mary's visitors – her friends were mostly church people, and from the gossip among them and the servants I heard what happened to the families of those Tolpuddle men.

'I wondered if you might have news,' said Will, his face grim. 'I suppose the wives have been ignored.'

'They haven't seen their men since they men left for work the morning they were arrested,' said Amelia. Indignation flashed in her eyes, 'They weren't even allowed to say goodbye when they left Dorchester, let alone before they sailed.'

'That is so sad...' Jane's voice shook.

'And you were right about Frampton's influence,' Amelia told Will. 'The wives tried to appeal for parish relief but he told his officers not to give it to them.'

'Fancy making them suffer for their men's offences,' cried Jane. 'How cruel.'

'That's what's worse,' said Amelia. 'Those poor, destitute women asked to put their children into the poor house while they went into service to earn their living. Then *they* were threatened with transportation!'

'What a world we live in,' said Jane. 'People struggling to survive on a pittance from one day to the next – after their fathers and grandfathers fought for King and Country, too. It's so unfair!'

'And this is England,' said Will bitterly. 'Country of laws and justice!'

Amelia nodded. 'Fortunately, members from all the unions are giving what they can to a relief fund. Those wives were starving by the time they received help. Now a shopkeeper from Bere Regis brings them money.'

'That's what the special committee is all about,' said Will. 'They'll accept donations from any sympathiser.'

'I dread to think what would happen otherwise.' With sarcasm in her tone Amelia added, 'Frampton's told the farmers to increase their labourers' wages now – so long as they're not members of any union.'

'Pity he hadn't done that before,' said Will. 'It would have saved a heap of trouble.'

When the meal finished and they relaxed in easy

chairs, Amelia turned her attention to her own business. 'Tell me about the shop,' she asked Jane. 'Has Hetty coped all right?'

'Yes,' said Jane. 'Hetty works hard to keep everything in order – *and* she has her grandmother to look after. She'll be glad you're home, she looks so tired.'

'And I miss her visits,' said Luke. 'Hopefully they will resume now you're back, Mrs Freer.'

'I hardly recognised Hetty,' said Will. 'She's so different from that shabby little scaredy-cat she used to be. She looks quite smart – almost pretty when she smiles.'

'Working for your mother has done wonders for her confidence,' said Luke, and she's made good progress with her learning.'

Will grinned. 'Old Biddy won't care for that.'

'No,' said Amelia, 'but she likes the wages Hetty takes home each week.'

The conversation turned to Will's work. When he explained his plans his mother said, 'How will you manage once you've spent your savings?'

Will shrugged, 'It'll take a while to get started,' he admitted. Then he changed the subject by asking after his sister and brother-in-law.

'They're coming back when Isobel's school term starts,' said Amelia. 'Will you still be here, Will?'

'I hope so,' said Will. 'The best seams are on Alan's land and we need to open a new vein. Dad's old map shows where to go deep for paving stone. But I must return to London as soon as harvest is over.'

'I thought you didn't need permission,' said Luke, 'so long as you don't dig up crops.'

'That's the custom,' said Will, 'but some farmer's bound to make a fuss, so I need Alan's approval.' He was really hoping that Sylvia would be with the Lackfords.

As soon as the newlyweds returned during harvest Will called to explain his situation.

'I've decided to start my own business,' he told Sir Alan. 'With so many district boards in London there's plenty of work from the parish vestries. They're responsible for paving the streets. I will need kerb stones and gutters as well as squares. I shall order from all the local quarries, but we must open a new mine as our own is worked out.'

Sir Alan raised a cautionary finger.

'I wish you well,' he said, 'but try not to upset the farmers.' Before Will could argue the case for the quarrymen the squire added, 'Listen Will, if you're going to export stone you'll need to lease a wharf in one of the East End basins. I'd like to invest in your enterprise.'

'There's no need, sir,' Will stammered, embarrassed. 'I would not take advantage of our connections.'

'Nonsense lad, we are family now. Besides, I have professional friends in Town who might help once they know you have my backing. I shall give you a letter of introduction.'

It was more than Will dared hope for, but Sir Alan waved aside his thanks.

'If you'll excuse me I must go and see shepherd Tom about the yearling lambs.' He tactfully left Will and Charlie on their own in the drawing room.

Will thought his sister looked thinner, but her eyes were shining and her face glowed with health. 'I must call on Ma,' she said. 'I have something to tell her.'

'She'll be glad to see you,' said Will. 'She worries.'

'I know,' Charlie said dismissively. 'Oh Will – Switzerland is beautiful – you should see the mountains and the lakes. Isobel is learning to ski, she loves it there already – ' Charlie stopped, 'What's up?'

'Where's Sylvia?' Once again Will faced disappointment.

Charlie gave him a knowing look, not without sympathy. 'Sylvia left us at Weymouth, and took the mail coach to London,' she said. 'Her parents are just as anxious about her travelling the Continent as our Ma is about me.' Seeing the disappointment on Will's face she put a comforting hand on his and said, 'Please tell Ma I'll come and see her in the shop tomorrow?'

Amelia expressed relief that her daughter and Alan had returned safely, 'What with all the goings on in France, and summer storms.'

'Yes, the storms held us up,' said Charlie, 'and we never set foot in France–' She hesitated, then added, 'Did you hear about the convict ship that got wrecked off Boulogne in August?"

'No. Was it bad?'

'I'm afraid so,' said Charlie slowly. 'We heard about it a few days after it happened – and I wanted to tell you while we were alone.'

'Why? What's it got to do with me?'

'Ma, she was the *Esmerelda*–'

Amelia gasped, '*Esmerelda*?' she echoed. 'Father's ship. So that's how they used her after she was sequestered.'

'She was driven on to a sand bar where the gale and high tide broke her up,' Charlie added. 'They say everyone was drowned.'

'What a sorry end to your grandfather's ship.' Amelia sighed, 'Well, she won't carry any more thieves and murderers. I can't say I'm sorry about that.'

'Now, Ma, I have some much better news.' The doleful expression on Amelia's face turned to joy as Charlie added, 'You're going to be a grandmother!'

'Charlie – that's wonderful! When?'

'Next spring – by Easter.'

Mother and daughter laughed and hugged each other.

'Fancy Will and Tommy being uncles,' Amelia said happily.

'You'll be the only grandparent,' said Charlie, and you'll see a lot more of him, or her, than either of the aunts will.'

Amelia made a comical grimace, 'I suppose Beulah and Adele will have to be invited to the christening. From what you and Will tell me about Beulah, I am not looking forward to meeting her!'

Charlie laughed. 'We'll cross that bridge when we come to it, but I'll make sure you have a more important place than either of them.'

With such welcome news, the fate of *Esmerelda* was soon forgotten.

Another poor harvest wasn't much to celebrate, but when Sir Alan decided to carry on with tradition Swanwick folk weren't about to let a holiday pass them by.

'It *is* Dick and Maisie's first anniversary of their marriage,' Charlie said.

At Lackford Hall Hetty sat with Dick and Maisie Farmer. Amelia and Jane sat with their relations, and Tommy and Sandy joined other youngsters. It was a simple meal of cold meat and pickles with jacket potatoes washed down with locally brewed ale or cider, of which there was no shortage. A toast was drunk to Charlotte Lady Lackford and her husband, and Sir Alan proposed a toast to Dick and Maisie for their first year of marriage. Then followed toasts to anything and everything to do with folks' livelihoods and the merriment increased. Meanwhile Charlie and Sir Alan mingled with their guests, exchanging greetings and news.

Later, when tables and benches were being moved aside to make space for dancing, and the musicians took up their positions, Hetty looked around for Will. His face bleak, he seemed to be the only person not enjoying himself. She guessed he was brooding over Sylvia and wished she could cheer him up.

Sir Alan and Charlie led the first dance then more couples joined them. Hetty hoped Sandy would ask her to dance. Just as she caught his eye, Dick pulled Maisie up. 'You'll look after the baby, won't you, Hetty?'

So Hetty had to content herself with watching. At least baby Arthur was asleep. By the time Dick and Maisie sat down again Sandy was with foreman Harris' daughter. Hetty plucked up her courage and went to talk to Will.

'I suppose you'll be going back to London, soon,' she began.

'I can't wait,' Will said, then tried to disguise his bad humour by telling her about his plan to start out on his own. His mood began to lighten seeing Hetty listening wide-eyed. She was easy to talk to and seemed genuinely interested in his work, and hearing about the local stone being used in London's grand buildings. Then he noticed how her kingfisher blue gown set off her glossy chestnut hair, the freckles on her rosy cheeks, and the way her wide smile lit up her green eyes. She wasn't so unattractive after all.

'You look nice,' he said.

'Thanks, Will.' Hetty blushed furiously, delighted to be complimented by him.

Near by Amelia saw how animated Will became in Hetty's company. The maid said something that caused him to laugh and her to blush as she looked up at him.

Amelia stopped telling Jane about her coming grandchild, and nodded in Will's direction. 'Will and Hetty have become well acquainted while I was away.' Her lips tightened, 'She can't take her eyes off him.'

Jane followed Amelia's gaze. 'I'm surprised Will's not dancing. I've seen several young maidens look hopefully his way.'

'He never was very sociable,' said Amelia, 'and London's changed him. With that awful smuggling business behind him he's more sure of himself. He's also making up for missing his education when he left school at nine.'

'He certainly knows all there is to know about stone,' said Jane. 'I think he'll do well, and he has the stables to fall back on.' She turned to watch the dancers. 'My nephew and your Charlotte are a handsome couple.' She sighed, 'You're lucky, Amelia, to have grandchildren to look forward to.'

'Yes,' Amelia murmured, watching Will lead Hetty into a dance. 'But I fear Will's hopes are better than his judgement.'

First he set his sights too high, on Sylvia, but surely he could do better than Hetty. Much as she valued her service, Amelia thought Hetty could never become more than a shop girl. She was looking forward to having grandchildren, but not by that maid. Will had connections now he was becoming a self-made man.

Amelia smothered a sigh. It was just as well he was going back to London. When she'd settled Tommy's school fees perhaps she could spare something to invest in Will's new venture. At least he had enough sense to get established before thinking about marriage. Hopefully, by then, he would find someone more suitable.

After Will left Hetty missed their little chats. She knew he longed to see Mistress Sylvia, and they were bound to meet when Charlie and Sir Alan spent the season in London. There would be no place for her in Will's thoughts while he mixed with high society at balls and dinner parties. I should be satisfied we're friends, Hetty told herself, and glad to resume my lessons with Mr Audley.

Luke sensed a change in her. 'Hetty's growing up,' he observed to Jane.

'She's nearly sixteen – at that romantic age,' Jane said. 'And she's attracted to Will, but he's too busy improving himself. Anyway, if he and Hetty … Amelia wouldn't like it.'

'Ah,' Luke sighed. 'What the young go through.'

Not only the young, thought Jane. She was not so young when she was wooed and won by the Hon. Simon Maltravers, only to find he'd married her for money. When she proved barren, he lost interest in her and gambled away her dowry. Having missed out on true love Jane sympathised with Hetty. Yet, given time, she and Sandy might … they were well suited, and had things in common. They'd spent their early years in the same orphanage, and now were part of the Freer circle. Perhaps a little matchmaking wouldn't go amiss. The only trouble was, Hetty was a young woman and Sandy still a boy.

Even so, Jane decided, it wouldn't hurt to bring them together whenever possible. The next occasion where that could happen would be bonfire night in November when the nation celebrated the saving of King and Parliament. Much as working folk despised that burdensome institution, the burning of 'Guy Fawkes' was a pleasure not to be missed. She would have a word with her nephew. An entertainment that took folks' minds off the poor harvest and the bitter winter months ahead would be appreciated.

Chapter Eight

Autumn 1834

⌒

Had Hetty known, her imaginings were far from reality. Spare time was a luxury Will could ill afford.

He thought disparagingly of how a young man in polite society might spend all day studying then take his ease after hours. But not him. He had to shake off his weariness after the day's toil to study in the evenings, so determined was he to be worthy of one day asking Sylvia for her hand in marriage.

As he'd expected, when he returned to London the builders' strike had floundered. His employer, who had lost business, was preparing to move on. He accepted Will's offer to buy his unused supply of stone, then, using Sir Alan's investment fund Will took over the yard and leased a wharf in Pimlico Basin.

It was a struggle at first but gradually Will's persistence paid off. He called at the first address Sir Alan had given him, the office of a parish surveyor, and obtained a contract to begin paving that district's streets. Next he went to the public house which he knew two of his former workmates frequented, and who were presently unemployed.

'Thought I'd find you two "clergymen" here,' he said to Jimmy Priest and Johnny Parsons, and explained what he wanted. They agreed to join him, and all three drank to the success of their venture.

That night Will wrote to his quarry foreman in Swanwick ordering paving stones. Fortunately, while he had to settle his expenses and complete the work before being paid, the parish vestry advanced the money for the stone. By the time he'd hired a horse and cart he had nothing left to pay his bed and board but he managed to sweet-talk his landlady into waiting for his rent. To chop wood for her fires was no problem, and on wash days he helped her to mangle the bed linen.

He called on more of Sir Alan's acquaintances. One was a speculator in house property; another, an architect, was none other than Sylvia's older brother Sidney Scott-Wilson. Hoping to make a good impression Will thought it best to keep to business terms. This new acquaintance fired his determination. He explained about the good building stone he could import from Swanwick, and how it would take a polish for use as ornamentation. 'London firms need window sills, and steps for grand buildings – then there's gutters and kerb stones …'

Young Mr Scott-Wilson approved of Will's enthusiasm. 'You are enterprising, Mr Freer,' he began, 'I'm sure I can get you orders. Let us hope your quarrymen can keep up their output.'

It felt good to pay out wages that first time and Will began to take his ease. He visited the London sights on Sundays and explored the dockland. Walking the slum-lined narrow streets reminded him of the thousand or more houses already demolished to make way for the new St Katharine's Dock near the Tower. The same thing would happen to these hovels if the railway bosses got their way. Only property owners were paid compensation. It was another example of the way the poor were downtrodden.

I'd rather be poor in the country than here, Will thought.

He pushed aside such thoughts as he strolled past Westminster Palace, home to Parliament. Being a Dorset stonemason with a pedigree harking back to the dim past, he was interested in the City's great buildings. He devoted part of his study time to reading about the historic buildings, and took pride in knowing they were built by men like himself with, perhaps, an ancestor among them. He saw nothing, however, to persuade him that Parliament's members were honourable. They arrived dressed, not in their Sunday best as he expected, but in everyday clothes. Some actually rode up to the House in muddy hunting gear, spurs, crop and all. And these were supposed to be his betters.

The Commons, he learned, used ancient St Stephen's Chapel that once served King Edward VI. Even older was Westminster Hall built in the time of William Rufus, son of the Conqueror. In fact, Will mused, it was the Normans' passion for building castles and great cathedrals that had given the stone trade its impetus.

One windy evening in mid-October he stayed late at his yard, sorting out orders and accounts in the shed that served as an office. Next day was pay day. Will turned out his pockets and found just enough cash to pay his mates. He locked the money safely away, padlocked the hut, and began walking back towards his lodgings. Head down, deep in thought wishing he could spare a bit more to give the relief fund for the wives of the Dorchester labourers he was jostled twice before he noticed the streets were unusually busy.

It was late, yet crowds of people were hurrying towards the river. He looked up. Above Westminster Abbey the moon shone in a cloudless sky. Then Will saw it, an unnatural red glow on the skyline. Too late for sunset, there was only one thing it could be – fire!

He heard the frantic clanging of a hand bell and jumped out of the way just in time. A scarlet and brass fire engine tore past, its crew yelling at people to get out of the way of the careering horses.

'What's going on?' Will asked a passer by.

'Westminster Palace is on fire,' the man cried. 'The Houses of Parliament are burning!' Swept along by the crowd Will found himself running until he reached Westminster Bridge.

It was thronged with people. Tradesmen's apprentices and college students clambered all over the parapet for a better look, their heads stuck out through the balustrades like gargoyles. Chimney sweeps and delivery men stood on carts jeering derisively. They seemed elated because Parliament was being destroyed. Will jostled his way through the crowd to see for himself.

Confusion was everywhere. Dragoons had been brought in to stop the crowd hampering the fire-fighters. Men's shouts relayed back what was happening as flames broke through the windows of the House of Lords and spread to the House of Commons. Fed by plaster-covered timber structuring, wooden floors and benches, low beamed ceilings and leaking gas pipes, it was an inferno. The crowd cheered and clapped as amid the smoke sparks shot into the air, fanned by the wind.

Will saw several fire engines assembled whose crews were trying to save the Law Courts. They used grappling irons to strip the roof so the engines could play on the interior. But the pumps were hindered when the out-flowing tide lowered the level of the Thames. Even so the river was crowded with boats and barges full of sight-seers.

Will craned his neck to see when several ministers and members of the royal family arrived on the scene. A business man pointed out Lord Melbourne, and Mr Hume.

When the chief fire-fighter spoke to the group the Duke of Cumberland ordered him to concentrate on saving Westminster Hall.

The desperate fire officer gesticulated wildly.

'The hammer beams in the roof are too brittle, they'll burn like tinder!'

He caused more uproar by directing his men to pull down the surrounding coffee houses and pubs to stop the flames reaching the ancient building. Even the politicians began to man the pumps while the firemen dragged their hoses up over the roof-tops to douse the beams.

Until then Will shared the same sentiments of the crowds who cheered each spectacular crash of walls or roof. It was here the rules and laws were made that caused ordinary men misery. Here was where they sat, those rich ministers who encouraged and influenced the fate of the Tolpuddle men. It served them right. Let them find out what it was like to have their lives destroyed, everything taken away!

But not all thought like that. Some of the spectators broke away from the crowd to help the overworked fire-fighters. They formed a human chain to the river, and passed buckets of water from hand to hand to be carried up ladders to the roof.

Will watched the grimacing faces of the men struggling at the pumps. In the reflection from the flames they looked like demons in a medieval painting. My God, it's like hell! It was then he felt for the men of old who built the Hall; of how they'd left homes and family to build this great City. So he volunteered to climb a ladder and help pass the buckets of water to the men clambering over the roof. The walls were thick, but dampening down the roof was the only way to save the building.

Hours passed that felt like days until at last, sweaty

and exhausted, Will became aware he was no longer being showered by hot ash. Glory be – the wind had changed with the turn of the tide! Even so, not until dawn when the fire was finally under control could he and the others rest their aching arms and shoulders.

Will's sore eyes were watering. His throat was parched and painful from choking on smoke and fumes. He went to the nearest public house to slake his thirst. It was crowded with jubilant bystanders as well as weary fire-fighters with smoke blackened faces and scorched hands. The general feeling was elation, and Will wished the ministers could hear the jokes and remarks that were bandied about amid raucous laughter. The habits of MPs had been purged, not by reform, but by fire.

Will downed his pint and stumbled away. The sun had risen by the time he reached his lodgings. Too weary and nauseous to care about losing a day's work he crawled into bed and slept.

He was woken at midday by insistent knocking on his door. He tumbled bleary-eyed out of bed, pulling the coverlet round him. He opened the door a crack to see his landlady stood there. 'Wh-what's up?'

'There's two gents downstairs wantin' a word with you. Your clergymen, so they say. Don't look much like clergymen to me!'

'Oh, crumbs!' Will suddenly remembered it was pay day. 'I'm coming, tell 'em.' He stumbled to the washstand, splashed his face in cold water and hurriedly got dressed.

'Sorry chums, I was up all night – at the fire–'

'So were we, guvnor,' said Jimmy Priest, 'lugging buckets of water around. Didn't see you in all that crowd.'

'We thought we'd be in trouble being late for work,' Johnny Parsons said. 'When we couldn't find you we came here.'

'Come on then,' said Will. 'Let's get you paid then go and see the damage.'

'Don't you want nuffink to eat?' queried his landlady.

'I'll be back,' Will told her. 'Don't feel like work today.'

His mates exchanged gleeful looks as they hurried to their stonemason's yard to collect their wages.

The smell of the charred ruins met them before they arrived at last night's fire scene. The smouldering shell of broken arches and blackened beams was an horrific sight. The House of Commons was unrecognisable, and the Lords' Painted Chamber was badly damaged. Among the pools of water and fallen plaster, sodden documents and works of art littered the cobblestones. Amid the rubble and ashes Westminster Hall alone stood whole. Workers picked their way through the debris, and soldiers carried bundles of papers and salvaged furniture to the Speakers Garden. Fusiliers on guard had orders to shoot any looters.

'Divine retribution for recent parliamentary reforms,' murmured Jimmy Priest..

'There is no House of Lords,' said Johnny Parsons, mimicking the way his 'betters' spoke. They are extinguished, Sir!'

Some folk had travelled from as far away as Brighton to stare. It seemed the whole world had come to gawp with wagons and horses trampling the mess. Feeling nauseous again, Will walked over Westminster Bridge while his mates went off to a pub. He hoped the breeze would refresh him. Among the newspaper men was a young reporter named Dickens, some of whose work he'd read, while an unkempt-looking elderly artist sketched the scene. Will was peering over his shoulder when a gentle touch on his shoulder startled him.

'Here you are, Will! We called at your yard but it was all locked up. Isn't this terrible!'

Will turned to see Sylvia, with her father by her side. Mr Scott-Wilson nodded.

'Sylvia! Er – good day, sir.' Will wished he didn't look so haggard, and wearing clothes that reeked of smoke. 'I was up 'til dawn,' he added apologetically, 'helping the fire-fighters – I felt too groggy for work, and slept all morning.'

He needn't have worried. Sylvia expressed only admiration for him.

'You were there,' she exclaimed, 'fighting the fire!'

'I was with the men working to save Westminster Hall,' Will said.

'And so you did!' Sylvia cried, as if he'd done it single-handed. Clasping her hands she turned to her father, 'He must come to dinner this evening, and tell us about it, mustn't he, father?'

'Yes, indeed.' Mr Scott-Wilson smiled agreeably, 'An heroic effort m'boy. Now we must be on, I have to meet Lord Kingsly and other colleagues – find out how the fire started.'

Sylvia kissed Will's cheek, 'See you this evening, Will.'

'Thank you, I look forward to it.' Will's heart sang. 'I'm curious to know what happened.'

He returned to his lodgings, still with the feel of Sylvia's soft lips on his cheek, and slept again. He awoke refreshed. After a wash and shave he put on his best Sunday shirt and suit.

The Scott-Wilson's 18th century house was soundly built of brick and stone, and less pretentious than the Kingslys' mansion. Will's practised eye noted the uncluttered rooms were finely proportioned with well-made doors and windows. A graceful staircase served the family while the servants used a back staircase. The furniture was dignified and pleasant, making Will feel comfortable. But his enthusiasm was dashed when his other in-laws arrived. The Kingslys were also keen to hear his version of events.

Sipping sherry before the meal, Will explained how he came to witness the fire, and the way the fire-fighters fought to save the ancient Hall. He toned down his description of the crowd's elation. The Kingslys wouldn't like to hear that. There would be enough adverse comments in the newspapers.

'Fortunately the wind changed,' he finished modestly. 'That helped the most.'

During the meal he asked Mr Scott-Wilson, 'Have you heard, sir, how the fire began?'

'Apparently,' said Mr Scott-Wilson, 'they were burning a load of old tally sticks, to make space in the Exchequer for the Court of Bankruptcy.'

Will remembered being taught at school about the ancient use of tally sticks as business receipts. The sum was notched on the stick before splitting it lengthways, and each person in the transaction received half.

'I knew such overcrowding would cause trouble one day,' said Lord Kingsly. His jowls wobbled as he shook his head, 'But I never envisaged anything like this.'

Will asked, 'If they were no use, why were the tally sticks kept?'

'They made good kindling for the palace fires,' said Mr Scott-Wilson while Beulah looked down her nose at Will for interrupting.

'Do go on, Uncle Mervyn,' said Sylvia, winking at Will.

'They should have made a bonfire in the Exchequer Yard,' said Kingsly, 'but the Clerk of the Works, the fool, decided they should be fed into the under-floor coal furnaces. In their zeal to finish work by five, instead of feeding them in a few at a time the stokers overloaded the stoves. By six the whole place was on fire.'

For a moment there was shocked silence around the dinner table. Then Beulah exclaimed, 'Really, I wouldn't be surprised if those workmen didn't do it on purpose – the way they all behave these days with their wretched strikes!'

'It's a pity they didn't give the tally sticks to needy folk for their winter fires,' Will retaliated. He managed to stop himself adding how stupid and blinkered he thought politicians were.

Beulah turned red, then purple as she looked at her husband as if expecting him to put Will in his place. Both were saved by the intervention of Sylvia's brother.

'Tell you what,' Sidney said suddenly, 'the government now has the opportunity to rebuild the Houses with plenty of space for all their needs.'

'That will come,' said his father, 'but at present they have to find somewhere for the House to sit for the next session.'

Will was thankful when the evening ended and he could return to his lodgings. He looked forward more than ever to seeing his sister when she and Alan came to winter in London.

Three days later the ruined palace debris still smouldered, and Will wrote to Amelia to say he wouldn't be home for Christmas. '*But I hope to spend Christmas Day with Charlie and Alan.*

'*They say the fire was the worst in London since the great fire back in the time of Charles II. The King offered the Privy Council the use of Buckingham Palace but they preferred to sit among the ruins of the Painted Chamber. They decided it would be best to fit up temporary rooms on the old site and have them ready for next Session. Thanks to me posh brothers-in-law my mates and me have more than enough work. There's plenty now for everyone.*

'The thing that bothers me most,' he finished, 'is what a set-back it will be for the cause of the Tolpuddle men. Their plight will be the last thing on MPs' minds.'

Chapter Nine

Winter 1834-35

∽

'Ugh!' Amelia Freer winced when she read about the rats scuttling from the fire. The distraction they caused, running over people's feet, gave pickpockets a lovely time.

'*I left my coat on one of the engines while I was helping the firefighters,*' Will had written. '*There was no money in the pockets, but I'm afraid someone stole the cambric handkerchief you gave me on my birthday.*' He was 20 in September.

Hetty was included in hearing Will's news but she didn't mention with what glee her gran received word of the terrible fire.

'Wish I'd-a bin theer,' Biddy cackled. 'I should love to a' zeen it. Zomebody must a' finished off what ol' Guy Fox started. An' about time, too!'

Jane Maltravers said, 'Bonfire night next month will seem quite tame.' She'd helped some young lads to make an effigy, stuffing with straw old cast off garments. They carried it around the village in a chair lashed to two poles crying, 'Penny for the Guy!' The collection was to pay for fireworks. On the beach, a pile of rubbish was added to each day for the bonfire. Finally, 'Guy Fawkes' was propped up on top.

Despite the dank misty evening the villagers appeared to enjoy November 5th more than usual. Hetty joined Sandy and the other youngsters whooping and squealing as they leapt away from jumping squibs. The spinning Catherine wheels were Hetty's favourite and she put her fingers in her ears when the crackers went off 'bang!' A huge cheer went up when the guy caught alight.

Amelia looked askance at Jane and her father and said wryly, 'They seem to forget that burning Guy Fawkes is supposed to celebrate the *saving* of Parliament.'

Ten days later Luke Audley came into the shop waving his paper.

'I don't know what this country's coming to. There's nowhere for Parliament to sit, and now the King has prorogued it again!'

Hetty had no idea what 'prorogued' meant, then Jane said, 'His Majesty seems to be in the habit of interrupting Parliament's sessions, making them stop and start.'

Thanks to her interest in the cause of the Tolpuddle men, however, Hetty was vaguely familiar with some of the great names being gossiped about in the papers. After old Lord Grey retired, Earl Spencer died and Lord Althorpe, who had supervised the saving of Westminster Hall, replaced the earl in the House of Lords. Meanwhile, it seemed King William and his parliament were wrangling. Lord Melbourne had to travel to the Royal Pavilion in Brighton, where the king had gone after inspecting the fire damage, to consult his majesty on re-organising the Cabinet. The king disapproved his choice of members.

'I suspect Melbourne didn't like it when Wellington was sent for,' Amelia said.

'No,' said Luke Audley. 'And his majesty has asked Sir Robert Peel to come back from Italy. It will be December by the time he gets back.' Looking at his paper he added, 'Seems quite a shock to some people. It says here that Melbourne blames the queen for the king's actions.'

'Fancy a man in his position insulting their majesties like that!' Jane exclaimed.

'King William was furious,' said Luke. He drove back to Town and dismissed the whole lot of 'em.'

Hetty gave a huge sigh.

'What's that for?' asked Amelia. The girl looked quite forlorn.

Hetty shook her head, 'If folks in high places carry on like that, what hope have the Tolpuddle men of a pardon?' She so wanted it for them, and for Will.

'That's what Will says,' said Amelia. 'He's afraid their cause will be forgotten.'

'And the trades unions have collapsed,' said Luke. 'Workers are afraid to join for fear of suffering the same dreadful fate as those labourers.'

★

Will and his mates were kept busy in the workforce, shaping blocks of stone and sawing timber to help fit up the Painted Chamber for the Lords. The earthy smell of stone dust, and scent of new wood, was sweet after the recent stink of smouldering debris. By Christmas the room was nearly finished.

Charlie and Sir Alan came with Sylvia to see how the repairs progressed. Will saw that his sister's thickening waistline was disguised by the velvet cloak she wore. She looked a real lady and he was proud to be her brother. Then he felt his colour rise at Sylvia's friendly greeting.

'My parents have invited you all to join us for Christmas dinner,' she said. 'Mother thought Charlotte should not be put to any trouble. It should be fun,' she added. 'My brother Sidney, whom you've met, will be there with his family.'

'You'll come, won't you Will?' said Charlie.

'If I don't have to work,' said Will. 'We still have the other room to sort out.' The second room had to be finished by February for Parliament's next session, and he was eager to resume his own business.

'Uncle Mervyn will see to it that all the workmen have Christmas Day off, so you must come. Besides,' Sylvia added, 'there's someone I want you to meet.'

Will looked forward to the occasion, especially as after church the Kingslys were to go to their own home to entertain Sir Mervyn's elderly parents. He would surely be able to find a few moments alone with Sylvia. His stomach knotted in anticipation. The person she wanted him to meet, he guessed, was probably a new business contact. Already his future seemed brighter.

On Christmas morning Will dressed in his Sunday best, and placed the presents he'd saved money to buy in his carpet bag. He'd gone to considerable trouble at the market in Portabello Road. He bought a crocheted baby shawl for Charlie and Alan, and an embroidered runner for the Scott-Wilson's piano. He hoped it would be acceptable. He'd searched for something special for Sylvia. At length he decided on a hair brush and mirror for her dressing table. They would remind her of him every day.

The Lackfords called for him in their carriage and drove to St Martin's-in-the-Fields where they joined Alan's relations for morning service. A tall stranger was with the Scott-Wilsons, he must be the person Sylvia wanted him to meet. The man had the easy familiarity of an overnight house guest so perhaps he was a relation.

Will's hopes of sitting next to Sylvia in church were soon dashed. He found himself in the pew behind with the Lackfords. At nearly twelve Hugh had grown tall and sturdy; auburn haired Isobel was fifteen and quite ladylike. However both youngsters were friendly and well behaved;

if they were bored, they didn't show it. They were indeed growing up.

To Will's annoyance Sylvia sat between her parents and the tall stranger. She turned to smile at him and nod a greeting. It wasn't seemly to chat in church, so Will had to wait until later for a proper introduction. During the service Sylvia's hat obscured her beautiful flaxen hair, but the scent of her perfume wafting back to him was a pleasure to inhale. When the liturgy required them to stand he admired her trim figure and rustling skirts.

Afterwards, when the congregation gathered to chat outside, Sylvia introduced the stranger to Will. 'This is my dear friend George Stanley whom I met on the continent. He's a government courier, recently returned from Italy.'

Some five years older than Sylvia, the courier was well built, handsome, and clean shaven with dark curly hair and sideburns. Will immediately felt self conscious of his own unruly thatch of tawny hair, but he looked the fellow in the eye as they shook hands and nodded. 'Please to meet you, sir.'

His mood lightened when Sylvia smiled at him and murmured, 'We'll talk later.'

As Sir Alan's carriage approached the Scott-Wilsons' house, Sylvia and her parents waited to greet them. Inside, presents were laid out ready to be exchanged, with port and sherry served before dinner.

Will felt twinges of jealousy seeing Sylvia being so friendly with George Stanley, unaware that Charlie was watching him.

Charlie nudged him. 'Those two have a lot to catch up on and think, Will, George knows people in high places. I'm sure Sylvia will persuade him to back the cause for the Tolpuddle men.'

Yes, Will thought, that must be it, George could prove

useful in gaining attention for the petitions. He was completely unprepared for the shock when at the end of an excellent Christmas dinner Mr Scott-Wilson stood up and announced Sylvia's engagement to Mr George Stanley.

'As you know, my daughter bore with great fortitude the tragic loss of her husband after only a few months of marriage. She deserves this chance of happiness and I am most pleased and proud. I look forward to giving her away a second time. Ladies and gentlemen, will you raise your glasses with me?'

The toast was drunk amid hearty calls of congratulations and tears wiped from smiling faces. With a heart-wrenching effort Will forced himself to go through the motions, whilst wishing he was in a bad dream. He felt even worse when Sylvia cried, 'Let's exchange presents now!'

Knowing her heart belonged to another Will feared his present was too personal and quite unsuitable. He had hoped she would guess his feelings for her, but not now. He felt such a fool, and wished desperately that he were anywhere but in that cosy drawing room.

Hugh and Isobel were a welcome distraction, crowing their delight as the gifts were opened. Sylvia accepted Will's gift graciously, seeming not to notice his embarrassment. 'What a lovely dressing-table set, Will,' she said gently. 'I shall put them with my trousseau.'

'What's up, Will?' Charlie's voice was soft with understanding as she manoeuvred him into a corner. 'I'm so sorry. I guessed you had feelings for Sylvia but you have to accept that a romance with her was not to be–'

'I should have known I wasn't good enough for her. I thought if I worked hard, built up me business – you know – like Granddad Warren–'

'You're too hard on yourself, Will. You must remember

Sylvia was the very first attraction for you, but you were *not* the first for her. She's been married before, and is a mature, experienced young woman. She's probably broken lots of hearts – unwittingly of course. I'm damned sure she didn't mean to break yours.

'She'll still be your friend, and I know she won't forget the Cause. So stop thinking you're not good enough. Sylvia just fell for someone else, that's all!'

As if to prove Charlie right, Sylvia and her beau came over to them. 'Will, George would like you to be his friend of the groom.'

Will thought he saw understanding in George's eyes. The man clearly wished to be friends. 'Sylvia has told me about your interest in the cause of the Tolpuddle men,' he said. 'I know one or two back benchers, and some journalists. We keep each other informed.'

'That's good,' said Will, swallowing his pain. If only circumstances were different he could like George Stanley. Instead, his envy felt like a knife thrust in his ribs. Forcing a smile he managed to ask, 'When is the wedding?' No doubt they need not have a long engagement.

'The last day in February,' replied Sylvia, her eyes shining. 'Just before Isobel goes back to finishing school. George and I will travel with her then start our wedding tour in Switzerland.'

'Oh, how romantic!' Isobel pirouetted on the spot, while Hugh declared that he was too old to be a page boy at the wedding.

Will sought solace from the carafe of red wine. Sylvia's parents were clearly pleased with the match, and despite his hurt he could not begrudge any of them their happiness. What he did begrudge was the thought that all his hard work and study was for nothing. He was still the underdog. At least Beulah wasn't there to gloat over his discomfort. She'd disapproved of Sylvia's association with him as much as she disapproved of Charlie.

He was grateful to his sister for staying close to him, and to Isobel and Hugh leading a hilarious game of charades with Sidney's children.

Conversation among the older people touched on politics and the disastrous fire. Sidney drew Will into the discussion. 'How is the fitting up coming along?'

'The overseer expects the work to be finished in a few weeks,' said Will.

'Sir Robert Smirke?' said Mr Scott-Wilson. 'He's an architect on the Board of Works. If he says the work will be finished on time, it will.'

Charlie gave a sudden sigh and leaned her head on her husband's shoulder. 'Are you all right, Charlotte?' he asked.

'Just tired, dearest.' Eyeing Will over her fan she smothered a yawn.

'Time to get you home, my dear.' Alan patted her hand.

'Can't we stay a little longer?' pleaded Isobel, 'We're having such a jolly time.'

Hugh nodded, imploring with his eyes like shepherd Tom's dog.

'Charlotte needs her rest,' said their father.

'I can drop them off when we go home,' Sidney offered.

'Very well,' said Sir Alan. 'What about you, Will? Are you coming, or would you rather stay on a bit?'

'No, I'll come now,' Will said, relieved. 'I have to be at work early tomorrow.'

The rest of the family came to the door to wave them off, and Will pretended he'd had a lovely time.

After they dropped him off on the corner of his street, he made for the nearest pub. To hell with the hangover he would suffer next day. It would be easier to bear than the misery in his guts right now.

Chapter Ten

February 1835

∽

'What's up wi' Will?' asked Jimmy Priest, staring after his boss as Will stomped into the hut that served as an office in their Pimlico yard.

'I dunno,' said Johnny Parsons, lifting his cap to scratch his head. 'He've bin like that since Christmas. Perhaps he've lost business while we bin doing government work.'

The two men were warming their hands over a charcoal brazier. With the temporary rooms for Parliament finished, they had money in their pockets for the first time that Will hadn't had to find. Paying them often left him short, but never short-tempered. Until now. He seemed immersed in building up his business with no time or patience for anything else.

'Just as well he's goin' home,' said Jimmy Priest. 'Let's hope he comes back in a better mood.' He decided to confront Will. 'Anything wrong, Guvnor? We thought you'd be glad to get back to yer own business.'

'I am, but there's a lot to do. I've organised a new load of paving slabs you and Johnny can deal with while I'm gone. I'm leaving you in charge, Jimmy.'

Will had made new contacts since the fire and secured fresh orders. At least he could thank his in-laws' connections for those. 'Besides,' he added, unwilling to mention his personal problems, 'I'll be in time for the Shrove Tuesday meeting where I mean to keep up support for the Dorchester labourers. They'll get little enough from the big wigs at present.'

'I'll be back at the end of the month,' Will told his landlady, as he paid his rent in advance. He tramped along the fog-shrouded canal path to the Thames where he would find a homeward-bound stone boat, now laden with coal, awaiting the tide. All the while he had to push thoughts of Sylvia from his mind, knowing that not until she and George were gone could he get on with his own life.

Everyone in Swanwick was pleased to see Will, but those closest soon noticed he'd changed. He was too solemn and spoke little – more like his old moody self.

'You never wrote to tell me if you had a good Christmas,' Amelia said pointedly.

'I was too busy helping to get those rooms fitted up,' said Will. 'I'm only here until I've been to the Company's annual meeting, I must be back in London with these orders filled by the end of the month.' He didn't tell his ma he was to be friend of the groom at Sylvia's wedding. That would be too humiliating. 'I'm collecting signatures on another petition for the Tolpuddle men.'

Amelia wasn't satisfied, 'Will's brooding about something,' she said to Jane Maltravers. 'He wasn't a bit interested when I told him how Tommy has settled in to his school in Dorchester.' She sighed, adding, 'At least he no longer resents his little brother being given a better education than he was.'

'He is being mysterious,' said Jane, 'but he's matured a lot, I think.'

'Will, you don't seem to have time to breathe,' said

Amelia one supper time. 'I need to know how Charlie is. Her baby's due in two months.'

'She's fine. Alan won't risk bringing her home by coach, the roads are too rough. He's waiting for calmer weather to bring her by ship. He can afford a passage on a packet boat and those cutters are fast.'

'Thank goodness,' said Amelia. 'I was afraid she would have her confinement in London, and I want to be with her.'

'Not our Charlie, Ma,' said Will with a glimmer of a smile. 'She's determined to have her baby in Swanwick.' To avoid awkward questions he made himself scarce, visiting the quarries to fill his orders. The men were pleased to see him. The bitter frosty weather had brought work almost to a standstill.

Will and Sandy rose very early on Shrove Tuesday morning. The feast day before Lent was a holiday. It was foggy and cold, the clammy sort of rawness that seeped through a man's clothes into his very bones. Hunched into their sheepskin jackets they set off for Corvesgate, joining other quarrymen on the way. The ground was frozen hard and along with some of their womenfolk the quarriers walked the five miles in just over an hour.

Sandy was proud to be included and looked forward to becoming a 'freeboy', but that wouldn't be for two years when he finished his apprenticeship. He looked at Josh Hort, the youngest member, who carried a new football under his arm ready for a traditional ritual. After the meeting it was tradition to kick the ball from Corvesgate along the old marblers' road used by the stone wagons in medieval times, to Ower, the main port on Poole Harbour for exporting stone. Sandy envied Josh having the first kick.

The meeting was held in the cosy warmth of the Fox Inn, where the men downed pints of ale while business matters

99

were settled and outstanding fines paid. The women took to the market stalls and the youngsters were let loose on the town. The ceremonious chasing of girls kept them warm. In and out of houses they went after the shrieking girls who weren't too sorry to be kissed when caught.

Despite his sombre mood Will found himself chuckling at the antics of the energetic youngsters. They seemed so alive, he reflected, compared with the thieving ragamuffins in the squalid back streets of London. Those who never saw a cow or a sheep, or enjoyed the pleasure of picking wild flowers. These local youngsters would soon be bringing bunches of fragrant primroses to their mothers, and at Easter the heady scent of cowslips would smother the mustiness of ancient church walls.

After the meeting the quarriers began their annual ritual, racing each other to kick the football along the causeway. In bygone days it was the custom to present the Keeper of the Ower Passage House with a pound of pepper in payment for the use of the port. Slow, flat-bottomed barges had to navigate their way between the small islands into the deep water of the harbour where the stone was loaded on to ships. Although the turnpike gates meant improved roads and Swanwick became a stone port in its own right, the Shrove Tuesday custom remained. After the age old ceremony more pints of ale would be downed.

As they neared the shore Will saw the market hoy pulling in from the far side of the harbour. The ferry boat was laden with passengers and their goods, and lobster pots piled up in the stern. Will watched idly as one of the crew jumped on to the landing stage to tie up. Here was a chance to seek more signatures for the petition. He smiled in amusement at the elderly woman clutching her spouse as heroically he bore her ashore piggy-back.

Will turned away so as not to stare as the man put her

down. As he did so he saw a crew member looking right at him. The glance from the man's steely eyes beneath brows flecked with grey seemed more than casual. What's up with him? Will wondered. Hasn't he seen quarrymen at Ower before? Perhaps not, he was swarthy looking enough to have come from foreign parts.

Will stared back and the man quickly looked to his business in the boat. Despite the dark hair streaked with grey and a short scruffy beard, Will had a fleeting idea he'd seen the man somewhere before. By the time he'd sought signatures from the passengers the hoy had pushed off again and he thought no more about it. He had other things on his mind. Having added to his petition, and with his orders filled, he must return to London within the week and face being friend of the groom at Sylvia's wedding.

The fog barely lifted all day but it suited Will's gloomy mood as he made his way back across the heath and over the hill to Swanwick, unaware he was in another's thoughts. Those of Abe Manuel, who helped crew the market boat between Poole and Ower.

Abe had been on the run for six months. After he escaped last August from the doomed *Esmerelda* he landed in the Romney Marshes, near Folkstone, where he scuttled the stolen boat he'd rowed across the Channel. It took all his time and cunning to survive, avoiding the watch houses. At first he'd gone from farm to farm foraging for food, taking eggs from hen houses or cheese from dairy houses. He'd stolen clothes from scarecrows, any rags were safer than convict garb, and spent many a night in a hedgerow to wait for the harvesters to start work in the mornings. While the teams sang to the rhythm of the scythes and their women and children bent to the task of tying the sheaves, he snatched hunks of bread and cheese from their nammet bags. His initial hunger satisfied, he hid during the day and travelled westwards at night.

He had to go further inland to avoid the authorities at Hastings, where the Revenue cutters were always on duty along the Kent coast. He knew all the hamlets that were safe havens with few questions asked. The militia who burned fishermen's boats to prevent smuggling were despised.

He took care to hide the marks of the irons on his legs when seeking work on the farms, stealing only when desperate rather than betray himself as an escaped convict. Once in Sussex Abe preferred to earn his keep along the coast, mending sails or fishing nets, and with his experience and know-how he was sometimes useful to the smuggling fraternity.

His progress along the south coast was necessarily slow, but by November Abe reached Brighton. Avoiding the main ports he worked his way through the winter helping with the herring season. At length he reached Christchurch in Dorset, then Hamworthy and for the last month had worked on the market boats. From there he intended to get to Weymouth, where he had brothers who would help him take ship for America, or Canada. But for now he must bide his time.

Although he no longer looked like a convict Abe had a shock when he saw Will Freer and the other quarrymen. He must be careful being so close to Swanwick, there were too many who might recognise him. Will Freer especially. They'd been in the same boat when Will first joined the old gang, and it was Will he saved when the lad was hurt whilst waylaying the informant who was later disposed of.

Perhaps it was a mistake letting him live.

★

To Amelia during the next few days Will seemed even more morose. The night before he left she weedled out of him what was wrong.

'Oh, Will, you must see that your kind of life would never have suited Sylvia. Pubs, skittles, music halls and the like. Nor would hers suit you. Would you enjoy musical concerts or sitting through grand opera sung in Italian?'

Will shook his head, 'I reckon you're right, Ma.' Changing his cultural tastes to suit Sylvia would have been hard going. 'I feel a fool as much as anything, so please don't tell everybody. I don't want folks staring at me and thinking I was getting too big for me boots.'

'Don't worry, son. I shan't say anything.' But Amelia needed to confide in someone so she told Jane, saying, 'I was afraid something like this would happen.'

Hetty was left to wonder why Will was so moody. Was he angry at the politicians for not caring about the Tolpuddle men – or was it because the farmers were annoyed with the quarrymen? She could understand that having endured another poor harvest and hard winter they were jealous of the quarriers' rights.

Will would protect the interests of his men, but the farmers were unhappy with land undermined by quarry workings. Sometimes the ground sank where the supporting 'legs' of old mines collapsed. Such land was only good for grazing, they couldn't plough to grow corn and make a profit from the high prices being charged.

Something else worried Hetty. Amelia seemed very cool towards her lately.

'Have I done anything wrong?' Hetty asked Jane Maltravers. Her self esteem was high because the locals respected her and treated her as one of themselves. 'Whenever I talk to Will, 'cause I don't like to see him looking grumpy, Mrs Freer interrupts like she don't want me speaking to him. I don't understand. She knows I'm good in the shop, and me learning's coming on. Sometimes I don't think she likes me.'

Recalling the last Whitsun dance, Jane knew Amelia didn't want Hetty getting too close to Will. But she couldn't hurt the maid by telling her.

'I think Will may have been let down in love, Hetty. It's only natural that Mrs Freer is upset for him, but she's also worried about Charlotte. She wants her home because the baby is due soon.'

'Didn't Will say Sir Alan is bringing her home by sea?' said Hetty.

'Yes, but how long must they wait for calm weather – without fog? It won't do for Charlotte to get sea-sick.'

'N-no, of course not.' Hetty was barely listening. So Will had been let down in love – did that mean he'd lost Sylvia to someone else? She felt her pulses race, so that's why Will was so dour of late! At first, while she felt truly sorry for his disappointment she was elated for herself. She yearned to be able to comfort him and say, '*I* love you, Will.'

Chapter Eleven

∽

The last day in February was cloudy but fine and for once there was no fog. Will put on his top hat and cut-away coat and walked to St Martins-in-the-Fields to take his place at the front pew beside George Stanley.

On the opposite side of the aisle, next to Sir Alan, Charlie smiled at him.

Encouraged by the look of understanding in her eyes, Will whispered, 'I'll be all right once it's over.'

Sir Alan's relations took their seats and Mrs Scott-Wilson sat beside Charlie. The younger family members filled the rest of the pew so the Kingslys had to sit behind. Will did not miss Beulah's disdainful expression and the glint of satisfaction he felt helped to allay his melancholy. She clearly still disapproved of his sister, and thought Charlie would never fill Lady Helen's shoes. If only Beulah knew the truth about Alan's first wife, he thought, she might not be so highty-toighty.

The wedding march began and Sylvia glided down the aisle on her father's arm. Will gritted his teeth and forced a smile until his jaw ached. The ceremony was a society event, and he began to feel acutely inferior among so many of the quality. He glanced at his sister, wondering if she felt the same.

Charlie stood with her head held high, her attention

focused on the bride and groom as if she couldn't care less what anyone thought. It must have taken all her courage to fit in with these people, Will thought, feeling more deeply for Charlie than ever before. He'd been so proud of her when he gave her away to Sir Alan, now he felt a desire to protect her from the likes of Beulah. He hadn't planned on attending the wedding feast but now he changed his mind. He would stay for Charlie's sake.

He was able to sit with the Lackfords to eat the sumptuous meal at the Savoy, and sensing that he and Charlie needed each other made him stronger.

'I'll come home as soon as your baby is born,' he promised when they parted.

★

Hetty heard all about Sylvia's wedding from Charlie who came into the shop the day after her return in mid-March. Sir Alan went on to Bridport to attend to his rope-making business. He would be away for some time.

'It was a *very* grand affair,' said Charlie, 'with all Alan's family and George Stanley's, too. I am glad I was there,' she added flippantly, 'Will was pleased not to be the only peasant being patronised by the quality.'

'Charlotte!' Jane Maltravers looked shocked, 'I'm sure Sylvia and her George were never patronising.'

'No, I know,' said Charlie, grinning. 'But you should have seen Lady Kingsly looking me up and down as if I had no right to be there.'

'I can imagine,' said Amelia. 'Anyone would think she'd never been with child.'

'Well, it's all over now,' said Charlie, 'so Will can recover his wits.' She smiled as she smoothed down her gown and rested her hands on the bulge beneath.

'Ooh, it moved!' Hetty stared in fascination.

'That's my baby kicking me,' said Charlie. 'Here, Hetty, put your hand so–' she placed Hetty's hand on her swollen tummy.

Next moment Hetty gasped, 'My, he must be strong – don't it hurt?'

Charlie chuckled and shook her head, 'The little rascal sometimes keeps me awake at night, especially on the packet boat.'

'You've come back none too soon by the look of you,' said Amelia, 'I wish you'd go home and rest.'

'Stop fussing, Ma. I'm fine, but I'll be glad to get rid of this bump and be normal again.'

'And you think Will is all right?'

'I think his pride is hurt as much as his heart,' said Charlie rolling her eyes at the ceiling, 'but he'll survive. He promised to come home and see my baby at Easter. He needs to open up his new shaft, anyway. At least by then the ground won't be so hard.'

The *Amelia Jane Boutique* was busier than usual. Customers came in to buy any little thing or just browse, hoping to hear news of Charlie's baby. 'How is your daughter?' Amelia was asked, or 'When is baby due?'

'Any day now.' Amelia replied shortly. She was tired of quips about her becoming a grandmother, they all wanted to be first to hear and spread the news.

A week into April she began to worry.

'The baby's late, I do hope everything's all right.' She couldn't help thinking of the babe she herself lost between Charlie and Tommy, and the grief she'd suffered then. To lose a grandchild would mean twice the suffering; grief for her daughter's pain as well.

'Don't worry, first one's always slow,' said Mrs Smith,

mother of seven children. 'And your daughter is well looked after with the doctor visiting every day.'

Her comment did little to allay Amelia's fears that the baby would grow too big with the risk that Charlie might not survive the birth. 'I wish Alan would come home.'

Luke Audley tried to take her mind off her daughter by talking about the wrangling in Parliament. Debates over matters of state went on long into the night. One motion was put before the House to abolish the malt tax which would help the farmers, but Sir Robert Peel pointed out it would have to be replaced by a property or income tax, so the motion failed.

'And they wonder why liquor smuggling still goes on,' said Amelia.

A few days later Peel resigned, Parliament was dissolved and by Easter Lord Melbourne had formed a new Whig ministry.

The upheavals in government meant nothing to Hetty. She thought only of Charlie and wished the baby would hurry up so Mrs Freer could stop worrying and being irritable. Then a week after the Prime Minister's resignation it happened. Hetty came back from her rounds to find Dick Farmer waiting with horse and carriage outside the shop.

Amelia greeted her breathlessly. 'Oh, thank goodness! My daughter's asking for me, she says the baby's coming. You'll have to stay here until Mrs Maltravers comes. I have sent a boy for her.'

'Don't you worry, Ma'am. I can manage.'

'Good girl,' said Amelia, relieved to see Hetty brimming with confidence.

By closing time Hetty and Jane were dying to hear. 'I shall go to the Hall and see what's happening,' said Jane. 'I'll let you know when I know myself.'

Hetty heard no more until she went to the shop next

morning. Jane was waiting for her. 'Charlotte had a little girl around midnight, and my nephew came home just in time.'

Hetty gave her wide grin, 'Oh, lovely! But are they sorry it's not a boy?'

'Not a bit. Charlotte is delighted it's a girl because she never had a sister and Sir Alan is just glad both are well. Now – Mrs Freer won't be in for a few days, she's staying at the Hall to look after Charlotte and help with the baby.'

Hetty clasped her hands, 'I'd love to see them, I must take a present.'

'Visitors will soon be allowed,' said Jane, 'why don't you take them some flowers?'

On Sunday Hetty rose early before the morning mist had lifted and went up to the fields near Will's cliff quarry where she knew the best cowslips grew. The hedgerows lining the dry stone walls were bursting with life. Blackthorn bushes were laden with tight mayflower buds, and clumps of primroses still nestled among their roots. Now and then a skylark soared into the sky ahead of her and yellow-hammers darted about with food for their young. Her senses filled with joy, Hetty laughed out loud at the lambs running to their mothers at her approach.

Humming to herself she picked cowslips until her back ached. As she straightened up to stretch she gazed down across the wares, and saw the mist was drifting out to sea.

A sudden movement on the cliffs caught her eye. What are those men doing, she wondered, it's a bit late for gulls' eggs. But they weren't scaling the cliff, they were in and out of the caves dug out by quarrymen back in old Boney's time. Then she saw a long-boat bobbing on the swells as men climbed into it. Further out she made out the shape of a barque looming in the mist. Smugglers!

With that unwelcome thought Hetty saw two men climbing up the wares and decided to make herself scarce.

She hurried on, afraid they would soon be near enough to see her. Then goodness knows what might happen. Seeing an elderberry thicket close to a stone wall where she would be well hidden she squeezed through a narrow gap between gorse bushes and brambles, heedless of scratches, and prickles catching her skirt. Struggling to smother her panting breath she watched and waited.

Within a few minutes the men came past. She recognised one as a farmer's son and guessed the other was a hired hand. Both men wore ropes slung over their shoulders to which were attached wooden kegs, one on the back and one on his chest.

Hetty smothered a gasp – tub men! So the cliff quarry was still being used for landings. Not daring to move she waited, and presently two more men trudged past. After what seemed like an hour, and no-one else passing by, Hetty came out of hiding, her hands scratched and her skirt torn where it had caught on brambles. She pressed her nose into her bunch of cowslips to let their comforting perfume settle her nerves.

'You bin a long time,' said her gran when she came home. 'I s'pose you bin to church?'

Hetty thought better of saying what she'd witnessed and pretended not to notice the whine in Biddy's tone.

'No, up cliff picking these for Charlie,' she said, showing Biddy her bunch of wildflowers. Proudly she added, 'I'll be first outside the family to see the baby.'

Biddy resented having the maid grow away from her, but seeing Hetty's face glow with such tenderness, she bit back the caustic remark she was about to make and sought sympathy instead. 'P'raps 'tis just as well you'm gettin' in wi' they volk. I fear I ain't much longer for this world. Climbin' them stairs do make me pant and me chest hurt.'

'Then it's just as well you only have to get up them

once a day,' said Hetty. She was determined to enjoy this special day. She ran upstairs, changed into her Sunday best, and put on the white gloves Jane gave her. They would hide the scratches on her hands. Then she took up her flowers and went out, calling, 'I'll be back in time for dinner, Gran.'

Feeling free from the oppressive home atmosphere she took a short cut through the woods to Lackford Hall. Tight bluebell buds were pushing up beneath gnarled oaks, and new ferns unfurled their fresh green fronds. In the hazel copses powdery catkins danced in the breeze, and Hetty savoured all the earthy woodland scents.

At the Hall the family was gathered round Charlie as she reclined on a day bed in the lounge. The new mother had just finished feeding her daughter, and Sir Alan with Jane and Hugh looked on adoringly.

Hetty blushed with shyness as she was ushered in but Hugh greeted her warmly, 'Hello Hetty, come and see my baby sister–'

'Give me the flowers,' said Jane, 'I'll put them in water.'

'Thank you, Hetty. They're lovely.' Charlie smiled up at her then nodded at the infant in her arms. 'What do you think?'

'She's beautiful,' Hetty breathed, gazing in wonder at the tiny curling fingers.

'Would you like to hold her?'

'Oh, yes please.' Wide-eyed with pleasure Hetty held out her arms.

'Here,' Sir Alan took the baby gingerly from Charlie, and gave her to Hetty.

Hardly daring to breathe Hetty rocked the child in her arms, enjoying her milky-sweet softness. Then she murmured, 'She needs burping.'

Holding the baby against her shoulder, she gently

rubbed the infant's back until she was rewarded with a good healthy burp and dribble of milk. Hetty chuckled and wiped the tiny rosebud mouth, then rocked her again. The infant gazed up at her, yawned, and fell asleep.

'You have a way with babies,' said Charlie. 'I shall come to you if I need help.'

Hetty didn't like to call Charlie by name in front of Sir Alan who insisted on calling his wife by her proper name. 'Yes, ma'am,' she said shyly. 'I'd like that.'

Feeling closely involved in a family for the first time in her life, Hetty couldn't help comparing the event with what her own lonely birth must have been like. Her breast ached with yearning. She'd been neither loved nor wanted for most of her life. But not any more.

Later, while preparing their dinner she told Biddy how she'd felt when she held the baby. 'They made me welcome, Gran,' she added as she dished up. 'And I be needed – in the shop, teaching maids to plait straw, and now I can help with babies.'

'Aah, mind thee don't bite off more than 'ee can chew, maid,' said Biddy. It wouldn't do for her granddaughter to get a swelled head. She'd want to marry and have kids more than ever now. Biddy feared Hetty would fall for the first man to make eyes at her, then be disappointed – or worse, once he'd had his way with her.

Chapter Twelve

Will did come home in time for Easter, laden with presents for the baby. Tommy was home and the family were invited to Sunday lunch at Lackford Hall. The brothers were each given a turn to hold April.

'Being an uncle is more grown up than being a brother,' Tommy said to Hugh, sounding almost as pompous as Hugh sometimes did. 'What's your sister's name?'

'I *feel* more like an uncle,' said Hugh, not to be outdone in importance.

'April May.' Charlie answered Tommy's question, 'Because she was born at such a lovely time of year.'

'I like that.' Something stirred in Will's breast as, hardly daring to breathe, he cradled the babe in his arms and murmured, 'My niece, April May.'

'It's a pity Isobel isn't here,' said Jane. 'Have you written to her, Alan?'

'Yes, saying I hope she won't be too disappointed at not seeing our newborn, but when she comes home for the summer April will be at a more interesting stage.'

'That's true,' said Jane. 'I'll tell her April is saving her first smile just for her.'

During lunch the conversation turned to other topics, touching on changes in government that could affect the country in general.

'Folk here are so busy gossiping about our families,' Will remarked, 'they're not bothered about what goes on in London.'

'Our folk believe people in high places know nothing about the way they live,' said Luke. 'Why should they care about changes in government?'

'Even less so, now the Whigs are back in control,' Sir Alan remarked. 'Lord Melbourne being back in office does not bode well for your cause, Will. Lord Russell is more amenable, but the king has no liking for him.'

'You're for reform, then?' Luke asked Sir Alan.

'As to that,' Sir Alan shook his head. 'I don't like this Poor Law. I fear the new style workhouses will split families. However, time will tell. It's true that some take advantage of the old system.'

'There's a chap called Thomas Wakley,' said Will, 'just elected for Finsbury.' The locale was one of London's places where public meetings were held after the reform bill failed to get through.

'I know of him,' Luke said. 'He's a Devon farmer's son who became a doctor and wants medical reforms. I believe he writes a journal called the Lancet.'

Sir Alan flashed Will a glance of enquiry, 'You think he'll join the fight for the Tolpuddle men?'

Will's grey eyes gleamed as he called to mind what he'd heard. 'I think Mr Wakley might lead the fight. He's one of eleven children, and once engaged in bare-fist boxing in pubs, so he really does care about working men. He's asking for more petitions to put before Parliament and I'm collecting signatures again. There are rumours in some papers about Orange Lodges,' he added. 'They say the king's brother is Grand Master of the organisation –'

Will was interrupted by Amelia. As a new grandmother the last thing she wanted was to talk politics.

'Charlotte, shouldn't you be thinking about April's baptism?' It was usual to hold the ceremony within two weeks of the birth.

'I've barely thought about it,' Charlie admitted. 'You'll want your relations to come, won't you, Alan?'

'Of course,' said her husband. 'I'll have a word with the parson about Whit Sunday. That should give us time to make arrangements.'

'Then I'll make sure the rooms are ready,' said Jane. 'Sylvia and George will be home by then, too.'

Will caught a glance from Charlie at the mention of Sylvia, but Sir Alan was looking protectively at her.

'I haven't told the family yet,' he said. 'But I shall. I'll send invitations when I've made arrangements.'

No doubt Lady Beulah would come, thought Will, if only to save face with the family. Knowing Beulah would want to be in London for the summer concerts favoured by the king and queen, he hoped the relations would not stay too long.

While Amelia looked after Charlie during her laying-in period and Jane was overseeing preparations for the family visit, Hetty enjoyed being in full charge of the shop. Especially when Will came in to collect signatures.

It amused Will to hear Hetty talking slowly to customers, clearly concentrating on speaking well. She seemed sure of herself these days, and was firm with the girls she taught. They were busy fashioning new summer bonnets. With him she forgot herself and spoke naturally, her cheeks flushed, her green eyes sparkling.

He noticed she took pride in her work, and her cunning in flattering the ladies when they tried on a bonnet made Will chuckle. She would utter the odd French word she'd picked up from his mother. "*Charmant!*" she would cry ecstatically, or *"Magnifique, madame!"* Anything that encouraged them to buy. When the customer left, pleased with her purchase, Hetty would lapse into the vernacular, then switch to posh when someone else came in.

Will also saw how fresh and natural Hetty was, compared with the painted ladies and grimy urchins of London. His heart warmed at the sight of her honest face, and he felt glad she was making a better life for herself.

Hetty signed his petition eagerly. She could write quite quickly now, and treasured the smile he gave her as he went on his way.

The only thing that troubled her was what she'd seen on the cliff top. She ought to tell someone, but who? Her employers were too busy and so was Maisie. Besides, she wouldn't want to worry any of them after that smuggling scandal last year, innocent though they were of any connection. There had been so much trouble and hurt when Mr Warren's gang was dealt with, yet keeping it to herself was difficult. She had no intention of telling her gran, old Biddy would want to join in. Hetty fretted over the matter for some days before deciding to tell Will. He would know what to do. Her chance came early one morning when she was passing Warren Stables on her way to work. He was there making a fuss of Hercules so she paused to say, 'Morning Will. You love that horse, don't you?'

She was glad he had something to love, what with his disappointment over Sylvia, and everyone fussing over the new baby. She only wished he could see she cared for him.

Will nuzzled Hercules' nose and smiled wryly, 'Yep, I miss him when I'm in London. I miss being here, too.'

'I reckon you'm homesick,' said Hetty, cocking her head to one side. 'But you'll come back and stay one day, won't you?'

There was a glint of determination in Will's eyes, 'When

my business is firmly established,' he said. 'And when the Tolpuddle men get the justice they deserve.'

Hetty sighed. 'If ever they do.'

'Oh they will, now Mr Wakley is on their side.' He told Hetty some of what had been said at Lackford Hall.

'He sounds like a good man,' said Hetty. 'I wish him well with that. So how is your London business? You've been away from it for a while.'

'I'm going there next week, but I'll be back for the christening.'

'Can you stay for the Whit Tuesday holiday?' she asked hopefully.

'I don't know yet, it depends.'

Depends on what, she almost asked, stabbed by jealousy. On what went on in London, or if Sylvia was going to be around? She dropped her gaze from his stare. 'Will, there's something I want to tell you. I must tell someone–'

'Go on, then,' he said, curious and ready to be amused. She looked so serious.

Hetty took a deep breath then explained how she'd seen local men using the abandoned cliff quarry. 'They were smuggling, but I don't want to get anyone in trouble, and I don't want no trouble either.'

She bit her lip and gazed at him wide-eyed.

'You've not told anyone else?'

She shook her head emphatically.

'Well don't. There's no need to worry, 'tis only petty smuggling. I don't blame folk for trying to make their lives a bit easier.'

Hetty gasped, 'You know about it?'

Will shrugged, 'I know some locals take in a few tubs from France or Jersey, but they've got enough sense to keep quiet about it.'

Hetty couldn't help feeling anxious, 'Oh, I hope you're

not mixed up in it again–' She broke off and flinched, seeing anger flash in his eyes.

'Of course I'm not! But who are you to tell me what I should or shouldn't do?'

Hetty gulped and stared at him, horrified at what she'd almost accused him of. Oh dear, she never meant to get on the wrong side of him. 'I ain't nobody,' she muttered, shamefaced. 'I – I care about you, that's all. I care about your Ma, too. She wouldn't want to see you mixed up in it again.'

'Well, she won't because I'm not, so perhaps you'd be good enough to mind your own business!'

'I'm sorry, Will – oh–' Hetty turned and hurried away, hot tears burning her eyes. Why had she opened her big mouth. All she'd done was remind him she was a nobody – less than nobody compared with Sylvia. I'm a fool, she told herself. Will would soon be gone and she could see no chance to make amends. Gran was right, she'd wanted and expected too much.

Will spent the rest of his visit tramping around the quarries gathering signatures and ordering the best stone for shipment to London. He'd been surprised more than shocked to be cautioned by Hetty. Still smarting from the wound Sylvia inflicted on his ego he'd lashed out at the first person to offend him. Now he regretted losing his temper with Hetty. She worked so hard, and pleased his mother. She didn't deserve his bad humour.

He felt worse when he discovered how unpopular he was with the farmers. They refused to sign his petition for Mr Wakley. The labourers were happy to make their mark, but the farmers complained about the quarriers not paying to transport stone across his land. Times were hard for them, too.

Will was in no mood to listen. 'And what if I were to say

I know you're dabbling in the trade,' he snapped, his temper spiking upwards. 'And using my cliff quarr to land your goods.' He ignored their blatant protests and denials. 'You mark my words – so long as you don't hinder my quarrymen your secret's safe. I'll turn a blind eye so long as – if you're spotted – you cut and run. There's to be no rough stuff.'

They resented being told what to do by him, but with his connections to Squire he could soon expose them to the law so they grudgingly agreed.

Will left for London unaware that Hetty was pining over the way they'd parted.

Hetty couldn't understand why she felt so miserable just because Will had told her off. Why should she care? What was the matter with her? Why did it hurt so much? He was sure to forget all about her, anyway, in the City.

Her work in the shop helped, but she was so sullen at home her gran guessed something was wrong.

Biddy tried to goad it out of her, 'You'm in love, bain't you, maid. No man ain't worth the way you'm feelin – fools the lot of 'em!'

Hetty never bothered to answer back and ran upstairs. She wasn't even cheered by Sandy when she met him coming out of the pie shop.

'What's up, Hetty? You look like you lost sixpence and found a farthing.'

He sounded sympathetic, not mocking like old Biddy. He was younger than her, although he liked to think of himself as a man and went to the pub on pay days. Now, seeing only affection in his puppy-like gaze Hetty decided to confide in him.

'You'm fond of him, ain't you?' said Sandy after she finished telling about the smugglers, and how she'd unwittingly fallen out with Will. Hetty was only one of

119

the girls he was considering might make a man a good wife. She liked children and had good childbearing hips, a point he'd picked up from his workfellows when they had occasion to notice a passing female. He admired her, for he didn't know which was worse, the orphanage or slaving for ol' Biddy. Hetty never complained like some of the wives he'd overheard the older men talk about. Not that they spoke much at work, heaving stone around made 'em too breathless, but when they took their ease at the pubs away from their crowded little cottages their tongues soon loosened with a few drinks inside 'em.

'I *know* Will ain't involved, and that's the main thing I reckon.'

'How do you know-?' Hetty began, then she frowned. 'Don't tell me you're in with 'em, Sandy?'

'Naow,' said Sandy. He tapped the side of his nose, 'They just pay me sixpence sometimes to keep a look out when they're delivering. I stand about and take me cap off then put it back on again if I see a preventive man or a constable.'

'Oh Sandy, do take care. Look what happened to them Tolpuddle men. They never did anything wrong, let alone smuggling!'

To her surprise Sandy put his arms around her and hugged her. 'Don't worry about me, Hetty. I'm going to be like Will one day then I might ask you to marry me!'

Hetty didn't know whether to laugh or cry. At least he felt for her. 'Then you'd have to pay the shilling to marry an outsider – although me granddad was a quarrier.'

'That's good 'nuff fer me,' said Sandy, taking a bite out of his meat pie. 'Cheerio, maid, see you later.'

Huh, thought Hetty, watching him swagger off. I'll be an *old* maid before *anyone* marries me!

As the days passed, Jane or Amelia would drop by the shop

to check all was well and were satisfied that Hetty was holding her own.

'I was afraid the customers might prefer to be attended to by yourself or Mrs Maltravers, ma'am,' Hetty said, the first time Amelia came in. 'But they just like to hear that Char – er, Lady Charlotte, and her baby are doing well. They like the new bonnets, too,' she added.

Amelia nodded her approval, 'That's good, Hetty.'

By the end of May Amelia was able to spend more time in the shop. One day she was looking over the accounts when Jane rode up to the door on her pony. She was breathless with excitement.

'Amelia, Sylvia and her husband have arrived. You are invited to dine with us this evening–'

'So soon! Oh my, 'tis well their room is prepared.'

'Isobel is with them. They travelled through France then sailed from Cherbourg to Weymouth. They took the packet boat and were dropped off at Swanwick. It saved going on to London then making the tedious journey back here for Whitsun.'

'How sensible,' said Amelia.

'Sylvia was so eager to see Charlotte and the baby,' Jane went on, 'she had the look of a broody hen as soon as she stepped out of the carriage. She's thrilled at being April's godmother.'

'Let us hope she starts a family of her own soon,' said Amelia, not without sympathy.

A sentiment Hetty echoed in her mind with all her heart. Once Mrs Stanley had a brood of her own, Will would hopefully get over her completely. Thank goodness he was away in London until Whitsun.

The coming baptism was the last thing on Will's mind. Agitation on behalf of the Dorchester labourers was once again rife, and some MPs kept the matter before the House. Mr Wakley gave his maiden speech the day before the King's birthday, attacking the decision to transport the six men, then he raised the scandalous matter of their wives and dependents being refused parish relief. Without the vote, he said, working men had no one to speak for them in Parliament where laws were made. Unless the Dorchester Unionists were pardoned, and brought home how could the man in the street ever expect justice?

Will was elated when he came home the following week. 'At last,' he cried to Luke Audley, 'an MP standing up for poor men's rights. Mr Wakley has proposed that the Dorchester labourers be brought back and restored to their families. He's called for a full debate next month.'

'It was a wise move to give the other politicians time to think on it,' said Luke. 'With such strong feeling throughout the country some action must be taken.'

'There are other MPs on our side, like Mr Cobbett and Mr Hume,' said Will. 'Even Home Secretary Russell is sympathetic.'

'I'm glad you could spare the time to come home,' said Amelia dryly.

'I might even stay for the Whit Tuesday Fair,' Will answered. 'To celebrate.'

When the Scott-Wilsons arrived at Lackford Hall the Thursday before Whitsun, Jane and the servants had their work cut out. There was no time for gossip, apart from noting that Lady Kingsly left it until the last minute to arrive on the Saturday morning, despite her son Robert being a godfather. Beulah gave the impression she was doing the family a great favour by coming at all. The roads were rough, the jolting carriage played up with her joints so that she could hardly move, and when they alighted to walk up the hills her personal maid had to help Lord Mervyn support her!

While her parents made sympathetic noises Sylvia helped the new house-keeper. The children pitched in, Isobel appointing herself nanny to April.

Sir Alan took the men of the family on a tour around his estate while the ladies gathered in the drawing room and took tea. Then Charlie showed them the nursery where they found Isobel bathing the baby, with Maisie's help.

'Who is that person?' Beulah asked, when she saw Maisie allowing her toddler to touch April. 'The wet nurse?'

'That's Maisie Farmer,' said Charlie. 'She's the wife of our head groom, and my personal maid. She's a great help.'

'You mean there is no nanny, nor yet a wet-nurse?'

'I don't want them,' said Charlie. Her grey eyes gleamed, awaiting Beulah's reaction when she added, 'Breast-feeding one's own baby is a pleasure no mother should miss.' She smothered a grin seeing Beulah's mouth open and shut like a landed fish. 'Also, apart from my mother, Mrs Hart the gardener's wife can be relied upon. Her eldest child is good with baby too. Mother's shop assistant will baby-sit any evening if need be. So you see I have plenty of help.'

Beulah turned to her sister Adele, 'Well really! I'm surprised Alan allows common folk to handle his new child. I've always said he needs more servants.'

'Yet you would have my baby wet-nursed,' said Charlie artfully. 'I've seen how happy our servants' children are, having been fed by their own mothers. How can it be a bad thing? I'm surrounded by women only too willing to help and advise me.'

Beulah watched with some alarm, Maisie's toddler playing and fussing over the baby. Charlie smiled, 'Young Arthur loves April. She keeps him happy while his mother's busy. We help each other. You must remember,' she added, 'there's no call for more servants ordinarily. It's not often the whole family is here at once.'

'I see that.' Beulah tilted her nose even higher, 'But surely you won't let April play with common children when she's older?'

'Why not? My husband has taught me that on a country estate like this we are one big family. Why employ strangers when we have folk we know and trust, who really care? Those like Maisie and her husband, who spent most of their young lives in an orphanage, look on this as their home. You've seen Mrs Marsh, our new housekeeper, and we have a kitchen maid.'

Beulah sniffed, 'Also from an orphanage, I suppose. Well, it wouldn't do in the City. What do you think, sister?'

Adele Scott-Wilson smiled, 'I think the proof of what our new sister says is right before our eyes.'

Just then Sylvia came in, 'Oh there you all are. Mother, Aunt Beulah, can you come? I'd like your approval of the seating arrangements and to see if I've laid the table correctly.'

Beulah raised a critical brow, 'I'll leave that to you, Adele. I must go and rest before I dress for dinner. I trust my room is ready?'

This last remark was laced with sarcasm. Charlie nodded, and sighed with relief at the retreating back of her sister-in-law.

Hetty came in to help Vinnie Hart, the gardener's eldest daughter, put the younger children to bed while Maisie and Mrs Marsh waited at table. After helping Cook finish up in the kitchen they had supper with the servants.

Hetty went home marvelling that the two sisters, Lady Kingsly and Mrs Scott-Wilson, could be so different. She looked forward to hearing all the gossip from Maisie after church tomorrow.

The christening tomorrow! She'd been so looking forward to the ceremony, but now, after her recent quarrel with Will she feared it would be no pleasure for her.

Chapter Thirteen

Whitsun 1835

❦

Hetty would have been hard put to find a seat in church had she not been with the singers in the gallery. The whole of Swanwick came early, cramming the pews to watch the arrival of 'the Quality'.

Sir Alan and his family were last to arrive. The rector, Mr Barton, greeted them at the door then led them and their relations up the aisle. A smiling Charlie cradling her baby in her arms, exchanged greetings from well wishers in the congregation. Isobel darted a sympathetic glance over her shoulder at her cousin Robert Kingsly following behind his parents. There was a whiff of Beulah's lavender water as beside Lord Kingsly, nose in the air, she sailed to the front like a galleon, looking neither to right nor left.

Isobel saved Robert a seat in the front pew next to Sylvia as they were to be godparents. Robert, now at university, had the look of a personable young man in the making. He blushed at the admiring glances from several young maids and received a wicked grin from Isobel. That minx would tease him mercilessly later.

As the organist stopped playing Mr Barton announced the first hymn. Everyone stood up, and in the gallery Hetty was glad Jane was at her side. She concentrated on her singing, and only when the hymn finished did she risk a glance at Will. A quiver ran down her spine when his gaze met hers with a brief nod. Her heart soared. She was so relieved the rest of the service passed in a blur. She knelt or stood at the appropriate places, sang automatically, and barely listened as the parson droned through the prayers. She paid more attention after the second lesson when Sir Alan and Charlie were led, with the godparents, to the font near the south door.

The congregation stood, turning to focus on the ceremony, and Hetty joined in the oohs and ahs from motherly watchers as Mr Barton took the sleepy infant in his arms. April May barely whimpered when he scooped the holy water over her head.

'Dearly beloved, forasmuch as all men are conceived and born in sin…'

As the baptismal prayers went on and on Hetty longed for the service to finish. It troubled her that if a child of a happy marriage like Charlie's and Squire's was born in sin, what hope was there for her – she who was never baptised …

At last it was all over and Hetty hurried outside to find Maisie. 'Oh, where's your baby?'

'Back home with Dick,' said Maisie. 'I had to help Charlie dress, and what a to do there was. Them two,' meaning Sir Alan's sisters, 'had their personal maids running round the Hall like headless chickens! Fussing over this and that, and how their kids was dressed. I bet Cousin Robert's glad 'tis all over.'

'I think he'll be glad to get back to university,' said Hetty, 'the way some young maids be preening themselves in front of him.'

'Ah,' Maisie grinned. 'They won't get too close with that dragon of a mother!'

Just then Jane Maltravers approached with her father.

Jane smiled. 'Hello, you two. Lady Lackford asked me to tell you, Maisie, that you're to take the rest of the day off. The family are all going to the Manor House Hotel for Sunday dinner, and Mrs Stanley will help her to undress later–'

'What about the baby?' asked Hetty. 'She'll need feeding soon.'

Lady Lackford will use a private room, and you know what Isobel's like. She'll see to April's other needs.' Jane lowered her voice conspiratorially, 'She adores the child and, I think, she enjoys provoking her Aunt Beulah.'

Luke Audley shook his head, smiling. 'See you in the shop, tomorrow, Hetty.'

They strolled away arm in arm to join the Freers.

'I'd like to be a fly on the wall at that dinner,' said Maisie. 'I reckon Squire wants to impress his sisters, especially Lady Kingsly. Imagine her face when he shows them where Charlie was presented to the Princess Victoria last year.'

'*And* gave her royal highness the bonnet *I* helped to make,' said Hetty. Pride surged through her at the memory. 'I reckon that ol' Beulah will be jealous, and more ob-obnoxious than ever–'

'Lor' Hetty, wot's obnoxshus?'

'It means unpleasant,' said Hetty grinning widely. 'It's one of Mr Audley's favourite words when he reads the news.'

For a while longer they mingled with the rest of the crowd watching the quality walk down the hill towards the hotel on the shore until Maisie said, 'I'd better get back to me husband and baby.'

She turned to go. 'And I must get back to Gran,' said Hetty. 'She'll want to hear all about it just so she can scoff. That's all her pleasure these days.'

Though she spoke of Biddy, her thoughts were with Will. She hoped he wouldn't feel too bad being near Sylvia again.

Maisie's prediction turned out to be correct. The first thing Sir Alan did before dinner was to show his guests the ballroom where the royal reception had taken place. Beulah seethed with envy throughout the meal. To think that a quarryman's wife and daughter had met royalty, while she, who attended all the great royal occasions in London had never been presented!

Will was soon caught up in a discussion among the older men who were enthusing about the latest plans for the rebuilding of Parliament.

'You're an architect, Sydney,' said George Stanley, 'shall you submit plans?'

'I hope to,' said Sylvia's brother, 'but the competition will be stiff, the Royal Commissioners have invited all architects to submit their proposals.'

'What are the criteria?' asked Sir Alan.

'The style of the buildings are to be either Elizabethan, or Gothic,' said Lord Kingsly as if the decision were his.

'Progress will be slow, I fear,' said Mr Scott-Wilson. 'It will take months for the plans to be considered and the choice made.'

Will listened intently, looking from one man to another. He was so interested he forgot himself and gave a low whistle. 'Phew, and it will take years to build.'

A grunt of disapproval caused him to see that he'd offended Beulah, her mouth was turned down like a horseshoe over her double chins: a common workman daring to join in gentlemen's conversation!

Positively shaking Beulah said, 'Then let us hope the workmen will do their duty, and not hold things up with their dreadful strikes!'

For a moment there was silence, and Will sensed that everyone knew her dart was intended for him. Just in time he caught a warning glance from Charlie. Being indebted to Sir Alan for investing in his business he must not quarrel with Beulah. Swallowing the anger that threatened to engulf him, he took his time to answer.

'Not much fear of that my Lady. The affair of the Tolpuddle Martyrs has broken poor men's spirits so that the unions have collapsed. It's a pity politicians cannot see, because of all the new industries, cottage industries are being destroyed. There are thousands living in poverty, as I've seen for myself.'

'Hrumph,' Mervyn Kingsly wiped his mouth with his serviette. '*Martyrs* indeed!'

'Yes, sir. That is how the newspapers refer to them–'

'Only those against the government,' said his lordship, jowls shaking. 'Now, young man, I don't think this is the time or the place to discuss such matters.'

Will closed his mouth. It was a waste of time trying to talk to 'respectable' people like the Kingslys who considered trade unions a threat to their precious 'Society'. He was damned if he was going to apologise for speaking out.

'Time to adjourn to the smoking room, I think gentlemen,' said Sir Alan standing up. 'Come Will, shall you join us in a glass of brandy?'

'Thank you, no sir. I have business to attend to at my stables before dark.' Any excuse was better than having to endure, or cause, further embarrassment to his family or Sylvia's.

'I'll just check on baby,' said Charlie, following her brother to the door. She wasn't going to let him go without offering him some comfort and support.

'Don't be put off by them,' she said squeezing his arm. 'They're going home tomorrow. We shall be able to enjoy the Whit Tuesday Fair without them.'

'That's a relief,' said Will, 'seeing as I promised our ma I'd stay for it.' Everyone looked forward to the holiday which was always boosted by a travelling fair that used a field overlooking the bay. Beulah would not relish mingling with a gang of gypsies.

As Hetty expected, her gran made derisive comments about the quality attending their humble parish church. Hetty had to admit the occasion made excellent entertainment for Swanwick folk. The christening of April May was the grandest event since Charlie and the squire were married.

After dinner and by late afternoon, seeing Biddy dozing in her chair, Hetty decided to make the most of the lovely weather and go for a walk along the seashore. Her way took her past Warren Stables and as if in answer to her curiosity on how Will was faring, he appeared.

She hesitated, and gave him a shy smile, wondering if he would want to speak to her. He looked a bit moody. Why was he here, and not still with the christening party? Perhaps he couldn't stand being around Sylvia.

Hetty was surprised when his expression brightened on seeing her.

'Hello, Hetty. Look, I'm sorry I was a bit rough on you last time I was home. I thought how nice you looked in church today,' he added.

Hetty blushed, 'Thank you, Will, but I wonder you still want to speak to me with all them posh relations to live up to. Be the party all over, then?'

'As for my posh relations,' he added, 'there's one or two I was glad to get away from. Beulah especially. I came away before I said something I'd regret. 'tis a relief to get back to me horses.'

To his horses, Hetty thought, not to see me. She was glad he seemed more like his old self, but there was a hard streak she hadn't noticed before.

'I mustn't neglect my business,' he went on, 'I'm gaining

success like my granddad – and by honest hard work. Why do you look at me like that?'

Hetty was frowning, and the light in her eyes told him she was bursting to say something. Now her eyes blazed as she plucked up courage.

'I think success is how much you'm loved and appreciated, not how much money or property you've got. I hope you ain't forgot how unpopular your Granpa Warren was. You don't want to be like him. I wouldn't want to be like my Gran, nor me Ma! And I certainly wouldn't want to be like Lady Beulah. Who would miss her if she suddenly vanished?'

She looked so quaint, her face fierce with scorn, that Will couldn't help picturing Beulah disappearing in a puff of smoke. He chuckled.

'Right 'o, Hetty, I'll try to be more popular than Grandpa Warren.'

Hetty was dismayed when she met Maisie and heard that Robert was staying for Tuesday's fair. Not that Hetty had anything against Isobel's cousin, but the Kingslys only allowed him to remain when Sylvia said she and her husband were staying on, too. 'Says she wants to spend more time with her lovely god-daughter.'

It was something more to upset Will.

Chapter Fourteen

Whit Tuesday 1835

For the first time that year Biddy didn't feel up to running the fortune-telling tent so Hetty helped Amelia and Jane on their stall. With the three of them they could take turns to visit the other booths.

Hetty shared in the more than usual excitement with Swanwick folk awaiting the arrival of their squire. This year he would be bringing his Lady and family – Charlotte, Lady Lackford was arriving in style.

Soon after nine Sir Alan and his party arrived, he riding beside the open carriage carrying his family and the Stanleys.

Isobel could hardly wait to show Cousin Robert around, while her father, as was customary, showered the onlookers with pennies. It was the signal for the traditional club march and ceremonies to begin. The town band with Sam Roper and his big bass drum to the delight of noisy happy children, led the procession to the Parish Church. After a short service the marchers processed back into town where they dispersed to make merry. Hetty bought muffins to take home to Biddy and watched for Will when it was her turn to look around. Having always been at her gran's fortune-telling tent before, she only now realised just how noisy it was near the pubs. The clamour of rowdy quarry boys enjoying the Aunt Sally and the thundering of hobnail boots on wooden boards at the skittle alley all but drowned out the band.

Hetty found Will and Sandy playing skittles watched by Sylvia and George Stanley. I should have known, she thought, biting her lip. She'd turned away and begun walking back to Mrs Freer's stall when she saw Charlie and Squire approaching with a perambulator. It was the first time she'd seen a hand carriage for carrying a baby and almost forgot to curtsy. She stared at the wicker bassinette on three wheels, two at the back were connected to a smaller one at the front. It had two handles with a bar between by which Sir Alan, in top hat and tails, was pushing the contraption.

Charlie called to her. 'Hello Hetty, do you like my baby *pram?*'

'Oh my lady, may I look?' Curiosity overcame Hetty's shyness and she crowed in delight at the sleeping babe inside. 'I never seen one of these before.'

'They're the new fashion in America,' said Charlie. 'Sylvia's brother designed this one specially, as a christening gift.'

'Marvellous for getting her to sleep,' said Sir Alan. Would you like to push it Hetty?'

'Oh, yes please, sir.'

The new experience made Hetty's day. She couldn't wait to tell her gran about it when she got home. She wasn't so sure about the dance that evening, and dithered about getting ready. The thought of seeing Will hankering after Sylvia was unbearable. He had such ambitions and would never see her, Hetty, as more than a friend. He only talked to her sometimes because she worked for his ma.

Nor could she face turning up at the Dun Cow alone, everybody she knew had someone to go with. She decided to stay home and read the book Mr Audley had lent her. It was a lovely romance written by a lady called Jane Austen. Of course, it was all about ladies and gentlemen who were not *really* poor … Hetty sighed, she could always dream … Charlie had married into the gentry, but she and her ma did have posh blood in their veins, so I suppose the same goes for Will … Oh, to hell with it all!

Hetty took her book from the shelf just as someone knocked at the door.

Biddy sat up. 'Who be that? Hetty, you tell whoever 'tis I ain't doin' business tonight.'

Hetty opened the door and saw Sandy standing there, twisting his cap in his hands.

'Evenin' Hetty,' he began, his face red under his freckles. 'I come to take you to the dance.'

Folk didn't like coming to Biddy's door, and Hetty guessed Sandy's mates had dared him.

'She bin gallivantin' round all day,' snapped Biddy, startled by such boldness. 'You don' want to go, do ye, Hetty?'

'Well, I wasn't going to bother,' said Hetty, darting a glance from Sandy to her gran. It wasn't likely Biddy would approve.

'Oh, come on Hetty, you'm missin' all the fun–'

'If she says she don't want to go, then she don't!' Biddy's glare was designed to send him on his way. But Sandy wasn't going to be jeered at by his mates for losing the dare.

'It's only once a year, Granma. You was young once weren'cha?'

Biddy wasn't used to being stood up to by outsiders, but there was something about this pimply youth she found disarming. He was like her Harold when they were young. Hetty was growing up fast, maybe there was hope for her among the younger quarrymen. All the older ones had known Harold. 'Aah well, maid,' she grumbled, resigning herself to what was possible rather than what might not be. 'You'd better take a shawl – and you, young feller–' as Hetty ran upstairs to fetch her bonnet and shawl, 'you make sure you bring her home safe and sound. No hanky-panky!'

'Yes, Granma, her'll be all right wi' me!'

No one had ever called Biddy Grandma before. To Hetty she was always 'Gran' at best, or, 'you horrid old woman.'

Biddy watched the two youngsters hurry along the path, then cackled to herself as she lit a fresh pipe and went back to her net braiding.

In the upper room of the Dun Cow Sylvia and George Stanley were amused by the frantic activity as Swanwick folk cleared space for the evening's entertainment. Will was helping to lower furniture out of the windows, while excited youngsters raced around the dance floor.

'How did this place get the name of Dun Cow?' Sylvia asked Charlie.

'The quarrymen name the different layers of stone they dig,' said Charlie, 'and Dun Cow is one of them. It usually forms the floor of a quarry, and sometimes it's a whiter stone called White Horse. But don't ask me why they're horse and cow,' she added with a laugh. 'Not quite like the balls in London, is it?'

They chuckled at the fiddler being helped up to his chair placed on a table.

'And you attend every year, Uncle Alan?'

'I like to join in the fun,' said the squire, linking his arm through Charlie's. 'It's traditional.'

'And as much a novelty as Sylvia and I having an aunt younger than ourselves,' said George Stanley smiling at Charlie.

'Come, Charlotte,' said Sir Alan, leading Charlie on to the floor, his blue eyes twinkling at her. 'Let us start this ball rolling.'

Will stood back and tried not to mind the ache in his heart as Sylvia and George followed. He'd lately managed to put Sylvia out of his mind, but being near her still pained him. He focused on Robert and Isobel who seemed to find the whole thing hilarious – and there were Hetty and Sandy joining in. Everyone was enjoying themselves. He looked towards his mother, thinking to ask her to dance when Sam Roper beat him to it. Even old Luke Audley was inviting Martha Hyer to partner him. Will put down his beer. He'd better join in or his ma and his sister might think he was still pining over Sylvia. Well he was a bit, but he didn't want their pity. Then he saw Jane Maltravers sitting alone. She was good to him and his ma, he would ask her.

'My, Will, folks will be talking about us next,' Jane teased, but accepted. The dance was a progressive reel where everyone changed partners after each set of movements. Towards the end Will danced a turn with Sylvia, who smiled at him seemingly unaware of his pain. He was relieved by the next exchange of partners, and when the music stopped he found himself with Hetty.

As everyone drifted back to their own partners Hetty stood still, looking for Sandy. He was with his mates, surrounded by girls their own age. Pretty Mary Dyke and Vinnie Hart were making eyes at the lads, but Sandy seemed more interested in Lizzy Harris, the daughter of his quarry foreman. Hetty was dismayed, realising he'd lost interest in her. She couldn't join them in case they thought she was barging in as if she had a claim on Sandy. Seeing an empty chair next to Mrs Maltravers she made to go to it, but Will put a hand on her arm.

'Hetty, stay with me, please?'

She saw desperation in his eyes and despite feeling he only wanted her company because he felt embarrassed by Sylvia's presence, she nodded and let him lead her to the corner where he'd left his beer.

'Would you like a drink?'

'Yes please, a lemonade.'

They sat together and chatted while the dancers in the next reel whirled past them. 'How's your new quarr going?' she asked. 'It's a new-vein isn't it?'

'Yes,' said Will, 'but we need to go deeper for good paving slabs. It should be producing soon.'

'And when do you go back to London?'

'Tomorrow. George and Sylvia have invited me to travel with them in their own coach.'

'Which will save you the usual fare,' she said, lowering her gaze so he wouldn't see her disappointment.

'Robert and Isobel will be travelling too. Robert has to get back to Oxford, and the Stanleys will see Isobel off to Switzerland. I'm more interested in what goes on when Mr Wakley's debate takes place in Parliament.'

The evening grew rowdier and merrier, but the thought of Will going away next morning made Hetty feel miserable.

At length she told Sandy she wanted to go home. But he was having too much fun, and too much to drink, trying to keep up with his mates.

'Not yet, Hetty, we get a half day off work tomorrer.'

'You promised my gran–'

'I said you'd be all right wi' me, and you be all right, bain'tcher? Stop actin' like you was me big sister.'

Hetty felt hurt and angry. Although she never took Sandy seriously, she resented being told he might ask her to marry him one day, then being treated like a nuisance. She lost all patience and shouted at him, 'You'll make yourself sick, you're too young to drink so much. You think you're acting like a man, but you're an idiot – and I don't need you to walk me home!'

'He'll be a man soon enough, Hetty.'

She spun round to see Will watching them. Having enjoyed little of the evening he was glad to find a reason to leave. 'Come on, I'm going now, I have to be up early. I'll walk with you.'

Hetty felt too miserable to argue. She half welcomed his company, yet would rather avoid it. So she stood by while he went to bid his mother goodnight.

He swayed slightly as he went, clearly having had plenty to drink but for reasons different from Sandy's. When she saw Amelia glance her way, with no smile, she knew her employer disapproved of her friendship with Will. I suppose she'll be sour towards me again at work. How stupid we all are. She thinks I'm after her Will, who I could love but can't have, and Will wanted Sylvia but couldn't have *her*. He certainly doesn't want me. I thought Sandy liked me, but 'tis no good taking notice of him, and I hate feeling so mixed up. Gran was right, no man was worth the way she felt.

They followed the path beside the stream with Will half-staggering and slurring his words when he spoke.

Huh, thought Hetty, he needs me if only to stop him falling in. She sighed, and muttered, 'There's no sense to anything.'

'Wassat you say?'

Hetty was surprised he heard her. 'I said, there's no sense to anything. We should all be happy, but we're not, are we?'

She wondered if he would speak about his feelings. After all, she only knew what she'd been told by Mrs Maltravers, or had overheard. Will's manner and behaviour told her the rest.

'Nope,' he mumbled, 'theer ain't no sense to nothing, especially our wunnerful gov'ment who punish the poor an' protect the rich.'

Hetty looked askance at him, remembering his remark about Mr Wakley. 'Do you mean the Tolpuddle men?'

'I mean all working men,' Will growled. They ain't got no rights, cain't vote or nothing. You should'a heard em' cheering when Westminster Palace burned down.'

Hetty remembered something she'd read in Mr Audley's papers. 'I thought you could vote if you had property.'

'Aah, when I'm 21, but thass not 'til nesht year.'

'Oh. Well, I expect your Mr Wakley will change things. He cares about working men from what I hear.'

They'd reached the edge of the wood and Hetty could see her cottage through the trees. There was a light in the window, so was her gran still up? Hetty didn't want Biddy to know that Will, not Sandy had walked her home.

'I'll be all right now, Will. Thanks for walking me home.' She smiled up at him to show she was grateful, and tried to hide the lump in her throat. 'I hope all goes well–' her voice broke on a sob. 'In – in London, and something happens soon to help the Tolpuddle men. Goodnight, Will.'

She turned to go, but he grabbed her arm and pulled her close.

'Poor little Hetty. I see how sad and lonely you are. I thought you and Sandy cared for each other.'

Hetty turned her face away from his beery breath. 'We are fond of each other, but only like brother and sister 'cause we were both in the same orphanage until me gran–' She couldn't finish because Will was crushing her in his arms.

She lifted her face to protest, 'Will – you're tipsy–'

Then he was kissing her, and somehow she didn't mind him being tipsy. But she knew he couldn't mean it, and began to struggle.

He stopped, and still holding her he said, 'You're like part of my family, so don't feel sad an' lonely. I like being with you, Hetty, 'caush you're int'rested in what I do, and you undershtand my work.'

'Oh I understand you, Will,' she said pushing him away. 'And I do like hearing your news, but just now I think you've had a mite too much to drink.'

'You sound just like my sister,' said Will. 'G'night, Hetty.'

He didn't see her tears as she fled towards the light in the window.

Chapter Fifteen

⁓

Next day, in the old cottage near the Freer quarry Sandy Mason spent his free morning nursing a hangover and cleaning up the mess he'd made being sick during the early hours. He felt bad, too, about breaking his promise to Hetty's gran. He'd let them both down, but at least there'd been no hanky-panky as Biddy put it, and he'd won his dare. It was one thing to be able to hold your head up with your mates, but another facing Hetty to say sorry before he went to work in the afternoon.

Amelia Freer rose early to see Will on his way. She'd persuaded him to spend the night in their house near the stables, meaning to speak to him about Hetty Cauldon. There wasn't much sense to him last night so she'd waited until they sat down to breakfast. Tentatively, because she didn't want a row, she said, 'Did I see you leave the dance with Hetty Cauldon last night?'

'We were both going,' Will said, stirring his porridge. He still felt hazy about last night and could hardly believe that after being besotted with Sylvia, funny little Hetty Cauldon was the first woman he kissed. It just proved he was drunk – yet he'd enjoyed the feel of her softness in his arms and the taste of her lips.

'I was sorry for her.' Will shrugged. 'Sandy was supposed

to take her home but he was having too much fun with his friends. She *is* older than him. I said I'd go with her so Biddy wouldn't give her a scolding, which I don't think she deserved.'

'I see,' said Amelia. Perhaps she was worrying needlessly, she should be glad her son was so considerate. 'I suppose Mrs Cauldon would be worried as it was the first time Hetty ever came to the Whit Tuesday dance.'

Her thoughts turned to that other worry, Will travelling back to London with Sylvia and her husband. 'What do you think of George Stanley?' she asked, eyeing Will with some concern. 'He seems a personable young man to me.'

'It's all right, Mother,' said Will knowingly. 'I've got enough to do without pining over what might have been. Besides, Isobel and Robert are coming, too, so we shan't lack in conversation.'

The sound of a coach and horses stopping outside roused them both. 'I left my things upstairs, Ma. Can you tell them I'm just coming?'

Her anxieties mollified, Amelia watched the coach drive away then went to open up the *Amelia Jane Boutique*.

When Hetty arrived she found Mrs Freer wasn't in a sour mood after all.

'Will told me how Sandy let you down last night,' said Amelia, intimating he'd pitied Hetty. 'I'm glad my son saw you home safely.'

'Yes ma'am,' said Hetty, thinking I bet he didn't tell her he kissed me. 'I was grateful, 'cause I promised my gran not to come home alone.'

She'd been relieved to find Biddy was already in bed, also touched that the old woman had left a candle burning in the window. Still feeling Will's strong arms around her, and his mouth on hers, she'd sobbed herself to sleep because he had to be drunk to kiss her. Yet she was glad she hadn't got Sandy into trouble, much as his behaviour annoyed her. So she was surprised when he came to the shop during his dinner break.

'I'm sorry about last night, Hetty. You was right, and I've had me punishment so please don't be cross.'

Hetty shook her head and resisted the urge to say, I told you so. He looked so pale and woebegone, and with those big puppy eyes she couldn't be angry with him.

'Very well.' She sighed to smother the giggle that bubbled inside her, 'I shall forgive you this time.'

'Thanks Hetty.' He grinned sheepishly and went off to work whistling.

★

Three days in a private coach was quicker than returning to London by sea. As Will predicted, Isobel and Robert kept the grownups entertained and bolstered his spirits. Besides, he was beginning to like George Stanley and the journey was a chance to get better acquainted. At least the roads were hard and dry. He listened to George enthusing about how the railways were progressing.

'One day they'll build one to Southampton, then it will be possible to reach London from Swanwick in a day, by paddle steamer and train.'

'Sounds too good to be true,' said Will.

He arrived at his lodgings in Pimlico late on Friday afternoon. By the time he'd delivered his petition to the Dorchester Committee it was gone six o'clock, so he went to find Jimmy Priest and Johnny Parsons in their favourite pub.

'Finished wetting the baby's head, then, Will?'

'Yes, thank goodness. How are things here?'

'We've got enough work on with the new contract for

paving the streets around Hyde Park. We're waiting to see what happens after the big debate. June twenty-fifth, 'tis set for.'

They were among thousands nationwide who were upset when Thomas Wakley's motion, that the Dorchester labourers be brought home to their families, failed. Mr Hume, who Will remembered as a march leader at Copenhagen Fields and who helped heroically when the Palace of Westiminster caught fire, seconded the motion. The MP spoke of the many petitions including eight from the Dorchester area, saying one alone bore 21,000 signatures. He estimated the total number of petitioners to be more than 800,000.

'Lord Russell wanted Mr Wakley to postpone his motion until he'd spoken to the King,' Will growled to his mates in the pub. 'But Mr Wakley refused. He said if his motion failed the people could never expect true justice from the government.'

Will's paper told how the member for Finsbury had spoken for an hour so passionately the House remained silent, which was unusual. Wakley explained the injustice of how little known or understood statutes were used to convict the men; how he'd met their wives and seen for himself the misery they endured. When he read aloud the farewell letter written by the leader, Loveless, to his wife, some members had shed tears. Wakley ended by saying that even if their oath of loyalty was illegal, the 'poor fellows' should not have been given more than three months hard labour. Yet when it came to the vote only 82 out of 400 were for the motion.

'He must have pricked the Home Secretary's conscience at least,' said Will, 'because Russell suggested the labourers be given a conditional pardon, and bring four of them home after two years. But Wakley wants them all home. He said the two leaders are good Wesleyans who studied and qualified to preach to their congregations.

'Perhaps that's why the vote went against him,' said Johnny Priest.

'More than likely,' said Will. 'I remember my dad saying how, in the old days, dissenters had to hide in the quarries to hold their services They've only lately been allowed to marry in church.'

Their sentiments were echoed when Amelia showed Will's latest letter to Jane and her father.

'Mr Wakley won't give up,' Will had written at the end of June, *he's warned the government that the agitation will continue, and be worse than before.'*

'I'm afraid Mr Hume can make no headway, either, not while there is still prejudice against dissenters,' Luke Audley said. 'Also, he worked hard to get the Combinations Act repealed.'

'So being a trade unionist is *not* against the law,' Jane remarked. 'But masters will only employ men who don't belong to a union.'

'Oh, it's all so confusing,' said Amelia. 'At least Will understands. He says that after travelling together for three days he's become friendly with Sylvia's husband, thank goodness. Apparently George Stanley has friends among the back-benchers who keep them informed.'

'I think Will is right,' said Luke Audley. 'From what I read, if Mr Wakley can't win one way, he'll find another. That man has something up his sleeve.'

'Will did mention Orange Lodges, whatever they are,' said Amelia. 'Something to do with Ireland, I think?'

'I believe the Order came into our country some twenty years ago, by soldiers who served in Ireland,' said Luke. 'Their members are strict protestant tories, set on opposing

Catholic emancipation which the government wants to bring in.'

'I don't see what any of that has to do with the Dorchester Martyrs, as some papers are calling them, said Amelia. 'Oh dear, I was hoping Will could soon be home for good.'

Luke looked at her benignly, 'He's not likely to, is he my dear? Not with his business growing in London.'

'No, I suppose not.' Amelia sighed, 'I don't think Will expected the affair to go on so long. He thought the Copenhagen Fields demonstration would be enough to sway the government. But that was a year ago and the Tolpuddle men are very low on the agenda. The whole business has worked in Will's favour, so he's hardly likely to go back to hewing stone.'

No, thought Hetty, sighing inwardly. Will is somebody now, business man, land and property owner. She felt despondent, and even more of a nobody.

Then Jane changed the subject, 'Our business is expanding, too.' Half teasing she added, You'll soon need a bigger shop, Amelia, if only for room to store the stock.'

'I've been thinking about that.' Amelia brightened, 'What if we take our surplus goods to sell at Poole market?'

'A splendid idea,' said Luke while Jane smiled agreement. Amelia turned to Hetty, who stood open mouthed in surprise.

'Well then, maid, how would you like a day away, in Poole?'

A day in Poole! The thought was both frightening and exciting. To Hetty Poole was the same as London. She'd never dreamt of such a thing.

'I don't know, ma'am. I never been out of Swanwick before.'

'I could go with you, for the first time at least,' said

147

Jane. 'Show you where to go, and what to do, make a few business acquaintances…'

'Oh, would you, ma'am?' Hetty had forgotten that Mr Audley was from Poole and Jane was brought up there. 'I – I'd have to see what me Gran thinks, she might not want to be left alone for so long.'

'Hm,' said Jane. 'It would be a long day, but you'd be home before dark.

'We could ask one of the girls to look in on her, make sure she's all right,' Amelia suggested. But when they were approached none of the girls wanted to do it, they were too scared of 'the old witch'. For all her resentment towards her gran, Hetty was too loyal to tell them that Biddy's 'evil eye' was a sham.

'Never mind,' said Jane. 'We'll think of something.'

The something turned out to be Sandy. He'd come to collect some chisels that had needed honing, from Sam Roper, and bumped into Hetty on her errands. She barely returned his greeting.

'What's up, Hetty? Not still mad at me are ye?'

Hetty shook her head. 'I've been offered the chance of a day in Poole, but it means leaving me gran alone too long. And knowing her she won't want me to go anyway.' She mimicked Biddy, saying, 'Thee's getting' too big fer yer boots, maid. I knowed that Amelia Freer would go puttin' ideas into yer head.' She scowled at Sandy's laughter. 'The girls I been training be all too scared to look in on her.'

'If I were you I wouldn't ask her,' said Sandy, 'I'd tell her. Say you bin ordered to go, and – and you'll lose yer job if you don't.'

'Well I ain't you, and I don't like telling lies.'

'Tell you what,' said Sandy, hoisting his bag of chisels over his shoulder, 'I'll look in on her for ye. I ain't scared o' her!'

He turned to go, but Hetty laid a hand on his arm. 'Would you, Sandy, really?' She recalled Biddy relenting about her going to the dance when Sandy called for her. Seeing the old woman's face was like watching dripping melt, her frown disappearing as a look of pleasure took its place. Yet doubt still nagged Hetty.

'You sure you won't break your promise, like last time?'

'No, 'course not. I'll enjoy buttering the old lady up.'

Some *lady*, Hetty thought. 'Well, if you're sure. Will you come with me after work, to tell her?'

' 'Course.' Sandy puffed out his chest in what he judged to be a manly way, and swaggered off, whistling.

Hetty smiled after him. 'Cocky little beggar,' she muttered.

The following Thursday, Hetty embarked with Jane and Luke on her great adventure. With the sun on her face and the tangy sea breeze bringing salt spray to her lips, she was mesmerised by the foaming bow wave as the little cutter sped across the bay with a brisk sou'westerly filling her sails. She had to hang on to her bonnet as they rounded the head. Big waves rocked the boat until she began to feel queasy but they were soon sailing smoothly again, and she cried out in delight at the variety of sea birds along the chalk cliffs. Long necked cormorants flew straight as an arrow then suddenly dived beneath the waves to pop up again yards from where they'd disappeared. The gulls scavenging after a fishing boat were familiar enough, along with their speckly-brown backed young ones, by now fully grown. One of the crew pointed out shags and guillemots, 'And them black gannets eat six times their weight in fish,' he told her.

The sailor chuckled at her obvious pleasure. 'Oh aah, 'tis all right on a day like this,' he said. 'But when there's no wind it takes hours longer. 'Tis quicker then to walk over the hill from Swanwick then along Holywell beach and take the ferry boat from the sand dunes. 'Tis only five miles or so.'

'I wouldn't mind,' said Hetty. 'But I shouldn't want to walk home again after a long day'.

They made good time across Holywell bay to the sand dunes at the entrance to Poole Harbour where a bobbing ferry boat was being rowed across and Hetty grew more excited.

Now the cutter was being steered against the wind as they entered the harbour mouth. 'Hold on tight,' said the captain. 'The current is strong here, we're head on into the wind and the tide be on the turn.'

Poole merchants traded with Newfoundland, and with the odour of cod oil, seal skins and whale blubber borne on the wind, and the sea being so choppy Hetty became nauseous. The more she held tight, the worse she felt. Then, just as she leaned over the side, wretching, they came into calmer water and her stomach cramps eased.

'Better now, Hetty?' said Jane. 'You were quite green around the gills, but the colour is coming back into your cheeks.

Hetty gave a wan smile, and began to take an interest in her surroundings. The quayside, with its tall warehouses, shops and taverns was barely visible behind the forest of masts and ropes where ships of all shapes and sizes were berthed. Hetty spied a church tower when she heard its clock strike eleven.

They eased past an odd looking mound sticking out of the water where men were busy with rakes. 'What's that?'

'It's a sand bank,' said her sailor friend. 'Those men be working the oyster beds. They send young oysters to the Thames estuary to fatten up for the London fish markets – Rightyo, watch yerselves!'

Sails were furled, and Hetty and her companions stood back as their boat manoeuvred between barques and schooners and the crew busied themselves with mooring ropes. Hetty craned her neck to look up at tall mast heads with their fluttering flags of different countries. Immediately the cutter was tied up the passengers were helped across a gang plank on to a flight of stone steps.

Hetty was glad to be on firm ground again, despite the seeming chaos around her. Amid the smell of oil and grease, men using creaking hoists and pulleys were loading or unloading. Cargoes of all kinds were landed and grouped according to their contents while merchants sat on barrels haggling. Crates were piled high, and fat round barrels were rolled down gang-planks into the vault beneath a warehouse. Hetty's mouth fell open as she stared anxiously at a man four stories up working a pulley in an opening at the top of a warehouse.

'Don't worry,' said Luke. 'He knows what he's doing, he'll not fall.'

Hetty hoped he was right.

'Come along my dears.' Luke sniffed the appetising aroma of bacon and sausages frying in quayside shops and stalls. 'I need refreshment.'

It was warm enough to sit outside so they bought coffee and meat pies. Ladies with parasols, and smart gentlemen, strolled among the market stalls examining the goods. There were summer fruits and vegetables, barrels of fish, and non perishable goods from France and the Channel Islands.

Hetty was fascinated by everything, especially the lamp posts which stood like unblinking sentinels at intervals along the cobbled street.

'They're gas lights,' Luke told her, 'to illuminate the docks at night.' He smiled at Jane, 'I am glad I came, it's worth every minute watching Hetty's face. 'You'd think she was in a foreign country.'

They walked along the quayside looking for a suitable spot to sell their straw-plait goods. When Hetty grew curious at each side street they crossed Jane drew her away. 'Don't go down there,' she warned. 'They're full of brothels, and slum tenements. Soon as sailors come ashore they spend their pay on booze; no young maid is safe with them.'

Hetty shuddered at the contrast. The harbour curved on for as far as she could see. The sound of distant hammering and the not unpleasant smell of tar and wood shavings hanging in the air drew her attention to ships moored away from the loading bays for repairs. The hull of one barque was being painted by men in a cradle slung on ropes over the side.

'Hetty, look!' Jane stopped at a big haberdashery stall where bolts of cloth stood on end along the whole length of a shelf. She began fingering the ribbons and laces on display. There were gold and silver hat pins, too, and flowers made from scraps of material. 'Wouldn't some of these make handsome improvements to our bonnets!'

'You interested in buying?' The challenge came from the buxom woman in charge of the stall.

'I think we might take back a few samples to show Amelia,' Jane said to Hetty. She began asking the woman how much the items cost, while Hetty lifted two bonnets from her basket to see which ribbons would match.

'This lace would be lovely on our wedding bonnets,' she said to Jane.

'That's Brussels lace,' said the woman, crossing her arms over her ample bosom. 'You won't get better.'

'I'll take a yard, please,' said Jane, 'and a dozen of those little mother-of-pearl buttons.'

Earlier, while they were drinking coffee, Hetty had

watched two sailors yarning, and noted the flat brimmed hats they wore. I reckon I could make some like that with straw plait, she thought. Now ideas flitted through her mind and she pointed out certain items to Jane.

'I'd like some of this, and that–' she began eagerly.

'Steady on,' said Luke. 'Don't you think you should report to Amelia first and decide what to buy next time you come?'

Hetty grinned sheepishly and nodded.

As Jane paid for her items the buxom stallholder looked keenly at her. 'If you're prepared to buy your haberdashery from me,' she said, 'I'll let you sell your bonnets and suchlike here. Be nice to have a bit o' company.'

Her proposal was readily accepted. 'We'll come again next week,' Jane told her, 'and bring some stock.'

'Next week!' exclaimed Hetty as they made their way back to the Swanwick clipper. 'I'll have to ask Sandy to oblige with me gran again.'

'If we come each week through July, said Jane, 'I think we'll be able to keep up with supply and demand.'

'And word will get round,' said Luke. 'By next year the Amelia Jane Boutique will have gained quite a reputation.'

Hetty didn't feel sea-sick at all on the voyage back, she was too busy thinking of what to say to her gran. She wondered if Biddy would approve of this new venture, and would Sandy be willing to spend time with her gran each week?

Chapter Sixteen

Summer 1835

⚬

Hetty needn't have worried, when she arrived home she was greeted by the savoury aroma of rabbit stew and Biddy was actually smiling.

It seemed she and Sandy got on very well. Perhaps, Hetty thought, it was because Gran never had a son that she'd taken a shine to him. He'd certainly won her approval by bringing her a rabbit he'd caught, and after he'd skinned it they both worked on making the stew.

'Thought you'd be back by sunset,' Biddy said. 'I asked nipper yer to stay fer supper.'

'How did you get on?' Sandy asked, and Hetty began to describe all the sights she'd seen, and how they'd made the acquaintance of a female stallholder.

'So, now you've bin out in the big wide world,' said Biddy, unable to resist a dig. 'Like as not ye'll become a real madam.'

Hetty ignored the remark, and rolled her eyes at Sandy. 'Mr Audley and Mrs Maltravers were very impressed with the possibilities.' Now was the time, she thought, to put her request. 'Mrs Maltravers thinks we should go a few more times – get me used to it – so long as the weather holds good.'

She was pleasantly surprised when instead of objecting

her gran said, 'It's all right wi' me, so long as nipper yer comes to call.'

Sandy said he would be glad to come again, 'I'll bring some fish next time, and maybe you can teach me to make a net for catchin' rabbits.'

Biddy cackled, 'Oh aah, thee'll be after smoking' me pipe next.' But she was nodding, and Sandy seemed genuinely pleased with the arrangement.

'I never expected to see her so happy,' Hetty said when Sandy took his leave. 'What's your secret?'

Sandy grinned, 'Just me manly charm.' Then more soberly he added, 'I ain't never had a gran, I reckon she'll do'.

Biddy was still in a good humour as she and Hetty prepared for bed. 'So, maid, what d'ye think o' the big wide world, eh?'

'It was quite an adventure,' said Hetty, her eyes shining. 'Jane will go with me next time, then I think I can cope on me own. They don't think I'll be sea-sick again – but tell you what, Gran, it must be awful for them as sails to Botany Bay. Just think o' them poor men enduring three months of it!'

Not all ships bound for Botany Bay were transporting convicts. Some carried fare paying emigrants, especially women looking for a better life. The colonies were short of women for most convicts settled there once they'd served their sentence.

Throughout July, while Hetty and Jane made their trips to Poole, Lord John Russell tried to organise free passages for the Tolpuddle wives to join their husbands. Although it failed, Thomas Wakley's long passionate speech had stung the Home Secretary into action. About the same time as Will penned his letter to Amelia, Lord Russell had written to the governors of New South Wales and Van Dieman's Land anticipating a favourable report on the conduct of the six Tolpuddle men. If he could persuade the King to use the royal prerogative of pardon it would overrule the statutes. But the best he could persuade His Majesty to was that four of them be allowed to return after two years, excluding the ringleaders.

Luke Audley shook his head over his newspaper, 'I fear Russell is fighting an uphill battle.' He and Jane were taking breakfast on their garden terrace. 'The wives are refusing to go unless their husbands send for them – and Russell has to contend with the Prime Minister. Lord Melbourne is quite indifferent to their plight.'

'Yes,' said Jane. 'It seems to me that his lordship never does anything. He ignores all the protests and believes in leaving well alone – but all is not well.'

'And Mr Wakley refuses to consider any compromise,' said Luke over the top of his paper. 'He wants them all home – my heavens–' He flattened his paper as he looked at Jane, astonishment written all over his kindly face. 'The man's even offered to stand security for their good behaviour, and financial support!'

'Well,' said Jane, 'that shows how much he cares.'

In August Mr Hume caused an explosive debate in the House by proposing a motion to condemn the Orange Lodges. His inquiry had found numerous English lodges were rooted in the army. The Orange Lodges, it was revealed, having been suppressed ten years before, were revived by the king's own brother, the Duke of Cumberland. When there was a public outcry Will and his mates were among the scandalised campaigners.

'The duke is grand-master of the Orange Lodges in England!' Will looked jarred, 'And – a declaration was made requiring secrecy in their proceedings *before* last year–'

'Meaning?' said Jimmy Priest.

'Meaning,' said Will emphatically, 'the declaration was

made before the Tolpuddle men formed their little society. It proves there's one law for the rich and one for the poor. The lodges are no different from the Dorchester labourers with their oaths of loyalty.' He paused for breath, he felt so angry.

'So,' said Johnny Parsons, 'that makes the King's brother just as guilty as the Tolpuddle men.'

'Yeah.' Will growled, 'I'd like to see him sent to Botany Bay, but his kind are beyond the law.'

His frustration was echoed in the House when Mr Wakley plunged back into the fray. He presented a petition directly linked to the Orange Lodges signed by 5,000 Bristol inhabitants. After such disclosures, the MP declared, the country would demand that the Tolpuddle men should no longer be punished. He quoted the 1797 Mutiny Act, an obscure law which had been twisted to convict the men, then added, 'It is time to end one law for the rich, and one for the poor!'

Three days later Luke Audley came into Amelia's shop waving his newspaper at her.

'I knew it,' he cried, 'Mr Wakley has stirred up a hornet's nest! The King tried to cover up his brother's actions by sending Parliament a message saying that while he deplores all secret societies, he supports Lodges and loyalty to himself!'

'How can he not be moved by the plight of ordinary labourers?' Amelia cried.

'I know,' said Luke. 'He encourages reform to stop corruption in high places, yet he's blinkered where this particular injustice is concerned. I can't see any sympathetic politicians letting the matter rest now.'

He was right. The next thing they heard was the secretary of the Orange Lodges was brought to the bar in the Commons and asked for the correspondence book in his possession. The man refused then absconded before he could be arrested, adding more fuel to the campaigners' fire. A debate followed on the motion that either members of the Orange Lodges should receive the same treatment as the Dorchester labourers, or those six men should be granted full remission.

The stubbornness of the House of Lords also stirred up the press, and the matter was discussed in public. Mr Hume was one of those who for years had exposed abuses of public institutions, offices, and management of public and crown revenues. At the end of the parliamentary session, one leading member threatened to propose a motion to take away the veto on all legislation measures. Which meant if the Lords rejected a bill that passed the Commons a second time, with royal assent it could still become law.

Will and his mates heard it all at outdoor public meetings while they worked on paving Hyde Park Corner. Cabinet ministers squandered too much public money, cried the orators, on things like creating offices for their sons then abolishing them and keeping the compensation pensions. Inequalities and abuses, they claimed, were rife even in the Church and the law courts. The Government cared only about the wealth the colonies would bring, rather than internal concerns like commerce, manufacturing and shipping. Reform was badly needed.

In September the King went in person to prorogue Parliament.

'The Lords must be glad,' Will said to his mates, his tone sarcastic, 'after such a long, toilsome session.'

'It's one way of delaying reforms,' said Jimmy Priest gloomily.

'Out of sight, out of mind,' agreed Johnny Parsons.

Hetty, meanwhile, enjoyed a busy summer travelling to Poole market on Thursdays, and in July she was asked to help with the children at the Sunday School picnic on the downs. Even her workmates Sarah Taylor and Mary Dyke showed Hetty respect when once they would have teased her about her lack of schooling.

By August Hetty was confident enough to go to Poole alone. She looked forward to seeing her new friend at the haberdashery stall, and hearing all Effie's gossip. Outgoing and outspoken, Effie liked bantering with the other stallholders.

It wasn't often there was no wind at all, but one Thursday Hetty was forced to take the other route to the sand dunes and be rowed across the harbour in the ferry boat. As she walked along Holywell beach she came to a wide stream that ran into the sea. She had to take off her shoes and stockings to wade across. It was so deep in the middle her skirt got wet when she had to lift her basket of straw-plait wares up out of harms way. She arrived at the haberdashery stall tired and cross.

'Just look at ye, Hetty Cauldon' cried Effie in amusement as Hetty tried to brush off the sand clinging to her damp skirts. 'Wait 'til it dries out, then 'ee can shake it off.'

'You can laugh,' said Hetty, grinning away her annoyance. 'Nobody told I about that pesky stream, it was deep wi' the tide in an' all. 'Twas all I could do to keep me goods from getting spoilt, an' I ain't looking forward to the return journey!'

She didn't notice a man staring at her from the shadows.

Abe Manuel had just emerged from his room in one of the back street tenements Jane had warned Hetty about. He'd overslept after drinking too much the night before and missed his morning crossing to Ower. He was in a foul mood, knowing he would have to contend with an irate master who would dock his pay. Abe cursed the thought of spending another winter hiding from the law. He was tired of this mundane way of life, earning a pittance by rowing back and forth across the harbour. If only he had the means he wouldn't stay here, or anywhere else in England. America was the place to be, or Canada, where a man could be free of English laws and taxes. But a passage, and getting himself set up cost money – far more than he could earn by honest means.

He was heading for the Ower boat's mooring place when he heard the woman on the haberdashery stall laughing at the maid she called Hetty Cauldon.

The sound of the name startled him out of his moody reverie. Was the maid any relation to that witch Biddy Cauldon, his old gang's smuggling accomplice?

Abe paused, pretending to watch men working on their boats while his brain raced with ideas. Wondering if the old woman was still around, he began to see a way out of his predicament.

As he expected, the market hoy he helped crew had left without him. Well, he would visit the bath house, get spruced up before it returned, and see what he could learn from that maid while he waited. He knew nothing of what had happened in Swanwick after he and his gang were caught. Were Warren and Maltravers still doing business? If so they could help him. Or had they been caught, too?

The afternoon wore on, and Hetty made only a few sales. She'd hoped for better as she didn't fancy carrying everything back with a long walk ahead of her – and having to cross that pesky stream again. She brightened when a stranger came to their stall and began chatting Effie up.

He had the weather-beaten appearance of a sailor with those eyes squinty from peering into the sun. Hetty briefly recalled Jane's warning, but although his clothes were shabby, they were clean and well mended with a neat patch here and there. He said he wanted to buy a bonnet for his wife, so he must be respectable. Effie handed him over to Hetty. 'You're just in time. Hetty yer is about to pack up and go home. The ferry boat be leavin' soon.'

Abe nodded at Hetty, 'Afternoon miss.' He pretended to examine her bonnets, 'Where d'ye live, then?'

'About a mile in from Swanwick bay, sir.' She was anxious to please him if it meant selling another bonnet.

'It'd be quicker for you to take my ferry boat to Ower and walk over the hill. No need to go all along Holywell beach.'

Hetty gladly accepted his suggestion.

Abe paid for a bonnet. It would do for a farewell present for his doxy when he'd completed his plans. 'Come on then, maid. I'll take you to the boat.'

They said goodbye to Effie who watched them go with a slight frown on her face. She nodded to a neighbouring stall holder. 'Thic maid be a mite too trusting.'

'Don't 'ee fret none,' said the man. 'He's a genuine hard worker, I seen him handling the boats.'

Hetty was curious to know more about this man who hadn't actually introduced himself. 'You know Swanwick, sir?'

'Aah. Used to visit when I were a boy. Had an old uncle there. He be long gone.' The lies slid easily off Abe's tongue. The maid was so gullible it was easy to spin her a yarn. He chatted about the cliffs and the birds, how his 'uncle' taught him to snare rabbits. 'I used to know a man called Freer,' he added guardedly, and hesitated as if trying to recall more clearly.

'The old Mr Freer, or the young one?' Hetty asked as he escorted her to the Ower berth. 'They were both quarrymen–'

'Were?'

'Yes,' said Hetty. She sighed, 'Will Freer and his father. The father died in a quarry accident, and Will is making a life for himself in London.

'William Freer – I had no idea. I remember him,' Abe lied, 'We fought together against Napoleon. A brave, good man he was. I'm sorry to hear he died so tragic like. And the son, you say, is in London.' He was sure he'd seen Will at Ower last Shrove Tuesday. The lad was one the few people who might recognise him. 'So the poor widow is on her own, then?'

Expecting Hetty to say that Mrs Freer had her father Henry Warren to rely on, Abe was startled by her next words.

'Yes,' said Hetty, 'but Mrs Freer ain't so poor. She runs a business making bonnets with her partner Mrs Maltravers.'

Abe started at the name Maltravers. The woman must be the wife of Henry Warren's partner in the 'trade'. Instinct cautioned him. He'd led this maid to believe William Freer senior was the only person he knew in Swanwick and he was dead. But he knew the young Will, Henry Warren's grandson.

Hetty was thrilled to meet someone who knew Will's dad from the French war. It would give her something to tell Will when she saw him again. 'And his sister,' she said, 'has married the squire–'

'What? How do you know all this?'

Hetty indicated her basket 'I work for Will's ma.'

'Ah, I see – and you say Mrs Freer is on her own. Has she no father?'

162

'Not any more,' said Hetty. 'Old Henry Warren died tragic, too, – er accidentally – at a quarry.' She just stopped herself from saying the old man had been shot, that would be too much to explain. It wouldn't do to tell this stranger everything. Hurriedly she added, 'Nobody liked him much.'

Now she was reminded of all the trouble Will had gone through she became hot with anger. 'It was all rotten ol' Maltravers' fault. Turned out he was mixed up in a smuggling racket and falsely accused Will Freer of murdering a coastguard. But 'tis true what they say, yer sins will find you out. Maltravers was killed, got run over by a loaded stone wagon.'

'Augh.' Abe's shocked intake of breath was genuine. The two people he expected to rely on were both dead.

The hoy from Ower was tying up and Abe pushed the unwelcome news to the back of his mind while he made his excuses to the master.

'But I've found ye a customer,' he growled.

He helped Hetty into the boat, and took his place at the oars. While he rowed, Abe wondered about old Biddy.

'Do you have brothers working in the quarries, too?' he asked Hetty.

'Oh, no. I live with me gran–' Hetty hesitated, not willing to go into detail about her background. 'That is since I – er lost me ma. I never knew me pa. We look after each other, me and Gran–'

'So you and her live alone?' This was better. Apart from Will Freer, Biddy was the only other person in Swanwick who knew him. It would soon be time to move on, he never stayed in one place long for fear of arrest. Now he could no longer expect help from Warren or Maltravers he needed time to think.

At Ower, he helped Hetty ashore and watched her take

the path that led across the heath and over the hill. He would pump her again next week – to decide the best time to find Biddy alone. If the old woman had money stashed away it wouldn't be difficult to relieve her of it.

Chapter Seventeen

Autumn 1835

∽

It had been a long day. Hetty had left home an hour earlier in order to catch the market boat from the sand dunes, now she arrived home an hour after sunset. She was so tired she almost fell asleep over her supper, not bothering to tell her gran and Sandy about the nice old sailor who had known Will Freer's father.

Nor did she get around to telling Amelia. She awoke next morning to find clouds had gathered overnight and it was raining. By the time she'd stoked up the fire and cooked porridge for herself and Biddy she was already late for work, and Friday was pay day.

'I'm sorry, Ma'am,' Hetty apologised, shaking her wet cloak. 'I overslept.'

'When did you get home last night?' asked Amelia. The girl did look tired.

'Not 'til after sunset, and I never had many customers. I earned just enough money to pay the ferry boat fares.' Hetty put the little that remained on the counter.

'In that case,' said Amelia, 'I don't think you should go again this year. We'll concentrate on our wedding bonnets for next spring.'

'Oh,' said Hetty, swallowing disappointment. She loved

her weekly outing, and Gran was less grumpy since Sandy began his regular visits. 'I told Effie I would see her next week–'

'Then you'd better write to her. Make it your first job.'

Hetty wrote a hasty message to Effie and took the note to the master of the market hoy. He would deliver it for her. Then she continued on her rounds to collect the girls' work and pay their wages.

It was a busy time, with harvest, and Mrs Freer fussing over her grandchild and expanding the business. With Amelia's approval, Hetty turned the cellar into a basement. As well as the straw plait work she and her assistants began braiding small nets for catching wild fowl and rabbits, something to interest the men. Hetty got the idea from watching her gran braiding. They'd actually managed to have a sensible conversation when she asked Biddy to teach her, and enjoyed each other's company. It was Sandy's doing, Hetty thought, and her heart warmed towards him.

She screened off the work area, and put items to attract male customers on display, moving them outside when the weather was fine. The girls in charge were an added attraction, banter being enjoyed by young men and maidens alike.

Sam Roper had plenty of work repairing farm implements and honing the quarrymen's punches and chisels. There were also jobs from the Warren stables, shoeing horses and checking that each gig and fly was kept in order. These were hired by well-to-do merchants who drove to Frometown to replenish their supplies.

Work progressed on Will's new quarry, although as he'd said, the men had to dig deeper. Care was needed to blast through a cinder bed with gun powder to reach the cap and new-vein seams for paving stones and roof tiles.

One person with a slight concern was Sir Alan. With the

advent of steam powered machines, and Mr Brunel building steam boats, he knew there would be less demand for ropes and sailcloth. While he was away in Bridport, or in court on session days, Charlie was busily happy with her baby. All in all, Swanwick folk were too busy to bother about what politicians were up to.

Doting on her first grandchild, Amelia spent most Sundays at Lackford Hall. She sat with Charlie and Sir Alan at church, then rode back with them in their gig.

'We're not going to London for the season this year,' Charlie told her when they were alone. 'Alan agrees that travelling with the baby is out of the question. I wouldn't dream of leaving her for someone else to look after, and besides, I haven't weaned her yet.' The tender expression on her face turned into a wicked grin, 'Just think, Ma, such bliss not having to endure dinner evenings with Beulah!'

Her ma smiled, 'I couldn't agree more after the way she turned up her nose at the christening dinner about my shop.' Amelia lifted her nose in exaggerated imitation, ' "Uh, fancy a *boutique* in a place like Swanwick!" I wanted to slap that supercilious smile off her face. No, without Beulah Lady Kingsly you can really look forward to April's first Christmas.'

'She'll be nine months by then,' said Charlie. 'She's already sitting up and trying to climb.'

'And Beulah won't want to come here,' said Amelia, glad that her immediate family would be home at Christmas. 'What about the Scott-Wilsons, and Stanleys?'

'Strange you should say that,' said Charlie. 'I received a letter yesterday from Sylvia's mother. She says as we shan't be seeing them at Christmas she and Mr Scott-Wilson would love to visit us in October before the bad weather sets in. I shall write and suggest they come after Harvest Home.'

'Yes,' Amelia agreed. 'Alan won't be so busy then, he'll enjoy their visit more.'

'We'll have a private harvest dinner party,' said Charlie. 'You'll join us, won't you, Ma? Jane and Luke will be invited, too.'

'I should like that,' said Amelia, 'if I'm not too busy. I must go to Frometown soon and buy a good supply of fresh straw to keep us busy through the winter.' She told Charlie of her plans to sell more stock at Poole next year. 'I've taken on more school leavers and we've turned the cellar into a basement where Hetty instructs the girls in net making and straw plait. They take bundles of prepared straw home to plait. It keeps the place much tidier.'

'Hetty is really coming on,' said Charlie. 'You've done wonders for her, Ma.'

'Not just me. Hetty's learned a lot from Jane, and Luke dotes on her like the grandchild he never had.'

By the time the Scott-Wilsons arrived at Lackford Hall in October, Charlie had organised the dinner party. Mr Scott-Wilson brought some London newspapers to read on the long journey, and when the men left the ladies after the meal, to smoke their pipes, they discussed the latest reports.

Despite a busy harvesting time nationwide, campaigners for the Tolpuddle men still found time to attack the Orange Lodges.

'I know you're following events,' Mr Scott-Wilson said to Sir Alan. 'You'll see the Home Secretary and the Prime Minister are at loggerheads, and Lord Russell is truly upset by what he sees as a travesty of justice.'

'Because lodge members still carry on making their oaths with impunity.' said Sir Alan, scanning the newspapers. Lord Russell had written to Lord Melbourne speaking up for the Dorchester labourers. He inferred that the Duke of

Cumberland – the king's brother – was far more guilty, and remarked disparagingly that the law did not reach HRH. Melbourne replied that he thought the matter was settled, and had no intention to do anything more for the men.

Still Russell persisted. None of the labourers were aware·they were breaking any law, he reasoned. All they'd done was act on the advice of union officials from London. As to the 'offence', two Acts of Parliament had to be put together in order to prove the thing was unlawful.

'The papers have a point,' said sir Alan, pursing his lips. 'If the Duke of Cumberland has done the same, justice should see that he too is punished.'

'Lord Melbourne thinks no one but he and his equals exist,' said Mr Scott-Wilson. 'Russell was irked by the PM's indifference – look there–'

He pointed to a paragraph giving the Home Secretary's written reply. 'He's told the Prime Minister that while he is in office the whole seven years will not be enforced, and Melbourne has told Russell he doesn't much care what is done respecting the Dorsetshire labourers ...'

'He is virtually giving Lord Russell a free hand,' Luke remarked. 'Perhaps that's a good sign.'

In the drawing room the ladies were more concerned with matters closer to home. Adele Scott-Wilson was bubbling with news she wished to share.

'I enjoyed the journey for once,' she began. 'The sun shone every day, and oh, the beautiful autumn colours on the trees. It was worth the journey to see them.'

'I'm sure that's not what you're bursting to tell us,' said Amelia, smiling.

'You're quite right. The reason that Sylvia and George didn't come was because Sylvia is pregnant with her first!'

'When is she due?' Amelia was delighted. Now she and Adele really had something in common.

'Next May,' Adele said breathlessly. 'This means so much to her, having yearned for children of her own. She won't risk travelling, so you won't see her 'til next year.'

Hetty was glad when she heard the news for several reasons, not the least being that Will would be home for Christmas. Mrs Sylvia's Stanley's happy event was bound to put distance between them.

Preparations went ahead as usual for Bonfire night, and a collection was taken up from the crowd for the Tolpuddle wives. Some folk could only afford a farthing, but everyone dipped into their pockets to find an odd copper or two. Local shopkeepers and merchants gave generous donations, and the money was given to Sir Alan who would pass through Dorchester on his way to Bridport.

'I shall be gone for some time,' he told Charlie as he made ready for his journey. 'When I finish my business I shall go down to Weymouth to meet Isobel, then we'll pick Hugh up on our way back. He'd arranged for Hugh to travel from Sherborne School and meet him in Dorchester. 'Ask your mother to write to Thomas then we'll fetch him home for Christmas, too.'

Six weeks before Christmas Hetty and Jane joined the other Church Singers to practice hymns and carols in Sam Roper's cottage next to his smithy. They were accompanied by a small band. Mary Dyke's father played first fiddle, Sarah Taylor and Billy Hart's fathers played first and second clarinets with Will's foreman Harris on the alto clarinet. Fred the cowman played the violin cello and Sam Roper completed the sextet on the bass trombone.

Hetty was delighted to be taking part in the tradition of carol singing around Swanwick, but she always hurried home after practice so as not to leave Biddy alone too long.

Then, a week before Christmas she became quiet and fidgety.

'Is something worrying you?' Amelia asked.

'It never occurred to me until now,' Hetty began, frowning. 'I shall be away much longer on Christmas Eve and I don't know what to do about my gran.'

'Mrs Maltravers and I have thought about that,' said Amelia. Mr Audley will spend the evening with me, and we thought we might invite Mrs Cauldon to join us. Mr Audley can pick her up in his pony trap.'

'Ooh, I don't know, ma'am.' Hetty sucked in her breath. Biddy would probably give a rude answer to the invitation. 'Me gran's not very sociable.'

'Perhaps Sandy could work his charms and call for her with Mr Audley. You never know, she might even enjoy the evening. Then you can be taken home together afterwards.'

Biddy's immediate reaction was as Hetty feared. But the old woman weakened when Hetty said 'There'll be a collection every time we stop to sing, and we all get a share.'

Then Sandy pleaded with Biddy that she didn't know what she was missing. He gave her no time to think. As she hesitated he said, 'Good. We'll call for you at six, now don't forget to wear your best bonnet.'

Biddy muttered and grumbled for the rest of the week, but when Luke and Sandy called for her she lapped up the fuss they made over her. It was a clear frosty night, the chill air turning the pony's breath into steam. Luke asked Biddy if she were warm enough when he and Sandy helped her into the trap. He gave her a muff for her hands while Sandy wrapped a blanket around her legs and placed her feet on a cushion. 'There y'are, Granma. Be that comfy enough?'

'Get on with ye, ye young varmint,' she cackled. 'I ain't

never bin so comfy in me life.' It was many years since she'd had a ride in a pony trap and she felt quite sorry when they arrived at Amelia's house. She puffed and wheezed making the most of the attention as Sandy helped her down and Luke took her arm to escort her inside. Hetty grinned after them and went to find Jane.

Amelia greeted Biddy politely, led her to an easy chair by the fire and told her she might smoke if she wished. When the old woman was settled Luke served her a glass of mulled wine while Jane slipped out with Hetty, and Sandy escaped with Tommy Freer to find their mates.

The Church Singers and the band assembled at Sam's cottage then marched to the nearest pub to begin serenading. After fortifying themselves with hot punch they did a round of the well-to-do inhabitants' houses, various tradesmen's and coal and stone merchants. From farmhouse to public house they went, wherever appreciative listeners would put coins in their hat. They marched down to the shore and the Customs House, then retraced their steps until they came to the rectory where Parson Bartlett's butler served them with best wine from the cellar.

It was the early hours of the morning before they finished at the inn near Sam's cottage. There they were joined by Will, who had come home for Christmas.
Seeing him Hetty felt too happy to notice her feet were numb from the cold. Sandy and Tommy stood with Will and when Hetty found herself placed close to them she couldn't resist glancing their way while she sang.

Her gaze met Sandy's and she blushed furiously to think he'd caught her ogling Will. She quickly looked away and concentrated on her song sheet.

Hiding a grin, Sandy nudged Will, 'Look at Hetty. She be singing her heart out. She aint got a bad voice, neither.'

Will turned his gaze on Hetty who pretended not to notice.

The last carol was *Silent Night*. It was Hetty's favourite, and she immersed herself in it. In her mind's eye she saw Charlie suckling her babe, the expression on her face tender and mild like the words in the carol. Hetty closed her eyes with the effort of singing as sweetly as she knew how. Warm from all her exertions, and an unaccustomed amount of wine, she did not see Jane watching her.

Jane hadn't missed a thing. How radiant Hetty looks, she thought, glancing at Will and Sandy to see if they noticed. Just which one is our Hetty sweet on?

Oh dear, it's just as well Amelia stayed home with Luke and Biddy. Will had put down his drink and was staring at Hetty as if spellbound, while Sandy stepped towards Lizzie Harris wearing the soppy expression of a tipsy youth.

The spell, if indeed that's what it was for Will and Hetty, was broken when everyone joined in a rousing chorus of *Oh Come All Ye Faithful*.

'Come, Hetty,' Jane said as the singers dispersed, 'We must collect your grandmother and take you home.' Seeing how tired but happy Hetty looked, she hugged her. 'Merry Christmas, my dear.'

It wasn't far to Amelia's, and Will and Tommy walked with them. Though befuddled with wine and weariness Hetty noticed Sandy was missing. 'Where's Sandy?' she wondered.

'Oh, he's gone all daft over Lizzie Harris,' said Tommy. Approaching adolescence, he still thought of girls as mere objects to be teased for a bit of fun. 'Said he was taking her home. I suppose he'll be kissing her next.'

'I wouldn't be surprised,' said Will, smiling at Jane.

'I hope he didn't drink too much tonight,' Hetty said.

'He made himself sick from the booze at the Whit Tuesday dance.'

Tommy sniggered, 'He might be sick over Lizzie when he kisses her.'

'Don't be disgusting,' said Will. 'I kept my eye on Sandy to make sure he didn't overdo it.'

'You kept your eye on me, too,' Tommy complained, 'and only let me have lemonade.'

Hetty had never felt Will's nearness more keenly. Stone masonry might seem menial to some, but Will was his own master. As a small contractor helping to improve the great City of London, he was important in Swanwick. But it was more than pride in being his friend that made her hang on to every word he uttered.

With her attention on him and Tommy, in the dark she didn't see the deep wheel rut in the road. 'Oops!'

She stumbled and would have fallen if Will hadn't caught her. She clung to him automatically as he steadied her, and oh, how strong his arms were, and his hands so big and warm.

'You all right, Hetty?' he asked. He sounded genuinely concerned and seemed quite sober.

'I think so. Thanks, Will.' She managed a sheepish smile, relieved that the darkness hid her rising colour. She felt giddy, with no desire to pull away as he continued to hold her arm.

'Ah, here we are,' Jane said, as they neared Amelia's front door. 'It is fortunate you didn't turn your ankle.'

She meant it kindly, but to Hetty it was like being doused with cold water. *She knows how I feel about Will. I'm sure she does.*

The thought brought Hetty down to earth with a jolt. She made to follow Jane and Tommy inside, but Will put a hand on her shoulder.

'Just a minute, Hetty.' They were close enough to make out each other's features as he turned her to face him.

'Yes, Will?' Hetty gazed up at him in confusion. It was hard being so near to him, knowing she could never measure up to Sylvia.

'I'm sorry, Will,' she faltered. 'I be the one who's had too much to drink. I ain't used to all that mulled wine and hot punch. I feel a bit stupid.'

'You don't look stupid, in fact I thought you seemed really happy tonight. And I never knew you had such a lovely voice. You were serene.'

Hetty's eyes widened in wonder at such praise. 'Oh – you are kind–'

Watching her face, Will felt something melt inside him. A strange sensation. 'Kind, be damned,' he said brusquely. He jerked her to him and kissed her on the lips. 'Happy Christmas, Hetty, you deserve it.'

'Ah, there you are, Will!'

Hetty gasped as Amelia's voice hailed them from the porch, her figure silhouetted against the light that spilled from the open door. 'Hetty, your grandmother is all rugged up, ready to go!'

'Ye-es ma'am, I'm coming.' Hot with embarrassment, Hetty hastily whispered, 'Goodnight Will.'

Chapter Eighteen

1836

Luke and Jane drove the Cauldons home on their way back to Underhill Manor. Biddy went straight to bed, but despite her tiredness Hetty took a long time to settle. She felt bewildered, apprehensive and excited. This was her best Christmas ever – and was it possible that Will felt something for her? The first time he kissed her she'd cried herself to sleep because he was tipsy and she'd felt humiliated. Tonight he hadn't drunk too much, he was concerned when she nearly fell down, and he'd wished her Happy Christmas – privately! Surely that meant something? And she'd responded to him. But what of Amelia?

Hetty guessed her employer got suspicious when Jane and Luke arrived without her and Will, then came to her front door and seen them kiss. *Oh dear.*

Whatever happened, Hetty thought drowsily, I shall always treasure his kiss. No one could take that precious moment from her. Will would never see her as beautiful – she just wasn't. But he said she had a lovely voice, and that while she sang she looked 'serene'.

The word was new to Hetty, it sounded like something beautiful. Next time she went to Mr Audley for tuition she would look it up in Mr Johnson's Dictionary …

She slept at last and only awoke when the church bells rang for Christmas Day's afternoon service. Then the singers had to perform again, this time accompanied by the organ. There was a full congregation, including dissenters who joined in to share the festive season.

After the service the carol singers' collection money was counted and interested bystanders clapped when the total was announced.

'Hetty, you're the newest and youngest member of our group,' said the lead singer. 'Why don't you distribute the money?'

The honour was unexpected, and Hetty felt embarrassed at being the centre of attention. Then she realised that most folk were busy discussing what they would do with their part of the proceeds. I shall have to give mine to me gran, she thought, seeing as it was how I persuaded her to go to Mrs Freer's for the evening. She'll reckon I had my reward from taking part – which admittedly, she'd enjoyed.

She blushed, seeing Will looking at her, but it gave her an idea. If she wasn't to keep the money her gran wasn't going to get it either.

Standing in the middle of the group she looked at the leader, took a deep breath and said, 'I'd like to give my share to the Tolpuddle wives. I don't reckon they're having a very happy Christmas.'

For a brief moment there was silence, then Sam Roper spoke up. 'That's a noble gesture, maid,' he boomed. 'An' I cain't think of a more worthy cause!'

'Aye,' someone shouted in the crowd, 'Well done, maid!'

So the proceeds were kept intact, and Rev. Bartlett said, 'Who will take this blessed gift to Dorchester?'

Will stepped forward. 'I can take it, I have business there in the new year.'

The money bag was given to him for safe keeping, and the crowd dispersed to enjoy the rest of Christmas.

Will walked Hetty as far as the Warren Stables and the tender look he gave her warmed Hetty to her core. She had pleased and impressed Will!

'Are you taking Tommy back to school, then?' she asked. She couldn't help being curious about his reason to visit Dorchester, for fear he might get into trouble by sticking up for the Tolpuddle men and their families.

'That, too,' he said. Ma wants me to look at the house her Aunt Mary left her, make sure everything is in order. I'll be around until February, for the Shrove Tuesday meeting, so if any repairs need doing I'll have time to see to them. The place will be mine and Tommy's one day.'

'Ah, I see,' said Hetty. What Will's ma really wanted, she thought, was to put distance between him and herself.

Early on a frosty morning in January, when the roads were hard, Will and Tommy drove to Dorchester with Sir Alan who was taking Hugh back to Sherborne.

'I have to stay for a few days,' Will told Sir Alan, 'so I'll take the mail coach back to Frometown.' He would go by carrier's cart from there to Swanwick.

Sir Alan gave him a warning look when they parted. 'Take care, Will.'

He meant for Will not to risk trouble over the Tolpuddle business. 'Don't worry, sir. I'll give the money to the agent who handles the wives' finances.'

Business was quiet in the *Amelia Jane Boutique*, but Hetty and the other assistants kept busy building up their stock. Easter was earlier this year, and as Mr Barton said it was the most important festival in the Church calendar. So it was also important to concentrate on the fancy bonnets that would be in demand by then. Many young couples liked to marry at Easter time, then there was the Good Friday Club walk, and a few weeks later the Whit Tuesday holiday.

'Will told me it was your idea to give the carolling money to the Tolpuddle wives,' Amelia said to Hetty that January morning. 'That was most commendable.' Her manner was always more pleasant towards Hetty when Will wasn't around. After all, the girl was likeable, just not a suitable match for her son. After seeing them kissing on Christmas Eve Amelia feared their becoming sweethearts.

'Thank you, ma'am,' said Hetty, wishing Will was someone else's son. It irked her to think that while Mrs Freer was fair to her employees, she looked down on them and especially on herself. She could not resist repeating something Mr Audley once said.

'It might not be much,' she began, 'but I always think that a little bit of help is worth a ton of sympathy. 'tis a pity them in Parliament can't see it that way,' she dared to add.

'Well, yes I agree,' said Amelia, surprised by Hetty's sudden flash of wisdom, and went to see how the others were doing.

Hetty wanted to ask when Will would be back, but decided it wasn't worth the risk of aggravating her employer. At least Dorchester was nearer than London, so she was sure to see something of Will.

Her hopes were squashed when the sky grew dark and it became bitterly cold as black snow clouds gathered. It snowed hard overnight, and with the roads made impassable there was no chance of Will coming home until a thaw set in.

Hetty, however, soon had more pressing concerns.

The damp and cold went to Biddy's chest and she succumbed to one ailment after another. Smoking her clay pipe made her cough and splutter, and she was more cantankerous than ever without it. When she began wheezing badly and Hetty feared it would turn to pneumonia, Biddy refused to let her fetch the doctor. All Hetty could do was dose her gran with their home-made rosehip syrup, massage her chest with cod oil and keep her as warm as possible. This was easier said than done with damp logs, and it meant taking time off work.

Gran Cauldon might not see another winter, Hetty began to realise. She tried to be nicer, and understanding. She made up the truckle bed downstairs and heated bricks to wrap and put under her gran's feet. Now the words she'd spoken to Amelia came back at her, only Biddy appreciated sympathy more than all Hetty's efforts to look after her.

When the quarrymen were unable to work, while many of them went fishing Sandy came in to relieve Hetty so she could go to the shop for a few hours each day. His presence had the effect of rallying the old woman and Biddy slowly improved.

Hetty found her fellow workers in great spirits. 1836 was a leap year, and they teased each other about which lads they would propose marriage to at the end of February.

'You gonna ask Sandy Mason?' Lizzie Harris demanded of Hetty.

'No I ain't,' Hetty retorted. 'He be too young an' flighty. Anyway, I'd prefer a proposal to come from the man, an' I got nobody in mind.' It wasn't true, of course. Even if she had the courage to ask Will, there was no possibility he would say yes, then things would be very awkward between them.

As it happened she never got the chance.

Will made it back just in time for the quarrymen's Shrove Tuesday meeting, the last week in February. By which time King William had opened the new parliamentary session. Will had heard enough during his time in Dorchester to renew his interest in supporting the Cause, and hastened back to London.

As soon as Parliament resumed, Mr Hume had raised

the matter of the Orange Lodges and forced a debate. Lord Russell backed him, saying all secret societies should be suppressed. The king issued orders to make membership of a Lodge within the army a court-martial offence, but Mr Hume still maintained that all lodges were illegal.

By March, it was known that an indictment against the Duke of Cumberland was being prepared for the next Grand Inquest of Middlesex. He was to be charged with being the head of an illegal society. That a prince of the blood royal should be tried by Petty Jury with the risk of his being transported, was unthinkable! There would be no peace for King William until he yielded.

In the House of commons on 14th March, in answer to a query from Mr Wakley, little Lord Russell took great satisfaction in announcing that His Majesty had been pleased to grant a free pardon to all six Tolpuddle martyrs.

The pardon was dated 10th March, almost exactly two years from the day of sentence. Within a week Lord Russell received a letter of gratitude from the Tolpuddle wives. Meanwhile the newspapers made a sensation of the government's misjudgement and defeat. Driven by the Radicals and trade unionists, they declared, victory was won by a nation-wide sense of justice rather than law. All fair minded men had reason to be jubilant.

Accompanied by a smiling Jane, Luke broke the news to Amelia before she heard it from Will.

Hetty bounced for joy. She beamed with pride when Luke said, 'And to think we all played a small part in their release by signing Will's petitions.'

'Easter will be extra special this year,' said Jane, 'particularly for the men's families.'

'It's a great triumph for the campaigners,' Luke said soberly, 'but it will take months for the martyrs to receive the news and be brought home.'

Chapter Nineteen

'Ere, get that down ye, matey.'

Abe Manuel pulled the blanket tighter around him to stop his shivering and taking the tot of rum from the hand that offered it, downed it in one gulp.

This was his second escape from a doomed ship – not his own doing this time and there were other survivors. Here in the north Atlantic he knew nothing, and would have cared less, about the jubilation over the pardon of the Tolpuddle martyrs.

He'd kept a lookout for Hetty Cauldon that Thursday, last August, but there was no sign of the wench. He was about to ask Effie about her, when the skipper of the market hoy gave the stall woman a note. Abe waited until Effie was alone then asked her.

'Yon maid won't be here again 'til next year,' Effie told him. 'This yer be her note to explain.'

Abe saw a glint of suspicion in the woman's eyes. She must wonder why a rough seafarer should be interested in the maid. Or was it something else? Had Hetty told anyone about him? Will's mother would know he was never a friend of her late husband. Perhaps she'd stopped Hetty from coming. Village folk never liked strangers. What if Mrs Freer spoke to the authorities and they came looking?

It was time to move on, business was slack anyway

while everyone was busy harvesting. The ferry master paid him off with no questions asked.

Abe had no trouble joining the Newfoundland fishing fleet. Whale blubber and sealskins were always in demand, and the cod fishing was plentiful off the Great Banks. Hoping to transfer to an American or Canadian ship, he'd passed the winter earning his living the hard way, and with no luck.

In early spring he found employment on a herring boat. It was then disaster struck. The ship was blown off course by a 50mph gale. For two days she was tossed and swamped by huge waves, and barely avoided being wrecked on the rocky coast of Greenland. Fishing was forgotten in the crew's strenuous efforts at the pumps to save the ship. When at last the storm subsided they began the perilous voyage back. By then the sea was infested with ice drifting down from the Arctic and they became stuck in it. Rescued eventually by a merchant ship trading with Newfoundland, Abe and his companions were now bound for Bristol.

'What'll ye do now?' one of the crew asked when at last they saw England's west coast on the horizon.

'Don't know yet,' Abe growled. 'I've had enough of the sea, I fancy being a landlubber.' He didn't intend to spend another winter like this last one.

'Eastertide be come an' gone,' said the man. 'There'll be work to be had at the summer fairs soon.'

'That'll suit me, mate,' said Abe, 'I worked with one years ago.'

A travelling fair would be ideal. The misfortune of the herring boat gave him ample plausible answers to any questions that might be asked. Also, with his beard grown long and twice as thick, he felt safe from any chance of recognition.

By Easter business at the *Amelia Jane Boutique* was booming. Then as things quietened during the lull until Whitsun, Hetty once again took the market hoy to Poole. Sylvia Stanley had given birth to a healthy baby boy early in May and Jane and Amelia were invited to the christening which was to take place on the first Sunday in June.

Mr Crabb the postman delivered the invitations to the shop where Amelia and Jane opened them together. Jane gasped, 'My goodness, I haven't been to London for a long time. It never occurred to me I should ever go again.'

'I haven't been since I was a very young girl,' said Amelia. 'I went there once with *Maman* to see Lord Nelson's funeral procession. Oh dear, I'm not worried about Adele or Sylvia, but I dread being scrutinised by Beulah and her friends.'

Has Lady Beulah got any friends? Hetty wondered disparagingly.

'Charlotte and Alan will be with us,' Jane was saying. 'I'm sure they can handle Beulah.'

They were delighted when one morning Charlie wheeled her pram into the shop. She lifted April out, and said proudly,   'Baby's just taken her first steps.' She held the child's hand as April bounced up and down on her feet, her little face a picture of triumph.

'My, isn't she lovely,' said Jane. 'Hasn't she grown!'

'She will be fourteen months by June,' said Amelia, crouching to catch April as the child took faltering steps towards her.

'Yes,' said Charlie, 'and Alan agrees she's old enough to travel. He says you must both come with us.' Eyeing her baby meaningfully she added, 'I for one will be grateful for your company!'

Thinking about the shop, Amelia asked, 'When shall we leave?'

'Alan says to complete the journey in time we shall have

to start immediately after Whitsuntide,' Charlie told her.

Hetty was to be left in sole charge of the shop, which she was already doing more or less, with Amelia busy packing and comparing notes with Jane.

The Thursday before Whitsun Hetty told Effie she wouldn't be coming to Poole again until July. 'I have to take care of the shop,' she said, and explained about Amelia going to London. 'Business will be slack anyway after Whit Tuesday 'cause nobody will have any money.'

'Yer,' said Effie suddenly, 'I just remembered. D'ye recall that bloke you met last summer and he rowed you back across t'harbour?'

'Yes,' said Hetty. 'He seemed quite nice for a rough old sea dog. Said he fought ol' Bony with the father of a friend of mine – er with my employer's husband, actually. Oh, I forgot all about him, and I meant to tell her.'

'He come looking for you after you stopped coming,' Effie went on. 'Then he disappeared, an' I ain't seen him since.

'Looking for me? I wonder why?'

'He never said, but I'd be a bit careful if I were you. You'm gullible, maid, and there was something about him I didn't like. There was never no sign of a wife, neither. I don't reckon he had one.'

Hetty shrugged.

'Aah well, he's gone now and I ain't likely to see him again.' But she couldn't help wondering why he should be asking after her. Mrs Freer wouldn't be interested now, she was too excited about going to London. Hetty decided that when Will came home she would tell him about the man.

Will had written to say he was coming home for Whitsun, and would miss the christening in London. It seemed there was a problem at his new quarry, and he felt it was more important to get that sorted.

Sandy told Hetty about it. 'We hauled up the first load o' stone from the new shaft,' he said, 'and when I split 'em they was all rough and uneven inside. I thought 'twas my fault an' I weren't half scared o' what Mr Harris would say.'

'What did he say?' Hetty asked.

Sandy grinned ruefully, 'He examined 'em an' said 'twasn't my clumsy hammerin' what spoiled 'em, but they ain't suitable for building.'

'So he sent for Will?' Hetty's heart leapt at the thought.

'Yep. Thought it were best he seen 'em for hisself. We cain't export rotten stone, 'twould be more than our reputation be worth.'

Hetty had to run the bonnet stall alone on Whit Tuesday so there was no time to wander around. Amelia's made sure of it, she thought, in case I go looking for Will. Well, there's still the dance tonight.

To her surprise Will came to the stall to see her.

'You on your own today, then, Hetty?'

Hetty blushed with pleasure and felt the colour rush to her cheeks. 'Aah,' she said, 'Your ma be busy with last minute packing. When did you get back, I never seen you in church on Sunday?'

Will grimaced, 'The coach broke down. We had to spend Saturday night and Sunday in Romsey. 'tis a pity it didn't go through Poole or I could have finished the journey by sea.'

The mention of Poole reminded Hetty she had something to tell Will.

'What did this man look like?' he asked when she'd finished her tale. 'Did he say his name?'

'No, and I didn't like to ask, although he wasn't dressed like he was one of my betters. His clothes were shabby. It was silly of me, I should have done.'

It amused Will to hear Hetty speak of her betters. He

186

never thought of her as beneath him, just a village girl. But her description, particularly the bit about his steely eyes, reminded Will of the man he'd seen watching him at Ower last year, and had since forgotten. Why did the man look away when he knew Will saw him? And why would he be looking for Hetty?

'If he really knew my pa, I should like to meet him. But you say Effie disapproved of him? You take care, I don't like the sound of this man. If you see him again, ask his name and let me know. Or tell Sir Alan.'

Will was niggled by suspicion, why he couldn't tell. Right now he had other things to worry about.

'How long are you here for?' Hetty asked.

'Until I sort out the problem at my new quarry,' he said, frowning. 'If the stone really is dud, it could ruin my business. I don't understand it, I'm sure my dad's map of the seams is right. Anyway, I'm going there now.'

He turned to leave, but Hetty had one more question.

'You coming to the dance tonight?'

He looked back at her and found her expression most appealing. Her green eyes were large, shining with hope. Her lips parted in an eager half smile, just enough to show her small white teeth. Although he'd kissed her to wish her a happy new year he'd had no idea of the effect he had on her. She really wants me to be there, he thought.

'I expect so,' he said with a teasing smile. 'I'd better show willing.'

Hetty watched him go with a warm glow in her breast. Surely he would dance with her, perhaps walk her home afterwards – and kiss her goodnight?

She was still smiling to herself when Charlie and Sir Alan came by, and had to stop her day-dreaming.

April was sitting up in her pram looking adorable in a little broderie-anglaise bonnet. She gave Hetty an idea.

'What if we made some small sun hats for children? I think they would be cooler than bonnets tied at the chin – when the days get really hot, I mean.'

'A splendid idea,' said Charlie. 'Don't you agree, Alan?'

She smiled at her husband and he nodded. 'They would be suitable for little boys, too,' he said. 'We can't let them go around in bonnets, can we?'

The two young women laughed, and Sir Alan began strolling on with the pram.

'Have you mentioned your idea to my mother?' Charlie asked Hetty.

'Not yet,' said Hetty, 'I only just thought of it.'

Charlie winked, 'I'll suggest it to her. It will give her something to think about, take her mind off Beulah.'

For Hetty packing up time couldn't come soon enough. Then the locals could prepare for the evening's entertainment at the Dun Cow, and the travelling fair would move on. She sometimes saw the odd stranger from the fair looking around, but took no notice unless they came to buy from her.

One woman who did buy a bonnet told Hetty they had to be at a place called Barnstaple in Devon for its July fair, so there was to be no hanging about. 'Good pickings there,' the woman said. 'Fair goes for a whole week!'

Amelia and Jane came to help with the packing up. Clearly trying to sound casual Amelia asked Hetty if she'd seen Will.

'He came by here,' said Hetty, just as casually. 'Said he was going to the quarr to look at dud stone. I think Sandy went with him. Are you ladies coming to the dance tonight, ma'am?'

'No,' said Amelia, 'Mrs Maltravers and I need an early night. Sir Alan is calling for us at dawn.'

No more was said, and Hetty never worked more quickly. She was in such a hurry to go home and get ready for the dance. She was totally unaware of the bearded man who lingered nearby, listening to every word.

When the travelling fair started on its way, no one noticed Abe Manuel slip away in a different direction, towards the woods below Lackford Hall.

Chapter Twenty

∽

At the quarry Sandy watched Will examine the stones. The lad was worried he could be out of a job if this new quarry proved to be worthless.

'Not all the stones be bad as them,' he offered hopefully. He was surprised to see Will's expression change to a grin.

'See these marks?' Will made Sandy look closely. 'These lines, dents and ridges were made by ancient creatures that got trapped and died in the mud aeons ago, before it turned to stone.'

Sandy peered closer. 'So what's that gurt snail thing?'

'That's an ammonite,' said Will. 'I've seen them at the British Museum, and I've read about 'em in books. They're fossils. You've heard of Mary Anning – she found all sorts of things on the beach at Lyme.'

'You know I cain't read much,' said Sandy. He pointed to another stone in disgust, 'What about this un, then? 'tis all humps an' hollows.'

Will laughed out loud. 'That's a dinosaur's footprint. Gurt monsters they were. Good job they became extinct millions of years ago.'

'You wot?' Bewildered by Will's sudden good humour, and the idea of millions of years, Sandy shrugged. 'Whatever they be, you cain't sell 'em to builders.'

'No, but we can sell 'em to museums – not just in this

country either. Fossil hunters and collectors will pay a fortune for these.'

Sandy stared at him. 'So, you ain't gonna go bust?'

'No, this seam is better than my dad thought. Come on Sandy, let's get ready for the dance, and tomorrow I'll write letters to men I think will be interested.'

Sandy was baffled with talk about creatures dying millions of years ago. He was just glad he wasn't going to be put out of work. 'I won't be calling for Hetty tonight,' he said, to get back to more immediate matters. 'I'm taking Lizzie Harris. Are you gonna take Hetty?'

'No, I don't think she expects me to,' said Will. 'Why do you ask?'

'Don't you know she's crazy about you? She's seventeen now, you know.'

'Is she?' Will grinned, 'She's missed her chance then, she never said anything, and 'tis leap year.'

'Well she wouldn't, would she? She's too shy.'

'I'll give her a dance, then.' Will hurried on, eager to tell his ma about the fossils.

'My, Will. You'll be famous.' It was the happiest Amelia had seen him since his disappointment over Sylvia. Then, when he spoke about the dance she added seriously, 'I hope you're not getting too fond of Hetty?'

Will stared at her. 'Hetty? I suppose I am fond of her, she's easy to be with and talk to. I don't have to mind my 'p's and 'q's with her, or worry about how I'm dressed. She understands about my work, and shows real interest. I've got used to Hetty being around, Ma, like one of the family. Why do you ask?'

'I was afraid your feelings for her might go deeper,' said Amelia, relieved. 'Only you're going up in the world, my lad. You already own this house and the stables, as well as your own business. You more than qualify for the vote, and in September you'll come of age.' She patted him on the shoulder, 'Then I shall put the deeds of my house in Dorchester in your name. You're a man of substance, Will, and I'd like to see you married to the daughter of a wealthy merchant, or banker perhaps. Someone more worthy of you than Hetty.'

Will stared at his mother. 'I'm too busy these days to think about marriage. I ain't thought about anyone since Sylvia.'

'Perhaps one day you'll meet a nice girl in Dorchester,' said Amelia, 'the sort of person I'd approve of.'

Will hid a smirk. 'I'll see what I can do, Ma. Right now I'm married to me work.'

He went to get cleaned up, amused to think his ma was worrying about who he might marry. Strange that she should be the second person within the hour to mention Hetty.

Will was never out of Hetty's thoughts. Especially this afternoon as she hurried home. What might the evening bring, she wondered, her stomach churning with excitement. Knowing Amelia wouldn't be at the dance keeping her eye on Will, Hetty let her fancy take flight. She imagined herself in his strong arms, holding hands as he walked her home – very late in the moonlight – pausing to kiss in the shadow of the trees. Mm, such delicious thoughts …

She was startled out of her reverie when, approaching her gran's cottage, she noticed there was no smoke coming out of the chimney. Gran's let the fire go out, she thought, mean old thing. Now I'll have to get all dirty lighting it again, supper will be late and I'll have to rush to get ready for the dance. She really didn't want a set to with her gran because that wasted time, and getting annoyed would spoil her looks. Such as they were. Hetty always forgot how plain she was when she talked to Will, and when he smiled at her she felt, well, *almost* pretty.

Trust old Biddy to bring her down to earth! Pity Sandy wouldn't be calling for her, now he had Lizzie Harris in tow. Gran always mellowed when he was around.

Hetty took some deep breaths to calm herself and was surprised to hear voices as she paused. Who could be visiting her gran?

When she opened the door Hetty's curiosity turned to shock. Her eyes widened sharply on seeing the stranger, whose huge bulk seemed to fill their tiny downstairs room. She recognised him at once, although his beard was long and bushy. It was the old seaman, only there was nothing nice about him now. He stood over Biddy in a threatening manner, holding the eye patch he'd snatched from her.

Hearing Hetty gasp, Abe turned and gave her an ugly leer. 'Ah, come on in, Biddy's little granddaughter.'

'What are you doin' here?'

'I'm an old acquaintance of yer gran's,' he said in a mocking tone.

'You two know each other?' Biddy croaked, her bony fingers clawing at the shawl around her shoulders. Hetty had never seen her so agitated.

'We met in Poole,' said Hetty, all thoughts of the dance gone out of her head. 'That day I had to walk all along Holywell beach. I forgot to tell you, I was too tired.'

'So you never told no one about me,' said Abe. That was more than he'd hoped for.

Hetty felt frightened, and angry. Effie was right about her being gullible, she saw now that she'd been far too trusting. She'd been a fool, but she knew better than to say she'd told Will about him. Trying to still her trembling she said, 'I asked what you want yer, Mister. And you never said you know my gran.'

'Me and yer gran go back a long way. Tell her, Biddy.'

'From the smuggling days.' Biddy's voice quavered, 'He were the mate on the *Esmerelda*.'

'Henry Warren's ship?' Hetty faltered, memories flooding back. 'You used to hide smuggled goods in our cellar, then the crew murdered coastguard Skinner and Will was framed for his murder.'

'That were nothing to do with me,' said Abe.

'I thought you'd all been hanged or transported–'

'Fortune smiled on me,' Abe sneered. 'I escaped, and now I'm on me way to America. But I need money–'

He paused to cast a sardonic glance around the room then turned back to Biddy.

'You were paid good money. I can see you ain't spent it on doin' up this hovel, so you must have it stashed away somewhere!'

Hetty was more angry than afraid now. 'How dare you come here to rob us!'

'I didn't come to steal, I come to ask for help but she won't give it.

'I cain't,' Biddy wailed, 'I ain't got no money.'

'I don't believe you.'

'If she has, I've never seen it,' said Hetty truthfully. Biddy would never tell her how much she'd hoarded, or where.

'So you don't know where 'tis, and she won't tell. I'm tired of asking nicely, so if you know what's good for you both–' He drew a hunting knife from his belt.

'I keep tellin' ye, I got no money!' Biddy cried again. 'Run, Hetty, run!'

Hetty wasn't about to leave her gran with this rogue. She took a step back as Abe came towards her. Desperately trying to think, she cried, 'You can have my wages I been saving, so long as you just go away!'

She made for the stairs to fetch the coins she'd hidden in her room, but Abe dragged her back. 'No ye don't, maid. Your few pennies ain't enough, and I ain't havin' you climb out yer winder and escape.'

He hauled Hetty back into the room, and clasping her around the neck with one arm he brandished the knife at Biddy.

'No,' Biddy cried, 'let her go – you varmint!'

'Find that money lickety-spit,' he ground out, shoving the knife against Hetty's throat. 'Or I'll do fer yer precious granddaughter!'

Paralysed with terror, her limbs limp, Hetty opened her mouth to scream. But no sound came. She could only stare at her gran like a dumb animal.

Wheezing and gasping, Biddy scraped back her rocking chair as she struggled to her feet. Prising up a loose flagstone she put her hand into a hole beneath and pulled out a leather pouch.

'Here,' she rasped, panting. The pouch jingled as she held it out with a hand shaking like she had the ague.

'Put it on the table then sit down.'

Biddy obeyed and collapsed in her chair with a hand over her heart. Her face was ashen.

'Now let her go,' she muttered painfully.

Surprise at the discovery of Biddy's hiding place steadied Hetty's nerves. She recovered enough wit to think how crafty her gran was, hiding the spot with her long skirts and blankets. Desperately trying to overcome her fear, she pulled on Abe's arm with both hands to relieve the choking pressure. What would he do now? He would have to put down the knife, or let her go, to pick up the pouch.

Abe kept hold of his knife, and loosing her suddenly, shoved her towards the corner where Biddy kept her braiding equipment. 'Get that ball of twine and tie the old hag up!'

Shock and anger rose above her fear, and Hetty found her voice. 'No,' she gasped. 'You got the money. Just go, and leave us alone!'

'I ain't got time to pussy-foot around,' Abe snarled. ''Tis either that or I'll have to kill you both.'

Hetty glared at him. Her mind working feverishly, she moved slowly to fetch the twine.

'Hurry up, you stupid maid!'

Biddy had regained her breath and was shrieking curses at Abe, catching his attention briefly. While he glowered at the old woman Hetty pounced on the ball of twine and threw it hard at his head.

'Do it yerself,' she cried and made a dash for the door.

Abe was too quick, and too strong. She'd barely lifted the latch when he grabbed a fistful of her hair and wrenched her away from the door. She screamed with pain, then he struck her a blow across the face with the back of his hand that sent her reeling. Her head hit the stone wall, and she fell senseless.

When she came to, Hetty's head was throbbing and her face felt sore. As she put her hands up to feel gingerly for any damage, she realised her hands were bound tightly together. She stared groggily at the wizened figure slouched in the rocking chair, all animosity between them forgotten. Gran Cauldon was the only family she had, and right now Hetty cared desperately about her.

Fearing Biddy had fainted, or worse, Hetty pushed herself up from a kneeling position. The effort made her head hurt more. Abe was helping himself from their larder, stuffing bread and cheese into his pockets.

'What you done to my gran?' Hetty demanded, her heart full of loathing.

'Tied her up, like you said. Now she can't get out and tell about us.'

'Us?'

'Yep, you're coming wi' me.' He threw her cloak around her, and grabbed the cord that dangled from her wrists. 'Do as you're told, or you'll be sorry. We've already lost too much daylight.'

Hatred made her bold. 'Why d'ye want me, I'll only slow you down.'

'You're my security,' he said. 'We're father and daughter, see? No one will suspect an old man travelling with his daughter. If you do as you're told, I might let ye go once I'm on board ship.'

Still dazed, Hetty had no strength to fight. All she cared about was her gran. With Squire and Charlie away, everyone would be at the pubs or the dance. There was no one around to help her. She decided to go along with this hateful man, the sooner to be rid of him. Thinking Abe must be going to take a boat from a cliff quarry, with a sob in her voice she cried, 'Hang on Gran, I'll run back quick as I can.'

Abe opened the door and stepped outside, dragging Hetty after him.

Chapter Twenty-One

⌒

They didn't go to the cliff. Abe led Hetty westwards along the empty road until they were several miles from Swanwick. Then he followed a farm track leading on to the downs that overlooked the English Channel. On and on they went, along the upper coast path, towards the setting sun. Any other time Hetty would have enjoyed the view, with the sun painting the clouds a glorious pink in its dying moments. Now she felt as if she were dying, too. Weariness and anxiety brought her to the edge of tears, but what was the use of crying?

By the time they stopped after three hours of walking Hetty had no idea where she was, she'd never been this far before. It was dark but for a waning moon and Hetty could see they were by-passing a farm. Tears of exhaustion she could no longer control slid down her cheeks and she stumbled with weariness.

Nearby was a spring where Abe let her scoop up the fresh water to quench her thirst, then he pushed her into a barn.

'We'll bed down here for the night.' He offered her some bread and cheese. At first she refused it. 'You better take it,' he said, 'you'll need your strength tomorrow. We got another half a day's walking to Weymouth.'

'Weymouth?' she gasped.

'Yep,' he said with a mirthless grin. 'And that's where you'll play your part as me daughter, to anyone we meet on the way. How d'ye fancy a new life in America?'

Hetty was horrified.

'No,' she cried, as apprehension uncoiled inside her. 'I'd rather die!' The thought of never seeing her gran or Swanwick ever again was unbearable. And Will, would he miss her? A sob of misery rose in her throat.

'Lie down and get some sleep, stupid maid,' Abe growled. He pushed her on to a pile of hay in the corner then settled himself next to her.

Hetty fought exhaustion to keep awake. She would find the strength somehow to escape when Abe was asleep. But how, when her wrists were tied and the other end of the rope was around his waist? She thought of Biddy tied to that chair. Her gran could be dead by morning. Grief, and guilt for not being nicer to the old woman played on her mind, while tears of sorrow and exhaustion wet her cheeks. Before she knew it, Hetty had cried herself to sleep.

She was woken in the grey light of dawn by Abe roughly shaking her.

'C'mon. Up ye get, maid.'

Still heavy with sleep, Hetty felt more cross than afraid. She began nagging him to let her go.

'You be safe 'nuff now. Why can't you let me get back to me gran. 'Twill be your fault if she's dead. You don't care nothing' fer nobody, do ye?'

She stopped short at calling him insulting names when he raised his hand. She didn't want any more bruises, so she glared at him instead. His mouth tugged into a grim smile, and there was a strange glint in his eyes.

He allowed her just enough time to kneel at the spring to splash her face and quench her thirst before making her climb the steep hill on the far side of the valley.

She plodded behind him, grumbling to herself to stem the fear inside her. Apart from all the trouble the rotten ol' varmint caused, he'd stopped her going to the dance, and seeing Will. And what about the shop? With Amelia and Jane away there was no one to open it. Hetty's only hope was that someone would miss her and find out what happened.

When they reached the top of the hill even Abe had to pause and catch his breath. Hetty glanced around and saw, not far away, an old shepherd sending his dog to round up some straying sheep. She wondered if she dared call to him for help, but Abe was watching her.

'I admire yer spark, maid,' he growled, 'but ye'd better keep yer strength fer walking. If I'm forced to free ye, you won't be goin' back to yer gran or anywhere else. The sooner we get to Weymouth, the better for ye.'

Hetty's fear rose to the surface once more. He *would* kill her rather than let her go.

By now the sun had risen in a clear blue sky, promising a lovely summer day. From where they stood Hetty could see right across to Poole Harbour, plain as anything, which only served to remind her of Effie's warning. How right she was!

The English Channel lay the other way, and to the west was a shadowy finger of land which Abe said was Portland Bill. He nodded in its direction, 'Aye, that's where Weymouth is …'

Hetty's heart sank. It looked such a long way still; she was so tired and hungry she doubted she could make it that far. Then it occurred to her that the farther they went, the more time it would give anyone following them to catch up. But what if no one came?

As Abe dragged her on she tried to imagine what might be happening back home. If someone went to Biddy's to find out why she wasn't at the shop, her gran would tell them what happened – if she hadn't died in the night. Oh, God, please let her be alive, and send someone to follow us … Perhaps they'll send the soldiers?

She trudged on, stumbling over grassy humps that marked the remains of ramparts of an ancient hill fort. Any other time she would have been interested, for Luke had taught her some local history. But now they were merely obstacles to be overcome and her legs felt like lead.

At length she noticed Abe studying the coast far below. Now and then he stopped to scan the horizon, as if hoping to see a sailing vessel heading into Weymouth Bay. Each time he paused she took the opportunity to look back to see if there were any signs they were being followed. At last she saw movement about two miles back. There were two riders. Her spirits drooped when they stopped as if admiring the view. Then they came on, again raising her hopes. Hoping Abe wouldn't notice she began playing for time. She hung back, dragging on the rope that bound her, to keep Abe's attention on herself.

'You might as well kill me now and be done with it,' she said, when he cursed at her. She tried to sound like she no longer cared, but inside she was quivering. 'I cain't go any further. I'll only slow you down.'

He glowered at her and tugged her forward,. 'We'll go down this path,' he growled, 'and along the bottom to the Cove. I'll find someone to take us the rest of the way by sea.'

Oh God, no! Down there, they would be out of sight of anyone following. And once they were out at sea Abe could throw her overboard.

Chapter Twenty-Two

⁓

At the Dun Cow Sandy was first to notice Hetty's absence. He began to feel guilty because he hadn't called for her, and asked around if anyone knew where she was.

'Either she was too shy to come on her own,' said Mrs Hart the gardener's wife, 'or her gran's not well. I do know Biddy was quite poorly last winter.'

'I hope it's not because I brought Lizzie instead,' Sandy said to Will.

'Shouldn't think so,' said Will. 'Not according to what you told me.' He recalled the expression on Hetty's face when she'd asked if he was going to the dance. Was she really fixated on him like Sandy said? He agreed that Hetty must have changed her mind for some reason, and as the other shop girls said, they would find out tomorrow.

He was surprised, however, to find that without Hetty the evening wasn't the same. The last time they'd danced funny, plain little Hetty Cauldon was blooming, and he'd enjoyed seeing her look so alive and happy. In the end he went home. He wanted to be up early to see his ma off to London, and make a start on those letters.

Amelia was already in bed, and Will sat down at the kitchen table. As he thought about the newly discovered fossils he visualised the quarry, smiling to recall the apprehensive look on Sandy's face. Remembering the lad's remark about Hetty he found himself comparing her with Sylvia. How different they were. Sylvia was well off and, though married now, would always be a good friend. Hetty was much younger, poor, and inexperienced in the ways of the world. Yet she too was passionate about the cause for the Tolpuddle men. His heart warmed remembering how, at Christmas, Hetty had influenced the church singers to give their collection money to the Tolpuddle wives. Sylvia would have done the same, but she could easily afford it, while it was some sacrifice for Hetty. Mrs Sylvia Stanley was charming and graceful. She moved in much higher social circles and had servants. Hetty never had any such advantages. She was homely, the sort who would put a man's slippers to warm by the fire while she cooked his supper... And he never felt like an idiot with her like he sometimes did with his 'betters'. The things he'd said to his ma earlier were all true, so why should Ma think the maid was unworthy? Because she'd been brought up in an orphanage, with little schooling? It came to him then that Hetty had never known her mother or father, and he thought about his own childhood. He could just remember sitting on Amelia's lap while she sang to him, or told him a story; how tender she was with Charlie as a toddler. His dad was loving too, especially with Ma when the babe between Charlie and Tommy died. He recalled how Ma spoiled young Tommy, then the pain of them all when dad died. Ma's love for himself was showing in her wish for him to be a 'man of substance'. Also, he'd seen Charlie and Alan with their baby... Darn it, there was so much love around when you thought about it.

He was lying in bed trying to sleep when the thought hit him like a hammer blow. Hetty didn't know what it was to be loved, yet she had so much love to give… and no one but old Biddy to give it to …

Will was up before the sun next morning to make sure his ma ate a good breakfast before her long journey. Amelia was excited and apprehensive, so he did his best to reassure her. 'You'll notice a few changes since you were last in London,' he told her. 'Charlie and Alan are sure to show you the sights.'

He said nothing about his thoughts the night before, he needed time to himself to decide whether it was more than just pity he felt for Hetty.

After he saw Amelia and the others off he sat down to write his letters. He'd just finished when there came a persistent knocking at the front door.

It was Lizzie Harris, his foreman's daughter, with Sarah Taylor and Mary Dyke, three of his mother's shop girls.

'Please, Mr Freer, there's no one to open the shop. Do you have a key?'

'Hetty's got the key, surely?' he said. 'Isn't she there yet?' A niggling doubt crept into his mind.

'No, she weren't at the dance last night, and now she ain't come to work neither. It ain't like her.'

'There must be something wrong. Either she or her gran must be ill, and they haven't been able to send a message..' Now Will did worry. 'I'll go and find out. Lizzie, will you go to the quarr and tell your dad I want Sandy to meet me at Biddy's? I may need him to run for the doctor if one of them is ill. You two, go home and wait for news.'

It wasn't far to Biddy's but he took a horse from the stables to save time.

Sandy arrived at the cottage to find Will with a distraught Biddy in his arms, trying to force brandy between her lips to revive her. The old woman seemed barely alive but she kept muttering something.

'Sandy, thank God,' Will gasped. 'Biddy's been attacked – take my horse and go for Doc Simpson – then ask Sam Roper to come.'

'Why – what–'

'I'll tell you later. Hurry, lad!'

Sandy was used to riding Trixie the quarry work pony, and was thrilled at the chance to ride Will's horse. He managed a canter and, after giving the doctor the urgent message, was breathless with excitement by the time he arrived at the blacksmith's forge.

'Sam, Will wants you at Biddy's,' he panted. 'Somethin' awful's happened. The doc's already on his way – I think Biddy's dyin' and Hetty be gone!'

The blacksmith took his foot off the huge bellows he was pumping, 'What – gone where?'

'I dunno. I only know Biddy's bin attacked. She's in a hell of a state.'

'Fetch me horse, lad.' Sam threw off his leather apron and washed his hands in the cooling tub. They rode back to Biddy's together, and found Doc Simpson's horse tethered outside. Will was looking out for them.

'We've put Biddy to bed, the doc's still with her. I told him you would stay here, Sandy, while Sam and I look for Hetty. She's in danger – I'll explain on the way Sam.' He urged his horse to a trot down to the highway, with Sam following.

Sandy frowned after them then went inside to find Doctor Simpson.

'What's goin' on, Doc?'

'It seems,' the doctor said in his low deep voice, 'that one of Biddy's old smuggling acquaintances came to steal money from her, and has kidnapped Hetty. Biddy was just able to tell Will about it before she lost consciousness. Poor old soul spent the night tied up in her chair. That villain had about 12 hours start. He'll be heading to Weymouth.'

'Weymouth?'

'Aye. He apparently has contacts there who will help him get to America.'

'Well I hope he gets scalped by them red Indians I've heard about,' said Sandy, bunching his fists.

'Let's hope he lets Hetty go before he boards a ship,' said the doctor. 'And pray he does her no harm. He's escaped the noose once, and been on the run ever since he survived a convict ship-wreck during the voyage to Botany Bay. He's got nothing to lose.'

Sandy whistled through his teeth. 'The rotten varmint. I hope Will kills him.'

'Steady on, lad,' said the doctor. 'Will's main concern is for Hetty, and right now my main concern is for this old woman.'

Sandy looked at Biddy then, and was shocked to see the grey pallor of her face. Her wrinkled cheeks were hollow, and there were big dark rings around her eyes.

'She already has a weak heart,' the doctor went on. 'I've given her something to make her sleep, so can you keep the fire going? Make sure she's warm. If she wakes try and get her to eat some porridge, or at least to drink some warm milk. I'll send someone so you can get back to work.'

'I'll stay as long as she needs me, Doc.' Sandy went to sit by the bed, and took one of the thin gnarled hands in his. 'Come on, Granma,' he said, 'Everythin's going to be all right, you'll see.'

Deeply touched by the orphan lad's affection for the normally cantankerous old woman, Doctor Simpson continued on his rounds.

Will and Sam galloped their horses along the road to the next hamlet, then followed a farm track to the top coast path where they could see for miles.

'How far d'ye reckon they could have got last night?' Will wondered when they stopped to study the terrain. They had a panoramic view of rolling hills and rugged cliffs above the Channel, but no sign of anyone walking anywhere in sight. In the far distance the shadowy shape of Portland Isle jutted out to sea like the bill of a monster bird. Ships, tiny in the distance, sailed on the horizon.

'They would have to stop when it got dark,' said Sam. 'By ten o' the clock I'd say, then be on their way about six hours later at first light.'

'And 'tis about ten now,' said Will glancing at the position of the sun. 'I don't reckon he'll go right into Weymouth by land. There's plenty of small coves and beaches where he might find a boat to take him to the harbour.'

'We'd best stick to the upper coast path,' said Sam. 'We can ride faster then, and maybe head them off.'

They rode on, stopping only to ask a shepherd or a furze gatherer if the pair were seen. Will felt sick with worry. If and when they found Hetty, would her gran still be alive? Would Hetty still be alive?

They came to a farm on the outskirts of a small village that nestled in a valley, a mile in from the sea.

'They might have made it this far last night,' said Sam. 'It wouldn't hurt to check that barn.'

'Someone's slept here recently,' said Will when they inspected the barn. 'Look how that pile of straw has been flattened, and there, do you see? Bread crumbs!'

They made enquiries in the village, but with no luck. 'You'm the only strangers I've seen in these parts,' said a man working on a thatched roof. 'You might try askin' the shepherd on yonder hill.'

Will and Sam had to ride up the next hill anyway to continue their journey along the downs. It was steep and they slowed their horses to a walk.

'It must have been Abe I saw watching me at Ower, last year,' Will said. 'I thought there was something familiar about him. Strange he should be the only one to survive the Esmerelda shipwreck.'

'What I don't understand,' said Sam, 'is how he survived in them shackles. The weight o' them would 'a pulled him under, let alone fighting a raging sea.'

'He must have got someone to free him,' said Will. 'He's crafty enough. It wouldn't surprise me if he didn't have something to do with getting the ship wrecked.'

'Then he's got the luck o' the devil,' said Sam. 'Only the devil could see all them poor souls drown while he escaped.'

'No wonder he's been biding his time,' Will said as they approached the shepherd.

The shepherd was sitting on a hillock, sharing his bread and cheese with his collie dog while the sheep grazed peacefully.

'Oh aah, I seen a man with a young girl, not an hour since,' he told them. 'She looked a mite tired, an' he was telling her to hurry, poor maid. Don't reckon he realised how their voices carried in the breeze on a hill top.'

'You don't know where they were headed?' Will asked hopefully.

The shepherd shook his head. 'Cain't say fer certain, but I did hear the Cove mentioned.'

Will thanked the man, and once more he and Sam spurred their mounts to a gallop. 'We've got to get to the Cove before Abe finds a boat,' Will called as they sped along. 'Once he feels safe, God knows what he'll do with Hetty !'

Chapter Twenty-Three

∽

They were halfway along the ridge when Will saw two distant figures at the end of the ridge. 'Sam, that must be them,' he cried. 'She's only half his size.'

When they reached the spot Hetty and Abe were almost at sea level. Towering above them was another steep hill, whose southern side had long ago slipped into the sea, leaving a sheer chalk cliff on a grey limestone base. At the foot of this precipice was a rough ledge, strewn with sharp rocks and boulders.

'That'll be a shorter way to the Cove,' said Will, 'but it will slow them down. Sam, I can catch them from here. Will you go along the track on t'other side o' this next ridge and head them off before that devil reaches the Cove?

Sam nodded. 'Take care lad. Thic bugger's dangerous. Just stop him getting any further until you see me coming the other way.' He turned his horse and galloped like the wind along the bottom track on the north side of the ridge.

Will kept his mount to a trot as he descended the incline, then dismounted at the bottom, rather than risk injury to his horse on the rocky ledge. It would be quicker on foot, for he was used to negotiating rocky terrain. From boyhood he'd had to climb the rock steps of steep quarry shafts and learned to spring up and down them like a mountain goat.

He soon had Hetty and Abe within sight, and in a few more yards he was within hailing distance.

For Hetty her nightmare journey only got worse. Weary and hungry, she slipped and stumbled several times. Abe was getting impatient, he tugged her along mercilessly.

'I told ye I'd slow ye down,' Hetty panted, annoyed as well as scared. 'I ain't never done you no harm, why can't ye let me be?'

She hadn't dared to look back since they'd gained the ledge as she knew Abe would hit her. She was frightened, too, of the sea crashing over the rocks; the channel swells were huge compared with the waves on Swanwick beach. Like a monster they slurped into any inlet, and the evil sucking sound made her shudder as each swell withdrew only to gathered monstrously again for another onslaught. And she hated being under the cliff, terrified of rock falls. Oh why couldn't horrid ol' Abe leave her be?

She fell again and Abe finally lost all patience. Dragging her up once more he raised his free hand to strike her.

Hetty flinched, putting her bound hands in front of her face, but the blow never fell. She heard Abe yell and looked up. He was holding his left ear where a stone had hit him a stinging blow. Then she heard Will's voice shouting, 'Abe Manuel, let her be!'

She swung round, unable to believe her eyes or ears. Will stood about fifty yards away, ready with another pebble in his hand. He came a step closer.

Abe let out a roar, 'Stop right where you are, Will Freer or I'll push the maid over the edge. Then I'll deal with you like I should 'a done a year ago!'

Will hesitated. There was no way he could save Hetty if Abe carried out his threat. 'Leave her, and go on,' he shouted. 'Spare her, and no one will stop you escaping!'

'Well now, there's a nice offer,' Abe sneered.

Will gasped as Abe drew his knife and for a moment it seemed he would stab Hetty. 'Tell you what I'll do, lad. She can watch while I deal with you first. *Then* I'll deal with her!'

Abe slashed the rope at his waist, and pushed Hetty roughly aside. Without her in tow he was sure-footed and started quickly towards Will, brandishing his knife.

Will backed up a few steps, drawing Abe further away from Hetty.

Hetty watched helplessly as Will dropped the stone and waited with his arms ready to stave off the coming blows. There was no one else around, not even a fishing boat, and she was terrified Abe would kill Will. The seaman was bigger and heftier, and used to fighting.

The knife blade gleamed in the sunlight as Abe lunged, but Will grabbed the knife arm, holding it away from himself. He tugged with both hands, pulling Abe off balance, but the smuggler recovered quickly.

Will was wiry and stepped lightly around Abe like a boxer, dodging the blows that would have felled him. As they circled warily, Will snatched up a piece of driftwood and aimed a blow at Abe's knife hand. It was a mistake. Abe dropped the knife to grab the stick, and cursing, pulled Will towards him. Next moment they were wrestling, each trying to trip the other up. Then Abe head butted Will who fell back dragging Abe with him. Momentarily dazed, Will found himself on the ground with Abe kneeling on his chest. Abe gave a rasping cry of triumph. 'I've got ye now, quarry boy!'

With Abe's crushing weight on top of him, Will could only struggled feebly as Abe put his hands around his throat and began to squeeze.

Hetty sobbed with anguish, seeing Will now helpless

against the cruel hands squeezing the life out of him. 'Oh help him, God. Please help him,' she whispered Don't let that ol' varmint win!'

As if in answer to her prayer Sam Roper appeared from behind a shoulder of rock. Hetty had never seen him move so quick. For all his size the blacksmith was sure-footed as Will. He leaped on Abe and pulled him back in a stranglehold. 'Struggle, and I'll break yer filthy neck,' he roared. 'Here y'are, boys, he's all yours!'

For the second time that day Hetty couldn't believe her eyes, her nightmare had suddenly become a fantastic dream. Soldiers of the Dorset Yeomanry were scrambling down ropes over the cliff face, and along the ledge from all directions. They soon had Abe manacled and were hustling him away.

The sergeant in charge remained long enough to loose Hetty and see that she and Will were not hurt.

'You all right, Will?' Sam put out a hand to help him up.

'Yes, thanks to you,' said Will. 'I see what you meant about holding that bugger up until you came, but I had to stop him hurting Hetty. Where did the militia come from, for goodness sake?' he added.

'I just happened to bump into them,' said Sam. 'They was out on patrol from Weymouth barracks. Smuggling's still rife in these parts.'

He nodded to Hetty as Will gathered her in his arms, 'I ain't never killed a man, but I would have then, but for them.'

Free from her bonds at last, Hetty rubbed her sore wrists where the rope had bitten into them. Nothing else seemed real.

'My poor Hetty,' said Will. He raised her hands to his lips, 'Let me kiss 'em better.'

'Will, oh Will,' she whispered, her eyes brimming

with tears of relief and exhaustion. 'I was so afeared for 'ee.' She tried to smile, but suddenly it was all too much. Her knees buckled, and Will caught her as she slipped into unconsciousness.

'You'll have to carry her now,' said Sam. 'Can you manage while I go back for me horse?'

Will nodded, and grinned as he hoisted Hetty over his shoulder. 'I've carried heavier loads. We'll meet you up top.'

He found his mare grazing peacefully where he'd tethered her, by which time Hetty was stirring.

'Ah, I was hoping you'd wake up,' said Will, lifting her into the saddle. 'I can't expect Floss to carry us both up this hill. Now you hold tight to her mane, and try not to faint on me again.'

'Please tell me I'm not dreaming,' Hetty said, as Will took the reins and began leading the mare carefully uphill.

'No, Hetty, you're not dreaming. You've come through a big ordeal, but you're safe with me now.'

Safe with me... Hetty savoured those words, and was glad Will was looking ahead and couldn't see her expression. At the top of the hill they waited as Sam galloped his horse up to them.

'We'd best go inland, and along the hill to Corvesgate,' he said. 'That way will be quicker and we can stop at the nearest inn for some refreshment.'

'Yes please,' said Hetty. 'I don't care if I never see th'English Channel again. And I'm starving.'

'That's a good sign, then,' Sam quipped. But it wasn't until they were halfway through a hearty meal that Hetty regained enough of her senses to ask, 'What about my gran? How is she?'

'She was poorly, but still alive this morning,' said Will. 'Doc Simpson took care of her, and Sandy stayed with her.'

When they were ready to continue their journey, Sam

said, 'I'll ride on ahead, and give them the news. It'll help the old lady to know you're safe. She was mighty concerned about you, maid.'

He cantered off, and this time Will mounted into the saddle, then lifted Hetty to sit sideways in front of him. It was of necessity that they should travel more slowly. 'Walk on,' he said to the mare as he shook the reins. 'You all right there, Hetty?'

'Mm-hm,' Hetty murmured, nestling against him. Perhaps this was a dream after all, and she hoped never to wake up. She felt so safe and content, and with the feel of Will's lips on her brow, she fell fast asleep in his arms.

Will rode slowly along the hilltop towards Corvesgate, enjoying the wide open space around him. He could see right across the heath from Frometown and beyond. What a contrast to the hustle and bustle he'd come to know in the City. To his right a patchwork of farmlands with their pastures and meadows sprawled across the valley to the downs above the Channel. Cornfields were already splashed red with poppies, and further east lay the quarry lands of Swanwick. The early summer afternoon air was warm and clear with the scent of new mown hay borne on a gentle breeze from the south. Directly ahead of him lay the ancient ruins of Corvesgate's castle beyond which the eastern ridge stretched away to the sea where even the white cliffs of the Isle of Wight appeared, tiny on the far horizon. To his left more heath land connected with Poole Harbour, and Holywell Bay where he'd first met Abe Manuel.

There were bad snowstorms that winter and *Esmerelda*, his grandfather's ship, took refuge in the bay. The few years since he'd got involved with the smugglers made it seem like a lifetime ago. Afterwards, while in London, his heart burned for Sylvia. He'd felt hurt and let down when she married another, but he knew it was their common interest in the cause for the Tolpuddle men that had drawn them together. The hurt eased, and he was glad for Sylvia that she had recently given birth to a longed-for baby. She had her heart's desire and they were still good friends.

Mature now, Will could smile at the dream he once had of being Sylvia's suitor. She had never roused his senses as looking at Hetty roused them now. Riding along with a sleeping woman in his arms was a new experience. There was a sense of intimacy in the way Hetty nestled against him, soft and warm, and trusting as a child. She didn't look at all plain with her eyes closed, long lashes curled on her cheeks, and her lips parted in a half smile of contentment.

She was so unworldly, and she was in love with him. That much was clear. He'd felt kindly towards her before, but this tenderness was new, this feeling of wanting to take care of her. A stirring of desire in his loins threatened to overwhelm him, so he urged his mare to a canter to wake Hetty as they neared Corvesgate.

Which the sudden jolting did. She opened her eyes and pulled away from him feeling shy and embarrassed.

'Oh, Will. I'm sorry to be such a nuisance.'

'You're not a nuisance, Hetty. I'm only glad you came to no harm. Are you feeling better, now?'

They'd stopped and dismounted where the mare could drink from the trough at the village pump. Here, within sight of the familiar hills of home, Hetty shed the last shreds of her dreamlike state. 'Yes, thanks. But I'm worried about my gran. How much longer before we're home?'

'We can take the highway from here,' said Will, 'and we'll travel faster if you ride pillion.'

'Yes, of course. How silly of me to fall asleep and waste time.'

'It was time well spent,' said Will, looking away from

her large open-eyed innocence which he was beginning to adore. He sprang into the saddle hen helped her up behind him. 'Hold tight, then!'

They set off at a canter and Will grinned with delight at the feel of her arms clinging around his waist. This too was new, this exhilaration from loving someone who loved and needed him.

It was then he felt the first pang of regret that he must soon return to London, and be away from Swanwick – and Hetty.

Chapter Twenty-Four

∽

They found Luke's pony trap on the edge of the wood, and outside Biddy's cottage Sam's horse was tethered to a tree.

Hetty slid down the mare's flank without waiting to be helped and ran inside. Will followed her.

'Ah, yer she is,' said Sam Roper as they entered. Luke Audley, who was sitting at Biddy's bedside, stood up.

'Your grandmother is very frail,' he told Hetty gently. 'The doctor said she suffered severe shock from being tied up and cold all night, and from worrying about you. It's been a great strain on her heart.'

'Oh, no! Is she …?'

'No, she rallied when Sam arrived and told her you were safe and on your way home.'

Hetty fell to her knees at the bedside, weeping. Her gran looked so small, she seemed to have shrunk in size since yesterday.

'Oh Gran, I'm here, I'm back,' she whispered brokenly, taking Biddy's limp hands in hers. It was so thin and frail, blue-lined with veins. With her other hand Hetty stroked the waxen forehead, and Biddy opened her eyes.

'Be ye all right, maid,' she rasped. 'Abe dint hurt ye none?'

'No, Gran,' Hetty whispered, smiling through her tears. 'I'm fine, thanks to Will and Sam. They soon gave him what for!'

The old woman gave a cackle that turned into a coughing fit.

'Here, Hetty–' Luke handed Hetty a tumbler of water. He gently raised Biddy's head from the pillow. 'C'mon Mrs Cauldon, take a sip to ease that cough.'

With a struggle and a grimace Biddy did so.

'I'd rather have me pipe,' she muttered as Luke eased her back.'

'Oh, Gran ...'

'Sorry, Mrs Cauldon,' said Luke. 'The doctor said no smoking until you're up and about.' He turned to Hetty, 'Which may take some time, I'm afraid.'

Biddy's hearing was still good, 'Doctors, pah. Fools the lot of 'em!'

'She sounds better already,' said Sam.

'Don't let her fool you,' said Luke. 'She's had a nasty ordeal. She needs time and rest to get over it.' He bent over Biddy to say goodbye, 'You behave yourself, now, Mrs Cauldon.'

He was rewarded with a rasping cackle.

'Thank you, Mr Audley,' said Hetty. 'And you too, Will and Sam. You've all done so much for us I don't know how to thank you.'

'You can thank us by taking care of yourself,' said Sam. 'You need looking after too, maid. Well I'll be off, back to me forge. Got some catching up to do.'

'Will you be all right, now, Hetty?' Luke asked.

'I think so,' said Hetty.

'I'll stay until Sandy comes in after work,' said Will.

Hetty gasped suddenly, 'What about the shop? Mrs Freer and Jane won't be back 'til next week.'

'I think the other girls can manage for a few days,' Luke said. I'll keep my eye on things.'

Hetty felt swamped with relief. 'Oh, thank you, Mr Audley. You are kind.'

'Not at all, my dear. You take as much time as you need'.

Hetty followed him to the door, 'Tell the girls to work on the wide-brimmed sun hats. The farmers' wives will like them for haymaking.'

'I will,' said Luke. 'Don't worry about anything except looking after yourself.' He nodded, donned his tall hat, and left smiling to himself. He'd noticed the way Will and Hetty looked at each other. 'I'll warrant this business has made a bit of difference to those two,' he mused as he made his way back to his pony trap.

Luke had thoughtfully brought some provisions so Hetty made them supper which they shared with Sandy when he came in. Before Will left he managed to get Biddy to drink some weak tea. That night Hetty slept in her own bed while Sandy took the rocking chair to be on call if Biddy needed anything.

For the next day or two Biddy seemed to slowly improve, and Hetty felt confident enough to manage on her own. It would be a week or two before her gran could be left for any length of time, and Hetty hoped when Mrs Freer returned she could work from home.

Meanwhile, she couldn't help thinking about recent events. Those few days were a nightmare – and yet – Will and Sam had been so kind, as if they really cared about her. She felt hot with embarrassment as she recalled falling asleep in Will's arms. That was sheer bliss. Of course she wasn't in her right mind at the time, after all she'd been through. 'My poor Hetty,' Will had said – because he felt sorry for her.

Nevertheless she would cherish the memory.

On Saturday evening Biddy had a relapse, and Hetty didn't dare leave her to fetch the doctor. By Sunday lunch time Biddy was struggling to breathe, but she managed to turn her head to look at Hetty. If there was any love in her expression the effort made it seem more like a glare. She raised a gnarled finger to beckon Hetty closer.

'I'm leavin' you this cottage, maid,' she panted. 'So you look after it – make sure you see to the fireplace – give the flue a good clean–'

'Oh, Gran,' Hetty whispered despondently, 'don't worry about things like that!'

'You hear me, maid? Promise!' Biddy wrapped her fingers around Hetty's hand. They were oh, so cold, yet how hard they managed to squeeze!

Tears rolled down Hetty's cheeks as she nodded. 'All right, Gran. I promise.' She drew her hand from Biddy's grip. 'I'm just going upstairs for my pillow, to make you more comfortable.'

She ran up the stairs, snatched her pillow and hurried back. She was just in time to hear Biddy's long rasping sigh, as the old woman's eyes closed. Her hand fell lifeless on to the counterpane.

'Gran! No, oh no!'

When Will and Sandy came in a few minutes later they found Hetty lying across the bed, sobbing her heart out.

'Sandy, fetch the doctor!'

Sandy hardly needed Will's bidding. He sprinted into town and within half an hour Doctor Simpson arrived.

'Her mind was wandering,' he said quietly, when Hetty told him sadly what her gran's last words were. 'It was only to be expected. But thanks to you she was at peace.'

'Let the maid be for a while,' he said to Will. 'I'll send the undertaker in the morning, but she shouldn't be left on her own.'

'I'll stay with her,' said Will.

'Here's some laudanum.' Doctor Simpson passed Will a small phial. 'Put a couple of drops in some hot milk, it will help Hetty sleep. She needs rest more than anything.'

Hetty turned from the still figure on the bed, and stared at them with big sad eyes. 'Thank you, Doctor, and you too, Will.

After the doctor left Will prepared supper. He scrubbed some potatoes and put them to boil while he beat some eggs to make an omelette. Then he went to Hetty and coaxed her away from the bed in the alcove. She was still numb with shock and sorrow, so he sat down with her on his lap and held her in his arms.

'I can't bear to see you so broken-hearted,' he murmured. 'You loved the old lady, really, didn't you?'

Hetty nodded. Between the sobs that wracked her she said, 'Gran was all I had, but she never acted like she loved me – all she cared about was the dirty old fireplace!'

Once again it struck Will that Hetty had never known love. 'There now, my lovely. Remember what the doc said, it was only to be expected that her mind would wander. I don't believe she never loved you, she worried herself to death after all.'

'I suppose that's true.' Hetty took the handkerchief he offered her and wiped her eyes. 'What was that you just called me?'

Before Will could answer, Sandy came in.

'I am sorry Hetty, I was fond of the old lady.' He gave Hetty a hug then went to the bedside to pay his respects.

How strange, thought Hetty, the way they all keep referring to my gran as the old *lady*, now she's dead.

Will was pleased to see Sandy, he would help to encourage Hetty to eat something. 'I was about to dish up supper,' he said. 'You'll have some won't you? We've plenty of spuds.'

'Yes, please,' said Sandy, giving Hetty his usual grin.

'Come on, then.' Will filled two plates. 'You must eat something, Hetty,' he said as he beat two more eggs for himself. 'You'll feel better then, won't she Sandy.'

He was right. She made herself eat if only to please them and did begin to feel better. She became aware there was something she meant to ask Will, but Sandy arriving had put it out of her mind.

Before he left, the quarry boy fetched in some wood for the fire and carried in some buckets of water from the pump outside. 'Anything else I can do to help?'

'Call in tomorrow, in case there are any errands to run,' said Will. Doctor Simpson is sending the undertaker, and Hetty needs time to recuperate. I have some business to sort out.'

That night, Will followed the doctor's instructions and insisted on Hetty sleeping upstairs in her own bed. 'I'll take the rocking chair,' he said, when she protested, 'then your gran won't be alone. And don't worry,' he added, seeing her anxious expression, 'I'll still be here in the morning.'

Next day he waited until Mr Grey the undertaker and his assistant had taken charge of the body. Then he said to Hetty, 'Will you be all right? Sandy will be in soon.'

Hetty nodded, and gazed wistfully at him. 'When are you going back to London Will?'

How she would miss him now!

She looked so forlorn he wanted to take her in his arms. 'Not until after your gran's funeral,' he promised. 'You'll need to go back to work then, if only for company and it's best to keep busy.'

'I expect you're right,' said Hetty. 'Meanwhile I'll sort out Gran's things, not that she had much, and clean this place up.'

'That's right, my brave lovely.' He kissed her brow, saying, 'I'll call in later.' And with that he was gone.

Hetty stared after him, feeling dazed and lost. She'd felt so close to Will during these last days, now left suddenly on her own she'd never felt so lonely.

Recalling his words she suddenly remembered what she had wanted to ask him, when Sandy had come in and she missed her chance. Was it only pity that caused Will to call her his 'lovely'? He had rescued her and treated her kindly, making her love him even more.

But soon he would be back in London and, with Amelia's disdain for herself, distant as the stars in the sky.

Chapter Twenty-Five

~

Hetty never thought she could miss her gran so much. She gazed around the room wondering what to do, then, seeing the empty bed in the alcove, she sighed. It was as good a place as any to start and didn't need thinking about.

She pulled off the covers and folded them, then took the sheets and pillow cases to the back house where she dumped them in the copper. It warmed her heart when she saw the pile of kindling Sandy had left ready, and the copper full of water. By the time she'd lit the fire beneath she felt less numb and her brain cleared.

Opening the door and windows to let in some fresh air she thought, no wonder me brain's fogged, it's too stuffy in here. She drew the curtain across the alcove and began sweeping and dusting. The June sunshine lit up all the cobwebs in the corners.

Hearing a tap at the door Hetty turned to see Mrs Hart, the Lackford gardener's wife, hovering in the open doorway. 'I've brought you a fresh baked cake,' she said, 'I won't come in 'cause I expect you'm busy.'

Hetty thanked her, almost overcome by such kindness. She'd just finished putting the room to rights when Maisie appeared with little Arthur in tow. 'Mrs Biggins sent this bread, baked this morning, and I've brought ye a jar o'me last year's blackberry and apple jelly.'

Maisie sat down for a chat, and Arthur's antics raised Hetty's spirits. 'Everyone's being so kind,' she said. 'I suppose they pity me.'

'No, it ain't pity,' said Maisie firmly. 'It's 'cause they likes ye, and want to make ye feel better. Now, I'll tell 'ee summat.'

'Oh, what?'

Maisie smiled and patted her stomach, 'I got news for Dick when he gets back.'

'Maisie, you're expecting again!'

'Yep. Arthur, yer, will have a playmate in a few months time.'

'How lovely, you are lucky.' Hetty felt glad for Maisie and Dick happily building a family, envious too. She no longer had even her cantankerous old gran.

'Listen, Hetty–' Maisie looked serious now. 'I know 'tis early days, but now yer gran's gone you'll have more time. I'd be glad of someone who could do a bit o' baby-sitting for me. Unlike our Lady Lackford, I ain't got no ma, or Aunt Jane.'

'No, of course you haven't,' said Hetty, 'I forgot you and Dick were orphans. Oh Maisie, you've really cheered me up – but I'm not looking forward to the funeral.'

'I'll come,' said Maisie, 'if you don't mind me bringing Arthur.'

Just then the parson arrived, and after they'd talked about the funeral Mr Barton said, 'I don't like to think of you all alone here, especially at night.'

'It won't be too bad now they've taken me gran away,' said Hetty. 'Will kept me company last night. He sat with me gran so I could have a good night's sleep.'

'Ahem,' said the parson sternly. He looked at her over the top of his spectacles. 'I think you should let my wife put you up at the rectory until after the funeral at least – '

Hetty felt bewildered and annoyed. Why should Mr Barton disapprove of Will being so kind? She supposed the rich parson thought of the cottage as a hovel, and didn't like to think of Will sleeping there. Abe had called it a hovel, and so it might be, but it was the only home she'd ever known. 'Oh no, please. I shall be all right, I have so much to do here. 'Twas me gran's dying wish that I look after this place. I can't break my promise.'

'Tell you what–' Maisie interrupted with a meaningful look at Mr Barton who had removed his spectacles and was polishing them vigorously. 'I could stay with Hetty while my Dick and the Master and Mistress are away. I don't have to be at the Hall until they get back.'

'That would be splendid,' said the parson, sounding relieved.

Maisie smiled at Hetty, 'I don't mind taking the truckle bed, and Arthur can sleep on the floor.'

'All right,' said Hetty, 'but I'll have to get used to being on my own.'

'That will come easier after the funeral,' said the parson as he took his leave.

The sheets for the bed in the alcove had dried nicely, and while they made up the beds Hetty asked Maisie, 'When are the family coming home?'

'By Wednesday, I reckon,' said Maisie. 'With my Dick driving them they don't have to wait for the mail coach. They'll start for home directly after Sunday lunch, and o' course they got the light evenings.'

Hetty was surprised by how many people came to her gran's funeral. Besides Will, Luke and Sandy, Maisie, Mrs Hart and Cook from the Hall were there, as well as the shop girls and outworkers. All people she knew, and their show of respect boosted her spirits. She knew Jane would have come had she been home, but she wasn't sorry Mrs Freer wasn't there for it would only have been from a sense of duty. Nor would Amelia like to see Will at her side, where he stayed throughout the burial. As did Sandy. When it was the quarry boy's turn to walk past the grave, he dropped in Biddy's clay pipe.

Hetty gave him a small smile when he said, 'She wouldn't want to be parted from it would she?'

Luke insisted on taking them to lunch at the White Horse, along with Will, Maisie, and little Arthur.

'Me and Arthur had best go home now,' Maisie told Hetty afterwards. 'I must do some baking before Dick comes back, and 'tis best you keep busy too.'

'Can you manage, Hetty?' Will asked. 'Only I'm expecting a visitor this afternoon. A professor who wants to see the fossils we found.'

'I'll be all right.' Hetty nodded, and tried to sound more confident than she felt. 'I have heaps to do before I return to the shop.'

'Then I'll see you later,' said Will.

Hetty hadn't realised how tiring grief could be. She went upstairs to tidy her room, then thinking *I'll just lie down for a bit* she climbed on to her bed. Before she knew it she fell asleep. When she awoke it was nearly supper-time.

She hurried downstairs, shovelled out last night's ashes then laid the fire ready to light. She was still kneeling by the grate when Will came in.

'What a picture,' he said, chuckling to see her smeared with ash.

'Oh, you,' she said, hot and cross with embarrassment. 'Stop laughing, Will Freer, or I won't invite you to supper.'

'It's a warm evening,' said Will. 'Don't bother to light the fire, How about I go to the pie shop while you get cleaned up? My treat.'

'Oh, that would be lovely, I do feel weary.'

While he was gone Hetty stripped off in the back house, threw her dirty clothes in the copper and scrubbed herself clean with cold water in the stone sink. Feeling fresher, she raced upstairs to put on a clean skirt and blouse. Then she brushed her hair until it shone, and left it loose.

Will was back already, with hot pies and a flagon of ale.

'Any sign of Sandy?' said Hetty, tucking into her pie.

'No, he's got to catch up on his courting.' Will grinned, 'He's afraid Miss Lizzie will be getting jealous of him spending too much time with you.'

'Oh for goodness sake,' Hetty grumbled. 'We were never more than just friends, and he really was fond of my gran. What about your visitor, has he gone?'

'He's staying at the Manor House Hotel for a few days,' said Will. 'He's really interested in our fossils, and wants to study the geology of these parts.'

'That's good,' said Hetty, wiping her hands in her napkin. 'He could bring business our way – buy up your fossils, and bring his friends here. Maybe with wives who will buy hats from the shop.'

Will looked at her appraisingly, 'It's good to hear you being so optimistic. You're doing well Hetty, in spite of everything.'

Hetty blushed at Will's praise. She couldn't bring herself to say how happy his presence made her feel.

'Maisie thinks your ma and everyone will be home tomorrow,' she said, trying to get back to practical matters.

'Hm, probably,' said Will. 'You won't mind being alone, now? I could stop over if you want.'

'Better not,' said Hetty, at the same time wanting him to. 'Otherwise Mr Barton will be looking down his nose at you being in my hovel.'

'Good lord!' cried Will, 'Is that what he said?'

'Not in so many words, but he sounded most disapproving when I said you stayed the night after me gran died. I'm sure that's how he thinks of this place.'

'Dear Hetty,' said Will, 'you mustn't think that. He's a kind man and means well. He just didn't approve of you having me as an overnight guest.'

'Why ever not – especially as 'twas in a good cause?'

Will chuckled at her heated tone. Touched by her wide-eyed innocence, he looked at her beneath half-closed lids, and said, 'He fears you're not safe with me.'

'But I never feel more safe in me life than I do with you!'

'Oh, Hetty. One of these days, my lovely, you and I are going to have a serious talk.'

Hetty stared at him. 'You did it again!'

'What?'

'Called me your "lovely".' She paid no heed to his saying they needed a serious talk, she thought he was patronising her. 'You called me that once before, and the day you rescued me I was your "poor Hetty". I don't like to think you feel sorry for me. I don't want your pity!'

'Come here.' She gasped as Will took her firmly in his arms. 'I never feel sorry for you,' he said, his lips brushing her forehead. 'I admire you. I call you my lovely because it's how I think of you these days, now I've discovered how much you mean to me.'

'You have? But – I – er–'

His arms tightened around her. 'You are lovely to me. If I didn't have to go back to London I'd ask you to walk out with me. Hetty,' he added, holding her at arms length to make her face him, 'Would you say yes, if I asked you?'

Hetty gazed at him, blinking back sudden tears. She'd often dreamt of this moment, and could hardly believe her ears. 'Yes, Will, I would,' she whispered. 'But what would your ma think? She hates me!'

Will threw back his head and laughed, 'Of course she doesn't hate you.'

'What is it, then? I reckon she thinks I'm not good enough for you – darn it, Will – *I* don't think I'm good enough for you.' Hetty choked back a sob, and knuckled tears from her eyes, 'I ain't just poor, I'm a baseborn. You must-a heard that.'

'So what? I was born out of wedlock myself–'

'Aah, but your ma and pa loved each other, they put right the wrong they did – and they *loved* you. No one loved me – oh Will, loving parents are precious. I can't come between you and your ma.' Hetty gulped, steeling herself to say, 'I'd be proud to walk out with you, but don't ask me to marry you–'

'That's my intention, as soon as I've sorted out my business in London–'

'I don't need a husband.' Experience of recent days had taught Hetty how fickle life could be. 'I have a good job, and my own place to live–'

'So you don't want to marry me?' Will cupped her face in his hands, 'Look at me, Hetty, and say it.'

Hetty felt threatened by a fresh urge to cry, 'No Will. Not without your ma's blessing.'

'I won't take no for an answer,' said Will releasing her. 'Ma values you in the shop, or she wouldn't leave you in charge. She trusts you, Hetty, and that's no small thing. I'll talk to her. She'll come round, you'll see.' Will stroked her hair, and dried her tears. 'When I come home from London I shall ask you again.'

Hetty looked up at him as he dropped a kiss her on her forehead and left. She watched him go, then with a sigh she slowly climbed the stairs. She must try and sleep, it would never do to turn up at work looking all haggard and miserable.

But her tired brain wouldn't let her sleep. She kept thinking that if only her gran had willingly given her money to Abe, they would all have been spared a lot of trouble – and Biddy would still be alive.

Then again, if Biddy had done so she, Hetty, would not have been rescued by Will, nor would they have become so close. With the feel of his last teasing caress on her brow she turned over and at last drifted into sleep.

Chapter Twenty-Six

❦

Hetty rose early next morning. Despite the lingering sadness of bereavement she began to experience a new sense of freedom. There was only half as much housework to do, and more time to spend on the vegetable patch. The fire was ready to light just when she needed it, and chopping wood was no longer a never-ending chore. By the time she arrived at the shop she felt quite cheerful – apart from a certain trepidation of facing Amelia now that Will had declared his feelings.

Luke and the girls welcomed her back and Hetty got them all busy making the shop ready for their employer's return. At lunch time Lizzie Harris' little brother came running in to tell them the christening party had arrived at Amelia's house. Luke immediately went to welcome them. After dropping Jane and Amelia off, Charlie and Sir Alan had driven on to Lackford Hall.

It seemed they'd all enjoyed the christening of Sylvia's baby, and mixing with Society – apart from the haughty Beulah.

'We had such an exciting time,' Jane told her father. 'And the architect to design the new Parliament buildings has been chosen.' She'd brought some London papers for Luke to read. 'I thought you'd like to see for yourself.'

'Thank you, my dear, much appreciated. But I must tell

you we've had our own bit of excitement here in Swanwick.' Luke explained about Hetty's abduction and how Biddy Cauldon had died from the shock. 'Your Will, and Sam Roper chased after that scoundrel, got him arrested and brought Hetty back.'

He decided not to go into more detail about the rescue, let Will tell Amelia himself. She was alarmed enough to hear her business was almost at a standstill.

'You must both stay for dinner so we can talk about things,' said Amelia, 'Mrs Harris is doing wonders in the kitchen, and I need to inspect the shop.'

It was nearly closing time when they arrived at the boutique. Hetty's apprehension eased when Mrs Freer seemed satisfied with progress, praising her good, reliable girls' progress on the sun hats for farmers' wives.

'Thank you ma'am,' they chorused, and Lizzie told her they were Hetty's idea.

'Ah yes, Hetty, Mr Audley has told me of your troubles,' Amelia said, kindly enough. To her condolences she added, 'So, now you have property of your own.'

'Such as it is, Ma'am. There's a lot needs doing, but I have the light evenings to work on it.' Mrs Freer's good mood seemed like an opportune moment. 'Did you enjoy your visit to the City, ma'am?'

'Oh, yes. It's changed a lot since I went there as a youngster. I'm glad I went, but happy to be back.'

'So now you've seen the London that Will knows,' Hetty dared to venture.

'Yes, I've seen some of the work he's been doing – where is Will, by the way?'

'I believe he's showing a fossil-hunting professor the finds at the new quarr.'

'Really?' Amelia turned to Jane with raised eyebrows, 'Perhaps this professor wants specimens for the British

Museum – my Will really is somebody these days. I have high hopes of him marrying well, the daughter of a wealthy businessman, or manufacturer.' Her eyes shone as she gazed at Luke and Jane, 'Just think – my daughter has married Squire, Tommy is doing well with fine prospects, and now Will – he should make a good match!'

'He has certainly realised his ambition to become a self-made man.' said Jane. She noticed Hetty had gone very quiet, and thought *oh dear, poor maid.*

'Do you think Will might settle in London after all, Amelia? Aren't you lonely without him, and Tommy at boarding school?'

'Hm,' said Amelia. 'I was thinking maybe Will could start up in Dorchester – he has the house there already – there'll be more chance of him meeting someone suitable. Also he wouldn't be so far away. Dear me,' she added, 'we should have shut up shop by now. Hetty, you and the girls go on, we'll lock up.'

Hetty almost choked on a sigh of relief. It was all she could do to stem her tears until she'd bid the other girls goodnight. It was a lovely summer evening with plenty of daylight still, but she hurried home and collapsed in a chair. With her head in her arms on the kitchen table she began to cry, hard hurting sobs she could no longer control.

Mrs Freer would never accept her for a daughter-in-law, for she could not measure up to being a business man's wife. She'd never thought of Will as more than a better-off quarryman who knew how to conduct business; not someone, like Amelia imagined, rising in society.

And suppose Will did change his mind about her, and bring someone else back from London to marry – how could she live with that? Why had she ever fallen in love with him? For two years she'd thought of hardly anything else but him. Now her dream was within her grasp she had to let it go. Life wouldn't be worth living if she made an enemy of Amelia by taking her son.

In that moment Hetty hated Mrs Freer. How could she go on working for her?

Knowing there was no one to see, Hetty gave in to all the hurt and anger she was suffering and wept until she could weep no more. When at last she sat up and gazed around the room she thought of her gran. Old Biddy had often traded on her sympathy, now she herself was indulging in self-pity. It seemed Gran was right, it didn't do for a base-born to expect too much.

It was then her gaze rested on the fireplace and she remembered her promise to Biddy. She spent the rest of the evening giving the fireplace a good going over.

Apart from clearing out dead ashes and laying the kindling, Hetty had never been allowed to check the chimney flue for soot. It was a dirty depressing job. How she wished Biddy's last words had been loving, rather than nagging about the fireplace.

The memory made her angry again and as she scraped away she dislodged a stone sticking out from the side of the chimney. It came away in a suffocating cloud of soot, and she swore as she wiped her face in her apron.

She picked up the poker to push the stone back into place. It wouldn't go, something was blocking the space. Fearing it might be a dead bird, or worse a rat, she wrinkled her nose and gritted her teeth as she put in a hand to feel tentatively for whatever it was.

Her fingers came into contact with something hard, it felt like metal. She found a corner to grasp and pulled out a small tin box. It was heavy enough to need both hands to hold it.

'What on earth-?' she muttered, and would have shoved

it to one side, but hearing it rattle curiosity got the better of her. She tried to open it, but the lid was tight. She grabbed a vegetable knife, and inserting its tip began to loosen the lid. It gave suddenly and she nearly dropped it when she saw what was inside.

The box was full of gold sovereigns. Hetty gasped, and wondered if she were dreaming. *No wonder Gran never let me clean the flue before, the crafty old miser!'*

Now her curiosity was satisfied weariness returned. She pushed the offending stone back into place and decided to leave the black-lead until morning. There would be time before she went to the shop.

She replaced the lid and carried the box upstairs. She would think about it tomorrow.

She was drifting into sleep when the thought occurred that Biddy must have saved the sovereigns from her smuggling days. Cleaning that pesky flue was the old woman's dying wish so – *her gran had wanted her to find that hoard*.

Which meant Biddy had cared about her after all. Knowing the way her gran thought that, *as a base-born I might never marry, Gran hoarded the coins to save me from the workhouse!*

A wave of grief and regret washed over Hetty. Tears came again and she cried herself to sleep.

★

Over dinner Amelia and Jane told Luke and Will all about their time in London.

'What do you think of the railways?' Will asked, and could see how impressed the two ladies were.

'They've completed one all the way from London to Birmingham!' Amelia exclaimed.

'And they are starting others in all directions,' Jane added. 'Such progress!'

'We'll have a railway come to Swanwick one of these days,' said Will. 'London is bound to connect to south coast ports.'

Amelia eyed him with a smile, 'Poole and Weymouth perhaps. I can't see it coming here. But Will, I want to hear your news. Tell me about this professor – is he buying fossils from you?'

'We're travelling back to London together,' said Will. 'So we'll discuss it on the way. He's very excited about our finds.'

'And Luke tells me Swanwick's had some excitement of a very different kind.'

'Yes,' said Will, eagerly. Here was his chance to mention Hetty. He began to explain how he'd discovered Hetty's abduction, and how he and Sam gave chase, 'We were nearly at the cove where we had to separate when we had Abe Manuel and Hetty in sight. We had to cut them off before Abe could find a boat. Fortunately Sam ran into a detachment of militia from Weymouth while I was fighting Abe.'

'My goodness! Were you hurt?'

'No, thanks to Sam coming to my rescue, then the soldiers took charge. But Hetty suffered a dreadful ordeal. Now she's recuperating, poor maid, from losing her gran.'

Amelia was alarmed to hear such sympathy for Hetty coming from Will. It seemed she'd come home just in time. 'She'll get over it,' she said shortly. 'I'm sure Hetty will soon get used to her independence, and enjoy it.'

'That will take time, Ma,' Will said defensively. He was startled by his mother's seeming lack of feeling for Hetty's grief. 'Losing her gran like that was a shock. I thought it my duty to stay with her that first night,' he added. 'She needed rest, but couldn't bear to think of old Biddy lying there alone.'

Both mother and son had forgotten they were in the presence of guests. Amelia's eyebrows shot up. 'You spent the night with Hetty Cauldon!' she cried, appalled. 'What about your reputation?'

'Mother!' Will resented the intimation. 'Hetty just lost the only family she had. I wasn't going to leave her alone after what she'd been through. She slept upstairs in her bed and I slept in a chair downstairs. Anyway, Mr Barton soon put his foot down, and Maisie came to stay with her until the funeral.'

'Well, thank goodness for that.'

'I'm surprised at you, Ma. Hetty is completely innocent. It never occurred to her that the situation was in any way improper–'

'Ahem,' Luke Audley coughed politely. 'My dear,' he said to Jane, 'I think it's time we went home.' He looked at Amelia, 'You must both be tired.'

Amelia nodded, 'Yes, of course. Please excuse our bad manners.'

Jane smiled and took Amelia's hands in hers, 'It has been a long day, and it was good of you to have us. We've enjoyed chatting about everything, I'll come to the shop tomorrow.'

Will helped them on with their coats then he and Amelia saw them to their carriage. While Jane gave Amelia a hug and kissed her cheek, Will and Luke shook hands, 'Good luck, m'boy. Take care.'

After waving them off, Will and Amelia returned to the parlour.

'Before you go to bed,' said Amelia, 'I'd like to hear what plans you have in mind, now that the campaign for the Tolpuddle men has succeeded.'

Will gave a casual shrug. 'I shall come home and settle down like I promised.'

'What about your London business?'

'I shall make Jimmy Priest and Johnny Parsons my partners; they're quite capable of running things their end. I'll have to go to the City now and then of course, but I'll be home most of the time so you won't have to worry about the stables or the quarr any more. Anyway, Ma,' he added, 'As soon as it's dealt with I shall take a wife. It's what you want, isn't it?'

'Yes, of course,' said Amelia. If they hadn't argued about Hetty she would have felt pleased. Now she was niggled by doubt. 'Do you have someone in mind?'

'Yes, Ma. I meant to tell you before I go back. I shall marry Hetty Cauldon.'

'Will, you can't!'

'Why ever not?'

'She's not connected, has never had a proper education–'

'Neither did I, Mother. Hetty has helped herself just as I had to. We have a lot in common, she understands me and my work. She'll make a perfect wife.'

'But Will, she is base born – she doesn't even know who her father was!'

Will could stay calm no longer. 'Ma, I never took you for a hypocrite. You disapprove because I spent one night in Hetty's cottage, yet you bore me out of wedlock. You must have done a bit more than spend time alone with my dad!'

Amelia gasped, indignation turning to shock. It was true, she and William had taken risks, and they'd paid dearly. And where would she be if he hadn't come back from the wars?

'I married a poor man for love–'

'Yes, you gave up wealth and title to live in poverty all your married life. Well, I love Hetty, and I don't have to give up anything – even if you disown me like your father disowned you. This house is mine, and I have my own business–'

He sounded so sure of himself. She made one more attempt to reason, 'And does Hetty love *you,*' she asked bleakly, 'or the prestige your position can give her?'

'If you must know, Hetty refused my proposal.' Will leaned over his mother, his eyes dark with anger, 'She won't marry me without your blessing!'

He stepped back, raising a finger at his mother. 'So don't tell me she's a fortune hunter.' As he stomped upstairs he called over his shoulder, 'You know what, Ma? You're a snob, just like Beulah Kingsly!'

Amelia sank into a chair feeling shaken and upset. *Fancy comparing me with Beulah!* The thought was more abhorrent than that of having Hetty for a daughter-in-law. And what if Will persisted? The mood he was in he could throw her out. She still owned the house in Dorchester, and she still had Tommy – but she would see little of Charlie and her grandchildren.

She was afraid of the scandal if Will and Hetty married, but her moving to Dorchester to start all over again would cause a worse scandal.

Painful memories flooded back. She might have *Maman's* aristocratic blood in her veins, but she was still the daughter of a smuggling ring-leader.

Despite the struggles, and the shame she'd born, she never regretted marrying William Freer. Recalling her love for him made her see again the joy on the faces of Charlie and Sir Alan. And now it seemed Will and Hetty were in love.

Amelia wished Sam Roper or Luke Audley were here to confide in. What was it Luke once said? Sometimes a person's hopes are higher than their judgement ... Was that her mistake? As for Sam, dear common-sense Sam, she knew what he would say: What do we want for our children? A better life, yes, but mostly to be happy ... Luke would certainly say the same, having seen his Jane unhappily married to that rogue Maltravers ...

Will hadn't even said goodnight. With a vexed sigh Amelia went to her bed.

She spent a restless night going over things in her mind, then rose early hoping to make her peace with Will. But he was already up and gone to the quarry. Fighting her frustration she thought, If I have to wait until he comes home tonight, at least I have more time to think.

How could she have been so blind where Will and Hetty were concerned? The maid was good and kind, she worked hard to improve herself, and was a real help in managing the shop during her own absences. And what patience she had, to put up with that cantankerous old grandmother and all the while persevering with her reading and writing. Hetty Cauldon would certainly make some man a good wife – but must it be Will?

It was a good thing her son was off to London tomorrow.

Chapter Twenty-Seven

Hetty woke early and realised afresh that her gran had cared about her all the time. Knowing she now had independent means boosted her confidence and renewed her strength. While she polished the kitchen range with black-lead (for she owed it to Gran to keep her promise) she thought about what to do.

She wasn't looking forward to facing Mrs Freer and had no wish to remain in her employ. How could she, knowing the woman's ambitions for her son? Apart from the reminders of Will she would suffer, to remain at the Amelia Jane Boutique would be awkward and embarrassing. *If Will has spoken to his ma I shall likely be dismissed anyway.*

Without her gran, and no hope of a life with Will, there was nothing to keep her in Swanwick. She could go away – find work in Frometown, or Poole. It shouldn't be too difficult now she had learning. With that thought she made her decision.

When Hetty arrived at the shop she said, 'Good morning, Mrs Freer,' then hesitated, seeing the look on her employer's face as if waiting for her to speak first.

She knows, Hetty thought. She clenched her fists and lifted her chin, 'Please ma'am, might I have a word in private?'

Amelia had meant to avoid the girl as much as possible –

go out as soon as Jane arrived, but Hetty was here first. She gave a stiff nod. 'Very well, come.'

Ignoring the curious stares of the other girls, Hetty followed Mrs Freer into the back room. Amelia sat down and left Hetty standing. 'You wish to speak to me about my son?'

'No, ma'am. I wish to give notice that I am leaving your employ.'

Amelia was unprepared for this forthright statement. She'd expected Hetty to be frightened to look her in the eye. 'Why is that,' she heard herself saying, 'has someone else offered you a position?'

'No, I am leaving Swanwick.'

'Oh?' Amelia didn't know whether to be relieved, or worried about what Will might say if he thought she'd driven Hetty away. She must play for time, get Hetty to finish the week, then leave while Will was in London. Let him think the girl didn't care when he returns.

All the same, Amelia couldn't help feeling responsible. 'What will you do, where will you go? How will you manage?'

Hetty thought better of saying she'd found Biddy's ill-gotten gains, 'I have a little money saved, ma'am, and I shall sell or rent my cottage.'

My cottage. Hetty swelled with pride. 'Now that my Gran has gone there's nothing to keep me here. I always wanted to better myself and thanks to you and Jane – I mean Mrs Maltravers, and Mr Audley I have. That's why I think I can find something, somewhere, 'cause I have the skills to be better than a servant.'

Surprised by this sudden burst of confidence Amelia said, 'Don't you like your work here? Are you sure you want to leave everyone you know?'

'I love my work here,' Hetty admitted, 'and I shall be

sorry to go.' *Oh dear, this is harder than I thought.* 'Now that I have learned to read and write I would like to start my own straw-plait school – perhaps in Poole where I already know a few people.' She could sell items on Effie's stall.

'You have been most kind to me, ma'am,' she added, fighting the rising lump in her throat.

Amelia recognised a broken heart, and seeing Hetty struggling to keep a brave face found herself warming to the girl. She saw again her much younger self, disowned, pregnant and alone. She too had been brave and bold, but she was taken in by Aunt Mary in Dorchester. Hetty had no-one.

The last icicle in Amelia's heart melted.

'Hetty, come, sit down.' She patted the chair opposite and when Hetty obeyed with a soulful look as if wondering what was coming, Amelia said, 'Is this to do with Will? Tell me truly.'

This unexpected sympathy from Mrs Freer weakened Hetty's resolve. 'Oh ma'am, Will has asked me to marry him – '

'I know, he told me last night,' Amelia said gently.

'He did? Well, I know you have high hopes for him and he does deserve better than me. That's why I have to leave, because I love him so.'

Hetty coughed to smother a sob, 'I couldn't bear to stay and – oh ma'am, you know what I mean. I might be dead,' she added, 'if it weren't for Will and Sam. After all that's happened, I must be content with what I have, and not expect too much.'

'And you love my son enough to do this – give up everything you know and start again?'

'Yes, ma'am. I never knew a mother's love, y'see, nor a father's. I reckon loving parents be precious and that's why I won't come between you and Will, not for all the fish in the sea!'

Hetty looked at Amelia, her green eyes large and imploring. 'All I ask, is a decent character reference to help me find a job until I get on me feet.'

For a long moment Amelia stared at her in silence.

An icy knot began to form in Hetty's stomach. Surely Mrs Freer wasn't going to refuse? A good reference was so important.

Amelia lowered her gaze as she stood up, to hide the sudden wave of emotion that threatened to swamp her. She swallowed, took a deep breath then held up her head to smile at Hetty.

'No, my dear, I shall not write you a reference because I won't hear of you leaving. It would break Will's heart. He is winding up his business in London to settle down. He means to start a new business here as a monumental mason and more than anything I want him to be happy. You have convinced me that you are right for him. You shall both have my blessing.'

Hetty gasped, unable to believe her ears. Then as Amelia's words sank in she jumped up, wanting to hug Mrs Freer. But she was too shy, and her knees went weak so that she had to sit down again.

'Oh, ma'am,' she managed to say at last, her voice quivering. 'You have made me so happy – '

'There's just one thing,' Amelia took Hetty's hands in hers. 'There was a time when Will's heart was absolutely on fire for Sylvia – that does not cause you any doubt?'

'Yes, I know. But they were only two of many whose hearts were on fire because of the injustice the Tolpuddle men suffered. The cause was all they really shared.'

'That's true,' Amelia said. 'Well, my dear, you'd best come to supper tonight and put Will's heart and mind at rest.'

At his new quarry Will spent the day making a final inspection of the seams, and gave his men last minute instructions. He would be leaving for London early the next day, so he bid farewell to Sandy and the other quarrymen then started for home. On the way he grimaced at the thought of facing his ma after what he'd said to her last night. He'd gone to bed angry and avoided her this morning. He did not want to leave home on bad terms, but how could they mend their quarrel? He would apologise for telling Ma she was like Beulah, but he still meant to marry Hetty.

Then he remembered something his dad once said: *The best form of defence is attack* ...

At home, hearing the murmur of voices in the parlour and thinking Jane must be with his ma, he went straight upstairs to pack. By the time he came down again, carrying his bag ready for the morning, he felt ready to swallow his pride and say sorry. It shook him a little to find her waiting at the foot of the stairs. For a moment they stood looking at each other, then she smiled.

'You're all ready to go, then.'

'Yes, Ma. Look, I'm sorry about last night. I shouldn't have said what I did, but I am serious about marrying Hetty – soon as I – '

He stopped as Amelia turned to beckon Hetty who had appeared in the parlour doorway.

'Don't you think you had better get engaged first, my son?' Both women were smiling at him. 'You tell him, Hetty,' Amelia said. 'I must go and see to supper.'

She disappeared into the kitchen as Hetty flew into Will's arms.

Epilogue

Two years later

~

'There they go!'

Will squeezed Hetty's hand as the second of two rockets shot into the sky. Hetty's squeal of delight was drowned by the cries of anticipation from the crowd gathered on Westminster Bridge. All heads turned towards Kennington Common.

It was Easter Monday, 16 April 1838. Four years ago Will had come with Sylvia to Kennington Common to join the common cause to free the Tolpuddle men. Today, having been invited to spend Easter with the Stanleys, he and Hetty waited with them to witness the celebration of the Dorchester labourers' homecoming.

Sylvia, being heavily pregnant, had left her two-year old with their nanny rather than bring the child out in the crowd.

'I'll be able to tell my little one that he, or she, was present on this grand occasion,' Hetty said. With one hand on her swelling stomach she smiled up at Will, her heart full to bursting.

Even more wonderful than this historic event, was knowing that none of her children would be base-born. She sighed with contentment, then had the grace to blush, recalling her first night of wedded bliss.

'I never want to hear you mention that word again,' Will told her during their wedding night love-making. 'When I'm finished with you, you'll be so legitimate … '

Hetty's cheeks burned at the memory – but now the parade had started. Each group of tradesmen, preceded by their colours, marched by to the stirring tunes of their brass bands. Huzzas were heard before the firing of the rockets, and now the cheering of the crowd came in waves as each contingent passed by.

Amid the procession, drawn in an open carriage by four white horses, sat the Tolpuddle Martyrs, doffing their hats and waving.

'And not a policeman in sight,' Sylvia murmured. 'How different from four years ago.' She meant that then the government had organised thousands of extra police and militia, who, it turned out, were not needed. The marchers and the crowd had been orderly and silent. Today they were orderly, but the noise was deafening as everyone cheered and yelled their good wishes until their throats were hoarse.

It took an hour for the thousands of trades representatives to file over the bridge. They paraded on, past the site where work on the new parliamentary buildings had begun, and on through the metropolis to the White Conduit House Tavern where the Tolpuddle men were to be entertained.

'How strange, that when the first martyr came home last year, the old King died a week later,' Sylvia said as the crowd dispersed. 'It was as if he'd been waiting to see his pardon carried out.'

George smiled indulgently at his wife, 'Most likely 'twas coincidence, my dear. His Majesty was ill for a long time, and I do know it was his ardent desire to survive until Princess Victoria reached her majority.'

'And now she is Queen,' said Sylvia. She smiled at Hetty, 'Shall the new Mr and Mrs Freer come to see the procession to her coronation in June? 'My baby will be born in time, what about you, Hetty?'

'It will be too near Hetty's time for travelling,' said Will, putting a protective arm around Hetty's shoulders. 'Swanwick will have its own celebration on the day, especially as the princess visited the place when she was fourteen.'

'Little did we know that only four years later she would be Queen,' said Hetty, a note of wonder in her voice. 'A new life for her, for the martyrs, and for us. Do you realise, Will, I will be nineteen by the time our child is born, the same age as Queen Victoria.'

Her laugh was jubilant, thinking of the new life inside her. 'It's a time of new beginnings for us all.'

Author's Note

In 1833 the general agricultural wage for Dorset was 10/-d per week. The Tolpuddle men were paid 9/-d. This was reduced to 8/-d, then 7/-d. Their families were close to starving when they were told their wages were to be cut to 6/-d. To avoid further degradation six men, two of whom were Methodist preachers, formed a friendly society, pledging not to accept work for less than 10/-d per week. But they were ignorant of the law. Trade unions were legal, but swearing an oath to secrecy was not.

Thirty years before, a great problem for the British Admiralty was manning its war-ships. When seamen were paid off, a working man might come home to find he'd lost his job. There was also a horror of life in the Navy with its poor pay, foul rations and severe discipline. (The log of one ship of the line, during the four weeks before Trafalgar recorded 25 floggings.) Hence the press-gangs which terrorised seaport towns during Napoleonic times; so a war-ship's crew was made up mostly of men impressed against their wills. As a result a mutiny occurred in April 1797 at Spithead. Each ship appointed two delegates and the seamen swore an oath of fidelity to the cause: orders would not be obeyed until their just demands were met.

On the 8th May Parliament passed a bill to augment their pay.

When another mutiny occurred on 22nd May at the Nore the government used force to put it down, causing bloodshed which led to the Incitement to Mutiny Act 1797.

The Act stated: '*Any person who shall maliciously and advisedly endeavour to seduce any person or persons serving in His Majesty's forces, by sea or land, from his or their duty and allegiance to His Majesty, or incite or stir up any such person or persons to commit any act of mutiny, or to make, or endeavour to make, any mutinous assembly, or to commit any traitorous or mutinous practice whatsoever, shall, on being legally convicted of such offence, be adjudged guilty of felony and suffer death.*'

These two Acts of Parliament were used to convict the six Tolpuddle Martyrs of treason when all they wanted was to stop their wages being cut further because their families were starving.